FEINT

FEINT

A NOVEL

MICHAEL G. SULLIVAN

Mind Harvest Press
COLUMBIA, SC

ISBN 978-1-946052-37-7 (ppbk); 978-1-946052-38-4 (ebook)

Editing, interior and cover design by James D. McCallister
(www.jamesdmccallister.com)

For Michael,
From His Friends

1

Mistakes are potholes in the uneven pavement of our plans. Even the shallowest can put even an experienced motorcycle rider into a steep ditch. If nothing else, Byron Round lay upon a bed stiff like a prison cot and took comfort from this familiar metaphor for his troubles. Little else comforted him. Not in his position. He'd kill to be out on the road again, the wind against his face. And, yeah—even two wheels in a ditch would be better than his current circumstances.

The past never far behind, he often found classmates from the seventh grade lingering in his daily thoughts, as if in a waking dream all the time. He could still name them in order of their seats, front to back—his had been in the sixth row, third from the front, and the scent of Miss Delaney's perfume as she bent over him to check his spelling would waft; it lingered still in his imagination. When he dared turn his head to the right, he could almost catch a glimpse of her full breasts, so mysterious and compelling at that age. He could still feel the heat that made his face glow in those days.

Had the voluptuous teacher ever noticed her student blushing? If he had to guess, he suspected Miss Delaney knew. Did that mean she secretly enjoyed teasing twelve-year old boys in the throes of hormonal change? Perish the thought. Monstrous, by today's standards.

But now that boy had become a stranger, one ruinously unaware of what lay ahead, and a symbol of innocence more than a genuine memory of Byron's true self. How many of our memories can we truly trust, anyway? We kid ourselves.

How disquieting to visualize that unknowing adolescent self, unmarked by all to come. A man's past—or in this case, that boy's future—follows him with its blue light on, its siren wailing.

Trust me, kid, Byron thought, *you'll never get away from it. Not on your life. Not if you tried.*

So much for comfort. Not here. Comfort had left Byron's life the ordinary Saturday morning when his wife Dianne disappeared. All she had said was that she planned to go shopping, as unremarkable a goodbye as could be imagined. But she never returned. Nor had any sense of normalcy in Byron Round's life.

His wife, a former childhood sweetheart, had spoken her intention that weekend morning more as a public announcement than as a remark addressed specifically to her husband. They had developed a kind of indirect language that allowed them to step around topics that were sure to wound. They had gotten so good at it that from time to time they were almost able to persuade themselves that they were, if not happy, at least not unbearably unhappy.

But those times were getting fewer and fewer for Byron. By then, when he could bring himself to look at Dianne, he would feel a rush of anger, like an in-coming tide about to sweep him away. The lies that brought them back together had been a type of infidelity—to the truth—more painful than the conventional sort. No question.

Byron had spent the rest of that morning cleaning the garage and carting bags of trash out to the curb. And with a history like Dianne's, when she didn't return home by five he became concerned. They had been scheduled to go to her parent's house for cocktails and dinner; Suzanne, her mother, had requested they arrive around six-ish. While not unusual for her to return home late, Dianne would never screw up plans made with her parents. Not after what she'd put them through already in life, Byron guessed. A shred of decency.

At first he telephoned the Kingsburys to ask if Dianne had gone straight there from her soon-to-become mythical shopping adventure, but Mrs. Kingsbury said they hadn't heard from her all day. She asked if everything was all right, but Byron could tell from her tone that the daughter had dished to the mother about the marital problems. No great leap.

After assuring her all was fine, he hung up with a knot in his gut. He couldn't think of anyone else to call because he had never met any of Dianne's friends. He suspected they were other addicts she had met in rehab.

Or former dealers. If not current. Byron tried not to worry—it was a misuse of the imagination, he'd heard it said.

AN HOUR LATER MR. KINGSBURY CALLED TO ASK IF THEY were still coming over for dinner. Byron told him Dianne hadn't returned yet, so he thought it prudent to wait at home.

Martin Kingsbury, with an immediate and knowing edge to his voice, suggested instead they call the police.

Byron, himself a former cop, knew it was too soon for that and said so. "Dianne'll be back any time now," he had insisted.

By then, however, his wife had already been dead, and wouldn't be returning anywhere ever again.

The thought still made his guts twist; he'd loved her since adolescence. Those relationships never fade, even with the occasional heartbreaks and betrayal that often come with lengthy friendships. And the way longtime friends yearn at the moment of departure from one another, Byron had begun missing Dianne that morning almost as soon as she closed the door behind her. Soon enough, he'd find out why.

2

At ten o'clock Byron telephoned the state police. He knew cop lingo to break through the filter and get responsive assistance instead of a brush-off—Saturday nights were busy. His history on the force paid off. The dispatcher said an officer would be sent to take a statement.

Trooper LeClair arrived around eleven-thirty. He apologized for taking so long and explained that he had been tied up at an accident scene on the interstate. Byron mentioned his own background in law enforcement, which precipitated a brief exchange about the details.

LeClair took out his pad and began to fill out the missing persons report. "Can you tell me what your wife was wearing the last time you saw her?"

The words *the last time you saw her* sounded ominous as Byron tried to recall what Dianne had been wearing. "A tan skirt and jacket, white blouse and blue shoes—flats. She was carrying a brown purse—no; more tan—with the designer's initials on it. And she was wearing sunglasses, large ones. They covered her face, almost."

The trooper wrote down the description. "Recent photograph of Mrs. Round I could have?"

"I've got several upstairs. I won't be a minute."

When Byron came back and handed the trooper two recent pictures of Dianne, smiling in both, he worried he might never see that face again. He felt certain now that she had scored junk and gone off to do it. But then, it was far from the first time he'd been in this position.

And, she always came back on her own. The days when Byron had gone out to track her down, to save her from herself, had ended. This fact he kept to himself.

"I'm sick with worry," he noted.

"While you were upstairs, I did a record check on Mrs. Round under her maiden name. Are you aware," he paused, pursing his lips with distaste, "she has several narcotics priors?"

Byron put his hands in his pockets. "Yeah. I know all about those."

"All the various other charges as well?" The trooper watched Byron closely. "Like solicitation?"

"Your records search is mistaken."

"How so?"

"Dianne's got a drug problem, no question. But, she's never been arrested for prostitution."

"There's no mistake."

"Are you certain?"

The officer held out his hands. "The records are the records. How long have you been married to her?"

Byron sat down in a corner. Sighed. "I didn't know about those."

"Names of any friends or known associates we, or *you*," he said with a pointed air, "could contact?"

"I don't." Byron knew that sounded strange. "We aren't social. And I don't have a habit."

"Not a single friend?"

"I considered that her old life. I thought she had left it behind."

The trooper wrote a note, seemed to underline it.

"But, Dianne's private. Our social life revolves around her family and people I work with."

"Mr. Round, as an ex-cop you know I can't release a missing person report until that individual has been missing for at least twenty-four hours. You see, most folks come home within that time."

Grim, Byron nodded. "I know the stats."

"Tell you what, sir—if your wife's still 'missing' this time tomorrow? You give us a shout then, and I'll put out the report." The trooper turned towards the door. "I wouldn't be too concerned, sir. She's relaxing at a friend's house right now. That's what I'd bet."

But he didn't think Dianne would be found at a friend's house. And he didn't think she was coming home, either. "I hear where you're coming from. Understood. But I think it's worse, this time."

"Addiction's a bear. I wish you luck with her."

"Thanks for everything."

Frustrated, Byron telephoned the Kingsburys to report what the trooper had said; her mother shrieked that the police should be combing every tenement in downtown Hartford.

Byron replied that they had bigger crimes to investigate than another junkie gone missing. "I remember feeling the same way when I was on the force. It's not personal."

"What cold bastards the police are. That *you* are."

"Ma'am? I'm not the one who developed a drug problem while I was overseas fighting for this country."

That settled everyone's energy. They weren't used to Byron speaking up like that.

Mr. Kingsbury got on the line asked in an oddly chipper tone if Byron wanted them to come wait with him, but he said no. He didn't want to see his in-laws, and equally certain they held no desire to see him.

After he hung up, he tried to imagine what they were saying about him. Perhaps they were calling the police right now to register an ugly gush of accusations. No, they couldn't betray him like that, at least not until they were certain of what had happened to Dianne. He wondered if it would seem odd that he had decided not to visit with his in-laws at a time like this, but was too exhausted to care and went off to bed.

3

On Monday, Byron stayed home from work in case Dianne returned. She didn't.

Mrs. Kingsbury arrived, and the two of them agreed this wasn't at all like Dianne, unless she was using again. Byron wondered if the Kingsbury's knew of Dianne's arrests for prostitution. How could they not? So they had concealed that from him, too. And Kingsbury seemed calm for a man whose troubled adult daughter had vanished.

Suzanne made sandwiches, and they waited together all afternoon with neither call nor appearance from Dianne. Byron hadn't changed his clothes or shaved in two days. He started to feel guilty —was there more he should be doing?

ON TUESDAY MORNING TROOPER LECLAIR CAME BACK TO tell Byron they had found his wife's car in the parking lot of a mall where she often shopped. Dianne was inside the car. The trooper said she had been dead for some time.

"Cause of death wasn't apparent," he said, "so the coroner will have to determine that."

"Understood."

"I'm sorry, sir."

"Yep."

"She just looked like she was asleep, sir."

Byron thought this added detail odd, like an answer to an unasked question. "I appreciate you telling me."

He telephoned the Kingsburys to tell them. Mrs. Kingsbury dropped the telephone. He could hear Martin talking in the background and swore he heard his father-in-law suggest that he thought his daughter's husband knew more than he admitted, but Byron tried to convince himself he'd misheard. Such a suggestion would make him look more guilty than he already did.

LATER, A SECOND STATE POLICE CRUISER CAME ROLLING down Willow Lane. Byron was surprised to see his former patrol commander, now Lieutenant Atkins, stepping out of the car.

"Tough day, Round. Condolences."

Byron put out his hand. "How did they find her?"

"A woman walking in the parking lot saw your wife slumped over the steering wheel and called us. She was already gone when the EMT people got there. I'm sorry."

"Where is she?"

"At the county morgue. They're doing the toxicology tests and then they'll release the body—I mean, your wife." He reached out and shook Byron's hand. "Anything I can do?"

"No. Thank you for coming out yourself to tell me." They shook hands again.

"After the funeral I'd like to drop by and talk to you some more, if you don't mind."

"Of course. I understand."

But Byron knew this wasn't good. The state police wouldn't send a lieutenant to follow up on what was, after all, only another drug overdose case.

THE NEXT FEW DAYS WERE LIKE A FILM GOING AT THE wrong speed: funeral preparations, telephone calls from his friends, an awkward wake at the Kingsbury's house, and everyone's unanswered questions about Dianne's death—Byron's included.

Worse and even more surreal, the media wrote lurid stories about covered-up drug use by a bank president's daughter. They hinted at a troubled marriage and even infidelity. Reporters camped out in front of Byron's house for days. They would scream at him and pound on the car windows whenever he drove out of the driveway. Pictures of Byron covering his face with his hands appeared on the front pages.

Three days later they had the funeral service at Trinity Church. Most of the attendees worked at the bank. They barely knew Dianne, but Byron knew it was important that her father see them all at the service. The Kingsburys were polite but distant. Byron thought it might be a result of their grief, or their knowledge the daughter and her husband had been quarreling at the time of her death. He wondered where Dianne's friends were. And wished he had a few of his own he could trust.

THAT MONDAY AFTERNOON, BACK AT WORK, BYRON decided to sell the house. He didn't want to stay there any longer. The scent of her perfume on the pillow next to him at night was enough to startle him with the reality that, this time? Dianne was gone for good. He tried to make himself feel nothing, like back in the field after a particularly ugly firefight.

He went up to Mr. Kingsbury's office to tell him about his decision to sell and move. Byron was his son-in-law in name only now. His concerns about Sunwest's compliance practices had driven a wedge between them even before Dianne's death. In any event, he rarely saw them now.

Taking the news well, Mr. Kingsbury said he understood and then excused himself, cold and brusque. "Late for a meeting."

N

A FEW DAYS LATER LIEUTENANT ATKINS DROPPED BY Byron's office, casual as could be with a pair of tall coffees, as though he was Byron's best pal.

He dropped the autopsy report on Byron's desk and began to ask some routine questions. At first he thought all this hysteria and attention came because the police always suspect the husband when a wife is found murdered, but the longer the questioning went on, the more certain Byron was that the lieutenant suspected guilt.

"Did you know she was still using drugs?" The way the lieutenant asked made it sound impossible that Byron had not known.

"No, I didn't." That sounded implausible even to Byron. "Of course, I knew she had some problem with drugs in the past." The lieutenant already knew about that, so no reason to be coy. "But she seemed fine ever since we got married."

Even Byron noticed he had used the words, "seemed fine." Was he trying to explain away his ignorance so soon?

"She died from an overdose of heroin. That's not the kind of drug habit a husband wouldn't know about."

"I can only tell you that I never saw any evidence of her using drugs during our marriage." How quickly he had shifted to the language of the law. Any evidence! Is this what his memories of Dianne were going to be like now? Little snippets of legal jargon pasted over their up and down marriage?

"You were a policeman. It's kind of hard to imagine she could be shooting up in the house and you wouldn't know about it."

"Maybe she never used drugs in our house." That seemed reasonable enough. A suburban housewife trying to hide her habit from her banker husband might very well only use when she was away from home.

"I got a warrant to search your house this morning. My people are there right now. They found drugs and needles in the bathroom and in her closet. Did you both use that bathroom?" The implication of that seemed clear enough.

"It was mainly her bathroom. I used the one across the hall." God, everything Byron said sounded as if he was trying to squirm out of a tight spot.

"But you did use it on occasion?"

"Yes, of course."

"Did the two of you own this house?"

"It's in both of our names, if that's what you mean."

The cop closed his notebook and glared. "If it's a yes or no question, you can save us both a lot of time by choosing one of those answers."

Byron, chastened, sat in silence. Innocent, he saw no need to clam up in front of a former colleague on the force.

"Now: can you tell me how a nine-hundred-thousand dollar mortgage gets maintained with no monthly payments showing?"

"When the bank bought Sunwest, I was given a kind of holiday on mortgages payments. As a kind of good-will gesture." Even Byron had to admit that sounded odd, but it was done all the time. "Nobody around here batted an eye, you know."

"No, actually I don't know. I've never had a holiday from paying my mortgage." The lieutenant said the word 'holiday' as though it were a disease. "Why don't you tell me how they work?"

"Well, often when two firms merge, there are side bar agreements to show the good will of the parties. Sunwest offered me a mortgage at an attractive rate and set a moratorium on payments for a period of time." To a policeman like the lieutenant, a situation this complicated couldn't help but look like evidence of corruption. Byron tried not to sound condescending. "It's industry practice. Really."

"How long was the moratorium supposed to last?"

"I'm not entirely certain. I'd have to consult my mortgage."

"Oh—I have a copy of it right here." The lieutenant was becoming tiresome.

Byron took the mortgage, a sheaf of legal-size documents with small print. "What the hell does any of this have to do with Dianne's death, anyway?"

"Let me ask the questions. So listen, I'm not too good at interpreting legal documents. Maybe you can show me where it says how long the 'moratorium' is supposed to last?"

Byron wondered where he had gotten that. The lieutenant had certainly done his homework.

He flipped through the boilerplate language in the mortgage to look for a note about the moratorium, but gentlemen often fail to write down such agreements. Anyone, including the lieutenant, should have understood that.

"It's not here." He handed the mortgage back to the lieutenant as if it had already been entered into evidence. "Typically, understandings of that nature are outside the written agreements."

"Did you carry life insurance on your wife?" The lieutenant asked this without looking up from the mortgage that he continued to study with feigned interest. He certainly wasn't being subtle.

Byron could hardly believe what he was hearing. It was such a painfully obvious attempt to establish a motive for killing Dianne that he almost laughed. "Yes, we had insurance on both our lives."

The lieutenant continued his charade of studying the mortgage. "In what amount?"

"I believe you probably already know the answer to that."

The lieutenant brought more papers out of his briefcase. Squinted at them and whistled. "Two million—jeepers. Sound about right?"

"It wasn't my idea."

"An unattached man could go out to lunch a long time on two-mil. Have himself a heap of fun."

The old cop's trick, Byron thought. Make the witness think you have the goods on him even if you don't. "No question. But again —it wasn't my call."

"That's a lot of money for a banker with a lot of debt and a wife with an expensive habit." The lieutenant's earlier expressions of sympathy for Byron's grief had been replaced by a policeman's flat questions designed to inflict the maximum discomfort on a witness. He watched to see how Byron reacted to each thrust.

"There—you said it yourself. Debt. The mortgage holder insisted on it." Finally, Byron had a solid answer for one of the lieutenant's unending insinuations. "As collateral for the loan on the house."

"Two million is a lot more than the amount of the mortgage." The lieutenant smiled. Check and mate.

"The bank insisted on one million dollars, but Mr. Kingsbury suggested two million. So there would be money left for Dianne in the event of my death. I ride motorcycles as a hobby."

"Understood. Only, it was her who seems to have died."

Byron held out his hands. "Yes. My wife. Who I'm grieving over right now."

"No doubt. You applied for the insurance yet?"

"My assistant did."

"When did she do that?"

"A day or two after the funeral, I suppose." Byron tried to recall when Martha had filed a claim, and now wished he had waited.

"Did you ask her to do that?"

"I don't remember. I think she did it on her own."

"Kind of odd, isn't it? I mean, a assistant making a decision like that without consulting her boss."

"We've worked together for six years. She'd know what—"

"—what you wanted done?" the lieutenant added, helpfully.

"What needed doing," Byron corrected. Then he thought of how it would look when the lieutenant questioned Martha. She was attractive and they were good friends, a relationship people often misunderstood. She and Byron had laughed at the rumors about them that used to swirl around the office. He hoped the lieutenant wouldn't hear them.

"Did you ever speak to Martha about your wife's drug problems?"

"I may have. I'm not sure."

"Did you ever discuss your marriage with her?"

"I'm sure that over the course of six years of working together, we discussed many things."

"May I take that as a yes?"

"You may take it any damn way you please." Byron had had enough of the lieutenant and his disgusting insinuations.

"Did you ever discuss Martha's marriage with her?"

"She's divorced." Byron only realized how damning that sounded after he had said it.

"Then I take it you did."

"I don't think I want to answer any more of your questions. Not without an attorney." Byron went to the door of his office and waited.

"I understand—the tremendous surprise and shock and awe at the loss of your wife, and all." The lieutenant made Byron's grief sound like a fraud of the first order.

"I'm sorry we had to meet again under such circumstances." Byron offered the lieutenant his hand. Shouldn't he be offering me condolences? "I have to admit I'm a bit confused. If Dianne died of a drug overdose, why are you asking me all these questions?"

"Your wife did die of a drug overdose, but not in her car."

"Then where did she die?"

"We don't know, but we do know somebody put her in that car. And that somebody is the person who gave her the drugs."

"Do you mean she was murdered?"

"That's what we believe. Do I know how, exactly? Not yet. But I will."

The lieutenant shut his briefcase with an ominous click, like the sound of a cell door closing. "And yeah, Mr. Round. I'd retain solid representation, if I were you. But left up to me, you'd be downtown continuing to answer questions. The law is the law, though. And you have your rights. But we'll hang out again soon. Bet on it." The cop, whom Byron might once have called a friend, left without shaking his hand.

4
____

In the foyer of the attorney's office, a converted townhouse, both client and counsel expressed regret Byron needed legal advice at all. The office being in West Hartford, less than a half-mile from where her body had been found, meant that her ghost had followed Byron down the sidewalk.

"But you hire litigators like me to alleviate worry. So that's what we'll do," Robert Taylor said, cocksure and smooth as silk. Six-foot-five and an easy three hundred pounds, his body and voice instantly filled any room. "Now, let's wander upstairs where we can 'chill' and 'rap' like the kids would put it."

"I appreciate you seeing me on short notice."

"Byron? Not only do I know people, I recall your history of on-time rent payments," said his former landlord. "That shows discipline and character. I like clients with character."

They had become casual friends years ago, when Byron had been a trooper and rented the Taylor's guest cottage for a few seasons. While the men appeared about the same age, Robert had always carried himself as older and more self-assured.

No surprise—such a bearing was part of the act: Considered one of the best criminal defense attorneys in the state, Taylor cut an imposing figure by design. His plus-sized suits and bearing shimmered with money and success, and with probing eyes and a circumspect demeanor—when he spoke, he made it count—his confidence preceded him into any room.

Byron, taking a series of deep, calming breaths, felt in good hands. They called Taylor 'Bob the Butcher,' a tenacious litigator hellbent on victory, exactly what an innocent man accused of murder would need.

TAYLOR'S BOOK-LINED OFFICE UPSTAIRS FELT WARM AND plush like a rich man's study. He gestured for Byron to sit facing windows that gave a scenic view of the surrounding neighborhood treetops.

But Byron, unable to shake the vision of Dianne lying dead only blocks away, trembled as he sank down. The fine leather sofa received him, felt like reclining on money, but offered little spiritual comfort.

"We're grinding some breathtaking beans this morning from Ethiopia, the cradle of coffee, if you will. Care to be dazzled?"

"Sorry. Coffee, the acid—I can't. My stomach's a wreck. Green tea, if you have any."

"As you wish. But I'd need a gallon of that to make it to lunch. No question."

The lawyer called down for the tea. He saw his client glance at the desk photograph—an attractive blond woman, well-tended and willowy, accompanied by an adolescent version of the same, a daughter as yet unborn when Byron had lived in their pool house.

"You recall my wife Maryann, and my daughter Nicole is now in junior high." As if realizing the situation at hand: "And, again—our condolences about," his eyes flitted to a legal pad, "Dianne."

"I appreciate that."

"A difficult time." Taylor squinted. "I'd be a wreck."

"Like I said. The coffee. My stomach's a mess."

"Right. A shock."

An assistant knocked and entered with a steaming cup. Byron

took the tea and a packet of sweetener from a young man in a crisp shirt and tie whose face betrayed irritation.

"Thank you, Matthew."

"No problem," albeit without sincerity. "Anything else? Biscuits? Scones?"

Robert, nodding with vigor but saying no-no-no, flipped to a fresh legal-pad page as the door shut with a thump. "He was being fresh, that little twerp. He knows I'm trying to cut back on the carbs."

"Understood."

"Now." As Taylor spoke, he drew columns with sweeping ink-strokes, compartments in which to distribute the case notes. "First, a little human boilerplate. How've you been feeling?"

"About Dianne?"

"In general."

"Fine as can be, under the circumstances."

"Tremendous. How about before this tragedy?"

"What is this—psychotherapy?"

Taylor smiled, patient. A prayerful gesture. "Please. I have my methods."

Byron sipped his weak tea and decided to add the sweetener. "In the days before she disappeared? Been in better moods and places. Sure. But life was fine. Or so I thought."

"Understood. You're still with the bank?"

"Yes." As the lawyer seemed prepared to jot down every utter-ance, Byron weighed the precision of his answers—he stopped himself from adding, *but I don't know for how long.*

"Relationship with the in-laws? Good? Or partly cloudy?"

"Rather distant, at least since Dianne's death. But, that's understandable."

Robert stopped writing. "Understandable—in what sense?"

"Well, they lost their only child to drugs, finally. What is there to say? Hell, I thought she was better this time for good. They're human beings. They're upset."

"Upset with whom? You?"

Byron could see Robert's interrogation tactic, pouncing on an off-hand comment and digging for subtext. "To some extent."

"Because—?"

"Dianne and I argued before she left that day." Byron didn't want to say more, not even to his attorney. "Perhaps she complained to her mother after leaving. Haven't a clue."

"A real throw-down? Or, a minor dispute over doing the dishes? Give me some context."

"Closer to the latter."

"Was that out of the ordinary?"

"No. But, not a big deal this time, either."

"What was it over?"

"I don't remember."

"It was that unremarkable?"

"We didn't get along so well anymore. All right?"

At that he stopped writing and scrutinized Byron's expression. "Many of the questions I'm to ask may seem painful, probing, unpleasant, and possibly all of the above. And as an ex-cop, you don't need reminding of what being sweated down by a couple of seasoned investigators is like."

"True."

"But unlike them, I'm not here to pin a crime on anybody. As such you must tell me everything, so we're not caught with our trousers down by unknown unknowns popping up in the prosecution's case."

At the mention of the word *prosecution* Byron's survival instincts flared, though he maintained a cool demeanor. "No. I mean, yes. I understand. Everything."

"Now—*what* were you quarreling about that day?"

Their plans for having a family, Byron now admitted; how he had learned Dianne had contacted gonorrhea, once, and going untreated for a time had left her unable to conceive. In the course of this discussion narratives about past drug use and arrests beginning in her late teens came to light, the attempts at rehab, the drama. Listening to it all tumble out, Byron understood why the police considered him a suspect. She had put herself through a number of ringers, as well as her loved ones.

"You didn't mention the arrests for prostitution. You either didn't know, or—well?"

Anger flared. An involuntary sweat broke out along his brow: "I admitted she had been arrested for the drugs. Accusing a dead woman of being a whore hardly seems—"

The lawyer rattled a sheaf of police reports. "Have a look at these."

Seeing Dianne's name on the arrest sheets made Byron feel punched in the chest. The charges **SOLICITATION** and **POSSESSION OF A CONTROLLED SUBSTANCE** leapt from the page in boldface type. "Still, it's ancient history. I helped her move on from the troubles."

Writing again and without looking at Byron, Robert spoke with a musing quality to his monologue: "But, you didn't mention solicitation specifically. You see, after you called, I requested a copy of her arrest records, let's see, once at the Hilton in Hartford. If memory serves from the police report, a manager called in the complaint." Robert handed Byron a copy of Dianne's arrest records. "Another pickup up off the street, when she was also charged with possession with intent, let's see, but that was bumped down to a misdemeanor. But still."

The attorney glanced from beneath arched, bushy eyebrows. "Because it's useful to hear how such matters get characterized by an individual in your position, and with such intimate history regarding the victim."

Byron, silent, pressed his lips together.

"But you already know the details without examining these reports. Don't you?"

"Yes," a single, hissing syllable.

It struck him: Now that she'd finally managed to get herself killed, was this all that would remain of his boyhood sweetheart? A yawning cavern of ache threatened to swallow him.

"She never mentioned it. And, I'm certain her parents don't know about those incidents, either."

Robert smiled. "Ah—but if you flip the page over, you'll find it says her father bailed her out."

"Wait—that can't be."

"Oh, yes. Both times."

Byron grappled with his reluctance to confirm this truth to his lawyer. Maybe because the facts exposed how easily the Kingsburys had fooled him, as well how easy he had been to fool? He took Robert's word for it, couldn't bring himself to read any more.

"I find it hard to believe he knew about those days." Why had no one ever mentioned it to him before the wedding? No wonder they were so glad to see him when he got out of the army—gone long enough to have missed her low points.

He remembered bumping into Mr. Kingsbury at the airport all those years ago, and how Martin insisted he come by to see Dianne. At the time, Byron had been surprised by Martin's enthusiasm—he had always felt Mr. Kingsbury didn't much care for him. And then all that talk about Dianne's being 'ill.' The three of them had lied to him from the beginning. If he were honest, he had to admit he had suspected this all along, even if he couldn't put it into words.

"Both her parents knew. But you can see why they chose discretion. Surely."

"No question."

But Byron didn't understand how they could have kept it from him for all these years. All the vacations together, the Sunday brunches, the talk about having a family; all of it had been a farce. He happened to be the old boyfriend who had been away when her life went off the rails, so his ignorance made him the perfect candidate to marry Dianne. What made him suitable to the Kingsburys was that he remembered their daughter as she had been, not as she was. Perhaps they saw her that way, too. A projection, more than the truth. The mind can play tricks when it comes to loved ones. Sometimes they make you so mad, Byron thought, you don't even think of them as people anymore. Or maybe that was only his military training coming back.

"You're sure you didn't know about the solicitation charges?"

Dry. "I suspect I'd remember that."

Robert pulled his chair closer to Byron. "Why do the police suspect you? Her purse and jewelry were taken, so it looks like a robbery gone wrong."

"As a former cop, my first suspicion would be a drug deal gone wrong—or some scumbag followed her into the restroom, tried to rob her."

The lawyer leaned forward. "Why do you assert she was killed in a restroom?"

"One of her shoes was found in the stall. A woman turned it over to store security. Whoever did it moved her—body," he cleared his throat, "to the car." Unable to hide his pain, Byron slumped in the chair and tried to find his breath. "After she became deceased."

"Tell me why the police suspect you."

He shook off the image of her lost shoe—forlorn, lonely, lost. "The lieutenant on lead was my old patrol commander."

"He knew Dianne."

Nodding. "Probably thinks I got sick of being married to an addict."

"Did you complain to him about her?"

Byron shook his head. "Not that I recall. Remember—she was worse than I knew."

"Thin. Usually the husband's having an affair or wants the wife's life insurance. Or both."

From inside his hands, Byron said, "Why don't you just ask."

"Are you having an affair, Byron?"

"No." Byron wondered why his former colleagues weren't treating this as a bungled robbery. "People at work might think so, though."

"Because—?"

"My assistant and I enjoy a cordial rapport. But nothing untoward. No affair."

Having said all that, he couldn't help but evaluate his relationship with Martha. Was it an affair? No. They had never slept together.

But in a fit of honesty, Byron acknowledged that in many other ways, they behaved with the closeness of a husband and wife, each marveling at the ease with which they could confess sins, enjoy a wry inside joke, sit together at times without speaking for extended periods. Is it cheating to be so close to a woman other than your wife? Byron no longer knew.

Robert leaned in, theatrical, and took a good sniff. "C'mon. Even I smell smoke."

"We spent a good deal of time together at work, and—look. We have lunch together every Friday. It's called friendship."

"Ever kiss her? An impulse?"

"Not a chance." Byron tried to sound indignant, but occupying the moral high ground, not one of his stronger traits.

"And how did she respond?"

Byron, irritated, barked a reiteration of his innocence.

"Will the cops find witnesses who'll report they saw you being affectionate toward the woman, your assistant?"

"Quick hugs in the parking lot, sometimes, at the end of the day. Nothing more. Friendship—even a lawyer has at least heard of it."

Sarcasm, obvious and justified. "Ever hug any other bank coworkers? At the end of the day, or otherwise?"

"All right."

"Well?"

"I haven't made other friends there. Not like her."

The sound of Robert's pencil scratching on the legal pad filled the room until he again spoke. "Right. Let's chat like a couple of grownup big boys—shall we?"

With a tight gut and the best poker face he could manage, Byron waited.

"Fair to guess that Martha is an attractive, younger woman?"

Why the hell was Byron feeling so guilty? He and Martha had never done, not actually done, anything sexual. Certainly he had thought about it, but you can't go to jail for that. "She's a woman, and she's younger. Sure."

Robert softened his tone. "Brother—you're not the first

husband to grab himself a taste on the side. Now, really. I need the facts."

"I didn't cheat on her. I didn't."

Wise old owl that he was, Robert's skepticism shown in his narrowed, probing eyes. "A different angle. Does it matter? We can discuss that as philosophers, if you wish. But what matters more is whether the prosecutor get assemble evidence to persuade jurors that you did the deed."

This is the world we're in now—a place where truth doesn't matter, where facts can be twisted like dough into any desired shape. "This is ridiculous. I'm being straight with you."

"But we both agree it could look as if you did."

Byron nodded. And maybe he had been in a way. Not the usual tryst where the lovers sneak off to a motel, but an affair none-theless, if he was honest with himself. All of Dianne's lies had eroded his affection for her over the years to the point where he'd become vulnerable to occasionally yearning for outside affection.

"Moving on. Carry any life insurance?"

"Some. Not much." He knew what Robert would ask next; also that he wouldn't like the answers any better than Lieutenant Atkins had.

"What's 'not much'?"

"Two million dollars."

Robert put down his pencil. Smiled. "That's quite a bit of not-much."

"Enough to risk killing one's wife over?"

"If you don't think so, then we must've grown up watching different television programs."

Again, the explanation, a recapitulation of the Kingsbury father's insistence: "When we took out our mortgage on the house, the lender insisted. We had to carry a million on each of us, assign it as collateral. I've been told it's common practice." Firm ground here.

"Be that as it may, I'm sure even you can see how the police will evaluate such a policy in light all of this. If they find out about it."

"The lieutenant already knows."

"You told him?"

Byron shook his head.

"How about the assistant?"

A grim realization settled onto his shoulders. "Knew about her, too."

"So who's feeding them information? In-laws, maybe?"

"Don't think so."

"But you don't sound confident.'

"There've been some problems at work. Mr. Kingsbury and I have seen some issues rather differently."

"What sort of issues?"

"Nothing to do with this case. It's work-related.'

Frustration simmered and the narrow eyes returned. "Mr. Round: you must let me be the judge of these matters. Now, what issues?"

Byron told Robert about his concerns with Sunwest and Mr. Kingsbury's cavalier response. He did not divulge about Martin's affair with Helen Stone, a side-issue Byron had uncovered in the course of investigating mortgage compliance issues. "You would see it's a garden variety dispute people have at work every day."

"That may be true, but with the police looking at you as a murder suspect...?"

Melodramatic, but he wasn't wrong. Nevertheless: "I've answered all of your questions with candor." It was true enough.

"A few more: will Kingsbury verify it was his idea for you to get the insurance policies?"

"I don't see why he wouldn't—it's true." Frustrated, Byron stood up. "Speaking of other questions: *you haven't asked me if I did it.*"

Robert glanced up, a quizzical knot to the brow. "That's because it isn't important. Either way, the accused is entitled to a zealous defense, and putting that together is my job."

"Aren't you a little curious?"

"This isn't about your guilt. It's about what the state can prove. They're not always the same."

He wondered if saying 'guilt' like that carried subtext. "Well, I didn't."

Robert held out his hand. "Tremendous. I believe you. Now, I have a thousand other questions—but they can wait. Not long. But for the moment."

They shook. Byron liked the clinical way Robert viewed the case. Good counsel. A feeling.

AT LAST HE FOUND TIME TO GRAPPLE WITH HIS STATUS as the prime suspect in his wife's murder. Everything he said would be thought through with enormous care. It was all a matter of interpretation, the spin the police would put on his words, his actions, even his thoughts.

Which sounded like paranoia.

Worse? When he was alone in the house, he still felt as if the police might be watching. He tried to recall every conversation he had with anyone who Lieutenant Atkins might interview. He mulled over all he told him; had he misstated anything, exaggerated anything, gotten dates wrong, names confused? Did he mention that Dianne and he had been quarreling, that they lived far above his meager salary, that she often disappeared for hours without him knowing where she was? But didn't that look like he was trying to blame her, his dead wife, for what had happened? And didn't that only make him look all the more guilty, the awful husband who had killed his wife and now was killing her reputation?

He thought about telephoning the Kingsburys to let them know he had hired Robert, but then he remembered the way they had concealed Dianne's arrest for prostitution, and he thought better of engaging them. With he and Martin already at dagger points over the Sunwest business, it was probably best to wait until the investigation wound through all this drama. He hadn't heard from them since the funeral, and Martin was avoiding him at work. How quickly their cobbled-together family had come undone.

THE NEWS WORSENED: THE NEXT MORNING ROBERT Taylor called to say the *Hartford Courant* was leading with a story about Dianne's prior criminal record, along with the fact that the police might arrest Byron. The article would also say Mr. Kingsbury would not confirm the story that it was he who had suggested his son-in-law buy two-million dollar's worth of life insurance on Dianne. Robert said that if Byron didn't kill his wife, someone was doing a thorough job of making it look as though he had.

How it all come to this seemed worse than a bad dream. Their history together went back so far—had Byron and Dianne been destined to go through all this strife together? He wondered.

5
——————

I t had been late in the school year when Dianne Kingsbury had transferred into Byron's homeroom class. Her family hailed from Missouri, only they pronounced it *Missourah*. Faintly exotic and Southern, from the way they spoke to the way Dianne and her mother dressed, to the way Mr. Kingsbury always stood when a lady came into the room, and with a general demeanor of conviviality, they seemed different from the people Byron had known there in Connecticut. Dianne stood out from the first moment he saw her. Smitten.

It wasn't long after first meeting her that he found himself scribbling her initials on the inside pages of his World History book. There it was—**LDK**—right next to the entry for *Decline of the Etruscans*. The L stood for Lynn, but she preferred being called by her middle name.

Dianne, always ready to tell a secret about herself. Almost immediately she confessed of being adopted, which she said lent her past a romantic air of mystery. Even as a teen, however, Bryon could hear a sarcastic edge to her words that masked some degree of pain at not knowing her birth parents.

Byron, on the other hand, agreed with sincerity that it must be wonderful being adopted—no one knew exactly who you were. You could be anyone.

⁂

ALSO EXOTIC WERE THAT MR. AND MRS. KINGSBURY smoked, which Byron's mother most decidedly did not. She thought it an expensive and dirty habit, bad for your health and, worst of all, she viewed it as a kind of chic wickedness indulged in by those with a penchant for the theatrical.

As such, he thought he might have taken up smoking soon after he visited Dianne's house for the first time. He wanted to be more theatrical too, or at least more than his mother was, which wasn't much. He loved the way Mrs. Kingsbury swanned into a room followed by plumes of blue smoke and the rakish way Mr. Kingsbury always wore a hat, straw in summer, felt in winter. The Kingsburys had style.

Byron's mother? She'd crept around the house like an unhappy mouse.

The Kingsbury home sat at the top of a steep hill in one of those new developments that had sprung up in a cornfield like mushrooms after a big summer rain. A modern one-story affair with large glass windows all around, you could practically see through it from the street when pulling into their driveway. Mrs. Kingsbury was an artist of some kind, a painter he thought, although he had never actually seen her painting. An easel sat in the living room and it always had a canvas with an incomplete image, usually a still-life—flowers in a vase, a bowl of fruit. Mrs. Kingsbury asked him to call her Suzanne, even though many years later when he would read her obituary he'd discover her name was actually Susan. He guessed that was her way of taking an artist's license with the ordinary name she had been given and adding a touch of glamor to it.

Suzanne. When she pronounced her name she'd emphasize the second syllable with a kind of breathy push that to him sounded French. And sophisticated too. If he closed his eyes, Byron could still hear her voice as she asked if he cared for a cigarette even though he was only twelve. He assured her his mother let him smoke at home which, of course, was not true. But he was tall for his age and, if you looked carefully enough, you could almost see the beginnings of a mustache on his upper lip. Byron became sure Mrs. Kingsbury thought he was older than his adolescent years.

Dianne hinted that her father had been lured to Connecticut by the promise of becoming president of the biggest bank in the state. In any case, they weren't sorry to leave Joplin—Dianne's real mother had a habit of popping up every now and then, and everyone found that disorienting. The Kingsburys hoped the move to Connecticut would put an end to it.

But Dianne kept a picture of her birth mother in her purse. Byron thought her mother looked rather disoriented, not at all like Suzanne Kingsbury.

BYRON'S MOTHER TAUGHT HIGH SCHOOL ENGLISH AND said she had students like him, who sat in the back of the classroom with surly expressions on otherwise blank faces and never raised their hands to answer a question, who often sniggered when other students, good students, raised theirs with what he thought was too much enthusiasm. He viewed good students as collaborators, little quislings helping out the fascist authorities, even as he remained unsure quite what a fascist was.

For his thirteenth birthday Dianne had given him a shirt, a gift his mother said was far too intimate for a girl of her age to give to a boy. He put it in his bottom drawer under his gym clothes where he hoped his hectoring mother wouldn't find it. He would take it out of the drawer each night after she'd gone to bed, wear it in his darkened bedroom thinking about Dianne. Then he would neatly fold it up and put it back.

But a few weeks later when he went to look for the treasured gift, he discovered it missing. He thought about questioning his mother, but he knew she would pretend she didn't know. He never saw it again. He hated the way he had no corner of the house he could claim as his own.

The T-shirt had been blue, and Dianne said she got it because it matched his eyes. No one had ever said anything even remotely like that to him before. For the next few weeks he looked in the mirror and practiced holding his eyes open wide and then, when he felt ready, he tried it out on Dianne. She seemed more puzzled than charmed and he stopped doing it. He wondered if she had ever guessed how much affection went into those clown faces of his. They were a clumsy pantomime of feelings he couldn't explain and she couldn't understand. They would go on like that for years, offering each other support at the wrong time or in the wrong way, but they couldn't seem to stop themselves from trying even when, as happened much later on, the bruises showed more clearly and refused to heal.

HER HOUSE WAS CLOSE ENOUGH, ONLY ABOUT FOUR miles from where he lived, and every spring when the snow melted he would again peddle his bicycle up those hills to visit.

Sometimes he and Dianne would push his bicycle to the top of Elm Hill and then, when she was seated on the handlebars, he would point the bicycle down the hill and jump on. As they started off, the bicycle would obey him when he pushed first on the right and then on the left handlebar, but as it gained speed, it seemed to get a mind of its own. He struggled to keep it on the road and when they hit a bump, the tires would lift off-road entirely, and Dianne would scream in mock terror. At the last minute before the end of the road he would apply the brakes and they would skid to a halt, her screams turning to laughter.

Afterwards, they would be so out of breath that neither of them could talk. When she got off the bicycle, she would hug him and wait for the excitement to leave her. As she stood still with her arms around him, he could feel her heart beating through her blouse.

They would spend the afternoon sitting on her porch, talking politely about school and other mundane details they didn't give a damn about, but they said them anyway because they thought her mother might overhear them. He wasn't sure what he wanted to say to Dianne, but whatever it was, it felt important. So they rattled on about classes and teachers they disliked, and what they would do when summer finally arrived. It didn't matter. He wanted to sit in the afternoon sun with her. He simply wanted to *be* with her.

Mrs. Kingsbury would come out on the porch with lemonade and cookies and the afternoon would slide by. Before he knew it, the sun would have gotten low over the hills and Mrs. Kingsbury would gently remind him that it was getting late. Riding that wonderful red bicycle home he would let it coast downhill as fast as it could go and think about Dianne. Mostly he wondered if she was thinking about him too, but she didn't seem like the kind of girl who would spend too much time thinking about one boy. His mother told him to remember that it takes two to tango, but he had no idea what she meant.

ONE AFTERNOON SUZANNE SAID THE VERNON ARTS Council was having a dance at the club on Saturday, and she and Mr. Kingsbury would like it very much if Byron and Dianne would join them. Suzanne always referred to her husband as Mr. Kingsbury when addressing guests in the house. Byron was about to say no when Dianne agreed that they too would be delighted to go. Byron did not know how to dance, and his one good suit no longer fit.

Saturday came, and the Kingsburys arrived at his house in their cream colored Buick with polished chrome bumpers. Mr. Kingsbury came to the front door and Byron could hear him talking to his mother in the living room.

He had asked her to take the plastic covers off the furniture, but she had refused. When Byron walked into the living room Mr.

Kingsbury stood up and the plastic made a kind of ripping sound behind him. Mr. Kingsbury pretended not to notice. Of course, Mr. Kingsbury was too polite to say anything about it, at least in front of him, but Byron was sure he must have made a remark about those damn plastic covers to Mrs. Kingsbury later. Like Dianne, Mr. Kingsbury also had beautiful manners.

When they arrived at the Wildewood Country Club, a valet opened the car door for the ladies and Byron followed Dianne out onto the gravel driveway. Mr. Kingsbury handed the boy the car keys and off the Buick went, squirming over the loose stones into the darkness. Dianne took Byron's arm with practiced ease and ushered him inside. The women were given corsages and the boys boutonnieres; everyone also got a name tags they were asked to keep on until after the awards ceremony.

Dianne wore a yellow dress with white daisies along her neckline. No one looked nearly so beautiful as she did. He had to stop himself from staring.

Byron, already perspiring, felt the back of his shirt sticking to his skin as they took their seats in the Grande Hall. He gazed in awkward silence as Mr. and Mrs. Kingsbury chatted with ease, seemed to know everyone. He hoped Dianne's father hadn't already mentioned the plastic seat covers to his sophisticated wife.

The waiters came around with drinks, and there were a lot of jokes about none-of-that for the children. They laughed, and Byron thought he could certainly use a drink, mainly because that's what adults always said when they were anxious.

The folks seated on either side of him asked questions about where he was going to prep school, and was Dianne his girlfriend, and who his favorite Impressionist painters were, but he only smiled and mumbled weak and indistinct answers about not knowing much about art.

He looked across the table at Dianne. She took a sip of wine from her mother's glass, caught him admiring her. She gave him a secret smile. He stopped giving a damn about the people chattering around him, and his place among them. His eyes came back to her over and over.

Once or twice Mrs. Kingsbury caught him at it, but she only laughed and whispered to Mr. Kingsbury. Byron thought how ridiculous he must seem to Dianne's parents.

THE BAND HAD BEGAN TO PLAY SOME LIVELY SOUTH American music, and Mrs. Kingsbury leapt to her feet and headed for the dance floor. Mr. Kingsbury followed and, oddly enough, seemed as eager as his wife to shake a leg out on the dance floor. Byron had never before known a grown man who enjoyed dancing. He had seen his uncle do so rather reluctantly at weddings, but only after the man had had too much to drink.

The Kingsburys were both tall and slender. They made an elegant couple on the dance floor. Mrs. Kingsbury seemed weightless as she bent backwards, her long black hair falling away from her pale face. With masterful assurance Mr. Kingsbury steered her though the heavy traffic on the floor. Their feet moved so quickly that they looked as if they were floating through the air. He hoped Dianne would not ask him to dance. With his mother's help he had learned the box step waltz, and as the Kingsburys whirled around the floor Byron rehearsed in his mind one-two-three, one-two-three. If Dianne did ask him to dance, he intended to do the box step no matter what music the band played.

Byron forced himself not to look in Dianne's direction and hoped the music would stop soon, but the band seemed to find encouragement in the Kingsburys' performance and played on with even more enthusiasm. Under the table Byron moved his feet in small squares, one-two-three. He was so busy practicing his surreptitious box step that he didn't notice Dianne standing beside him. Byron froze in mid-box step.

"Could we go outside? It's too hot in here."

He thought he heard her ask if they could dance. "I really don't dance very well."

"I said, 'Can we go outside'. I don't dance, either."

"Oh—yes. Thank god." He was so relieved to find that he

wasn't going to be publicly humiliated on the dance floor that he practically leapt out of his chair. "I couldn't hear you over the band."

"They're too loud."

"Your parents dance quite well," Byron's words were swept away by another blast from the brass section and he followed Dianne out onto the patio.

As soon as they got outside, he felt better. The darkness seemed to erase all the people in the ballroom behind them. They walked down the steps that led to the back lawn and out on to the grass away from the clubhouse until they were out of reach of the music and the lights shining from the porch.

They strolled the finely manicured ground of the country club without speaking and Byron didn't dare look at her, but he could feel her beside him and suddenly they were on the golf course. They heard crickets in the distance and walked on. Nothing he would ever do later, not even during the war, would take half so much courage as it took to put his arm around her on that walk, and nothing ever again would be so ferociously erotic as her hip swaying beneath his trembling hand. Dianne. His first love.

6

Byron had first slept with his high school sweetheart in the guest room of his mother's house. It was the only room in the house with a double bed. Mrs. Round had banished that particular piece of furniture from her own bedroom three days after Clarence Round had abruptly left the dinner table one evening, ostensibly to buy some ketchup, but never returning from the errand. Without being told, Byron had never mentioned his father's name again.

Byron had been trying to talk Dianne into sleeping with him for some time. She had never exactly said no, her hand always finding its way into his trousers often enough for him not to push the point further. But you can only do that for so long, and after a while Dianne said she was thinking about 'it' too.

So was Byron. Always. Every time he took off her bra he could sense they were getting closer to... he wasn't sure to exactly what.

They waited until Mrs. Round was away at a teacher's conference in Rhode Island. When it was over, neither of them said anything. But it had been a bit of a disappointment for both of them. Still, they came away wanting to try again. And again. The thought of staying together a whole night, finally, doing it and doing it—what a fever dream. Someday.

LATER, WHEN THEY BEGAN HAVING SEX IN HIS MOTHER'S car, they would lower the windows and let the night air cool down their sweat-soaked teenaged bodies. Byron would smoke a cigarette, and Dianne would lean against his shoulder. Sometimes they fell asleep like in the old song, and he would get her home after her curfew hour.

Once, Mrs. Kingsbury waited for them in the kitchen, pacing and smoking. He thought she had guessed what was going on. He wasn't good at lying yet, so he hoped she wouldn't press him about what they had been up to. He was sure he would have confessed everything immediately and begged Mrs. Kingsbury to forgive hm.

How absurd. Why not ask a dog to apologize for barking? But he didn't know then how the world was organized in such a laughable way. Life is clown-college. Your pathetic pratfalls, your tears, your broken hearts, they only make the audience laugh all the harder. And they should laugh too, because you are never more ridiculous than when you imagine your little tragedies merit even one genuine tear. But it would take years for the Kingsburys to teach him that.

IT WAS AROUND THAT TIME THAT HE BEGAN TO NOTICE the Kingsburys didn't seem to care for him as much as before. They were still polite, of course, but he could tell the climate had changed. He guessed they knew what Dianne and he had been up to. That was bad enough, but to imagine that they were at it each time he picked her up at her house must have been too much for them.

At last Dianne reported her mother had asked if they were having sex, and naturally she lied and said no. He prayed Mr. Kingsbury was not going to pull him aside for a similar chat.

"Do you want to stop?"

Dianne bit her lip. Shook her head. That led to a more direct expression of her feelings. A stark sense of naughtiness seemed to add intensity to the sex that afternoon.

HER PARENTS' SUSPICION ENDED UP NOT MATTERING. The bank where Mr. Kingsbury worked promoted him to senior vice president and they moved to Simsbury, a suburb where executives cluster around golf courses and good restaurants and expensive shops, their children went to private schools, and they paid heavenly dues at clubs like Wildewood. And just like that, Dianne was gone.

She telephoned to report she liked her new school, and that her father had bought her a car. Byron asked when he could see her, but she said she was busy helping her mother decorate the house; and she had joined some clubs at school that left her with little free time. When they hung up neither of them said "goodbye." That seemed too jarring and too true.

What had happened? Maybe nothing. Or maybe he simply hadn't yet learned to trust his instincts.

"YOU'RE LUCKY THAT GIRL'S OUT OF YOUR LIFE." MRS. Round spooned peas onto his plate. "Now maybe you'll concentrate on your schoolwork."

He tucked the peas one-by-one under a mound of mash potatoes and said nothing.

"I'm speaking to you."

Byron stared at his plate, as his father used to at dinnertime. "Yeah. I'm real lucky."

"Don't be sarcastic."

He filled his mouth with ham. Not answering his mother seemed less rude than speaking with his mouth full. This was etiquette triage.

"I only meant that now that she lives in Simsbury," Mrs. Round nudged a piece of pie in his direction as a kind of peace offering, "you won't be seeing quite so much of each other. And you'll forget all about her. At your age, this trifling puppy love will one day seem like nothing."

"May I be excused?" Without waiting for an answer he brought his plate to the sink. Asking to be excused was a kind of ritual more than anything. It was a tip of the hat to his mother's fondness for a long-ago, more courteous era.

"You may," Mrs. Round said to his back as he went up to his room.

There they lay on his bedside table: the good-as-new Algebra book, *Conversational French Edition Trois*, *Modern American History*, which didn't seem terribly modern to him, and his least favorite, *Gray's Anatomy*. He had discovered that Algebra and French were cumulative. You couldn't ignore your studies for a month and then plunge in and expect to catch up. He was too far behind now for his usual sprint before examinations.

He had always admired how disciplined Dianne was about her studies. They never discussed what they would do after high school because there were too many other, more interesting subjects to explore. But he felt certain Dianne would go to a very good college somewhere. He hadn't given much thought to what would happen if he didn't. He thought life would go on as it had.

THE NEXT SATURDAY HE TELEPHONED DIANNE AND asked if he could come by to see her. She didn't seem exactly delighted by the idea, but he insisted until she finally agreed. He thought once they saw each other again, all would be fine.

As soon as the sun went down the temperature followed it. His motorcycle always started reluctantly in the cold. He wheeled it out into the driveway and pressed the starter. Nothing. Damn. He tried again. Still nothing. He cussed his motorcycle bloody.

Collecting his wits, he put the bike into second gear and rolled down the driveway towards the road to pop the clutch. With a chest-clearing cough, the engine came to life. He opened the throttle just enough to feed the carburetors, and off he went.

It was about thirty miles to Dianne's house. As he crossed the Bissell Bridge it began to snow. He had to keep his head down or the snow would build up around his eyes. The single headlight struggled to light the way through the increasingly wet snow. With no other cars on the road, he started to enjoy the ride, although feet and hands were frozen as he pulled into the gated Kingsbury driveway.

As he pulled up the drive, Byron saw Mr. Kingsbury taking out the trash. He looked up, startled, then continued on. He tossed the slick black bag into a green street bin.

Kingsbury looked smug, strolling over with his arms folded and chuckling. "She said you might come by tonight, but I thought you'd think better of it."

"Why's that, sir?"

"Why, my boy—with the weather, and all."

"It's not too bad." Only then did Byron realize that he was coated in snow from head to foot. Even he could see how absurd he must look. "Not to see Dianne."

He looked disappointed. "It will be cold when you turn to head home, too."

"I heard the snow's supposed to let up." He hoped this bit of optimism on his part might erase the scowl on Mr. Kingsbury's face. Instead, it only seemed to confirm his low opinion of Byron. "Besides, I'm used to it."

"What? Nonsense. They're calling for six more inches. Whoever told you that took you for a fool, son. You better wise up, or this world's gonna eat you for breakfast." At that he went back into the house, turning at the last and beckoning Byron with a reluctant, limp wave.

Byron, brushing the snow from his coat and jeans, followed up the salted walkway to the Kingsbury's big new house. He must have looked like he was near death, because when Mrs. Kingsbury met him at the door she insisted he undress and get into a hot shower. The thought of being naked in Dianne's house within five minutes of arrival gave him a terrific erection he fought to leave alone. He thought of baseball players and their stats, and his excitement faded.

Afterward the shower, which indeed felt wonderful, Dianne brought him a pair of Mr. Kingsbury's pants and a shirt to wear. Downstairs, the formerly sardonic Mr. Kingsbury offered him a glass of brandy, and it was then that Byron noticed how enormous their latest house truly was. Dianne still looked the same even though she had let her hair grow long and wore it pulled back with a pink ribbon—no, she looked more beautiful. He had always thought pink was a good color for her.

Mrs. Kingsbury, sipping wine, said they had attended a dance at the country club they now belonged to, but she didn't say with whom Dianne had gone.

Byron tried not to wince at the thought of his girl dancing with someone else.

"Well, I've got work early in the morning, so I'll say goodnight."

"On Sunday? I thought you were playing golf, Daddy?"

Kingsbury cut his eyes at his daughter. "Where do you think the fathers of the world do the world's business? It isn't always in boardrooms and offices."

With that he kissed Dianne on the forehead and went off to bed. Mrs. Kingsbury said Byron must stay in the guest room so long as his mother agreed it would be foolish to drive back under these treacherous conditions. Assured his mother wouldn't care one whit, she put an extra blanket on the guest bed and said good night.

At last Dianne snuggled next to him on the couch. He wanted to kiss her, but restrained himself. Maybe it was that her parents were thirty feet away on the other side of a wall or two, but he thought it might be more.

Instead they talked about school—how much she liked her swell new car, the differences between the schools, and then he noticed she twice mentioned a boy named Trevor Long. Trevor this; Trevor that.

Shaking with anger, Byron asked if she had gone to the dance with this Trevor. She said yes. He didn't dare ask if she had slept with him. His guts twisted with snakes.

"I better be going." When Byron stood up, his knees felt weak. He wasn't used to brandy. That's all it was.

"That's crazy. It's freezing out."

"It's cold in here, too."

She blinked her eyes. Bit her lip. "You're staying in the guest room. No arguing."

He agreed, and they said good night. A quick peck on his cheek. The heat from her soft lips lingered. He thought he might weep.

Tossing and turning, he knew he would never sleep with Dianne in the next room—and maybe never again—so he lay there watching as snow tumbled down in the light of a streetlamp in the side yard.

After an hour, however, the door opened and Dianne appeared, an angel in silhouette. She crawled into bed beside him. He had almost gotten to sleep. It felt like an unfolding dream.

"You mustn't make any noise." She put her finger to her lips and kissed him.

"I'll try." He drew her to him. "I love you, Dianne."

"Hush," she said, climbing on top. "You know I love you, too. It was just a dance."

Neither would sleep much. Some dreams do come true. But when Byron awoke, she was gone. It would not be the last time.

IN THE MORNING DIANNE ANNOUNCED SHE HAD BEEN accepted at Russell Sage College in upstate New York. An exclusive and expensive women's college, they only took the most qualified students. She said he would come and visit. He was glad it wasn't co-ed. Relieved as heck.

In June, Byron got his report card, and with so little interest in his subjects, he wound up with a string of Fs. That caught him a bit off guard. He thought he might at least have got a "D" in History. Nope. His mother had been wrong again—not even losing Dianne had helped his studying habits.

And worse, he never made it to visit his first love at her fancy college. Not after making a hard decision, one other guys often do after receiving failing grades like Byron's: he didn't go to college, and with the war going on across the ocean, that meant dumb motorcycle grease monkeys like him ended up in the Army. Maybe he'd be a mechanic, at least, and not infantry.

7

War is a little island you're on while the rest of the world is off somewhere out over the horizon ordering pizza and watching the game. After shipping out to Vietnam, Byron Round learned this fact fast and hard.

It was late afternoon when his unit got to the river, but the sun was still high, so he lay down in the tall grass and dreamed of Dianne. He tried to imagine what she was doing—he pictured her brown eyes, flat and unrevealing, but in certain moments going soft and loving. Her lips, full; her scratchy, sexy voice. Her lean body, the swell of a bony hip, the downy small of her back.

Did she ever think of him now? Ever wonder what he was doing, ever remember those now faraway times together? As time passed, it became apparent they had been children, then, with groping hands feeling their way into adult life. It all seemed like a fairy tale, one with an unsatisfactory ending.

He woke with a start and a dry throat, realizing he was a long way from making out with Dianne in Connecticut. Shaking off the rude wake-up, he ate some canned peaches Dean had shared, a luxury out in the field.

The pleasure, short-lived: when Byron looked up from the last bite, his buddy, now motioning with silent fury for him to get his ass in gear.

The sun now starting to set and with rifles in hand, Byron and Dean crouched low in the grass as they made their way towards the rushing water. The sound of the river clearing its throat as water tumbled over rocks would cover any noise they made.

When they were within thirty meters, Dean signaled him to get down and they waited. They had been to this spot before and never seen anything, but you never know. They kept a sharp eye on the tree line across the river.

ABOUT TWO HOURS AFTER SUNDOWN, BYRON THOUGHT he saw someone coming out of the tree line. The man looked to be about his age, maybe a bit younger. Eighteen, Byron guessed. He was wearing a white shirt and dark pants rolled up almost to his knees. He was carrying a long object in his hand; a bamboo fishing pole, perhaps, as the man also appeared to have a creel hanging from his shoulder. The native walked down to the river, looking right and left as he went along, and then sat down on some rocks. He cast his line into the water and waited.

After a moment it occurred to Byron that the man had not bothered to bait his hook. The young fisherman was there to catch a delicacy other than the inedible carp that filled that part of the river.

But they were fishermen too, and as any good fisherman will tell you, it takes patience to catch what you're after. An almost-full moon had emerged so Byron lowered his head, but that made it difficult to see through the blades of elephant grass.

When he looked up, he thought the fisherman had left, but he caught sight of him again. He had simply moved a few meters up stream. Either he waved his arm over his head, or Byron imagined that he had, but Byron wasn't imaging the three men coming out of the trees behind him. And they weren't carrying fishing poles. No, those were the unmistakable short barrels of AK-47's.

The fisherman dropped his pole and took a rifle from one of the other men. No need for make-believe now that they felt certain no one was around to observe them.

The four enemy soldiers waded across the river in a single file. Byron knew enough to wait until the lead man stepped on to near shore, and he could feel Dean and the rest of the squad getting ready off to his right.

When the fisherman stepped out of the river, he was no more than twenty-five meters from them. Byron could see his face clearly in the moonlight. He was handsome in that raw, country way, and for the first time Byron, his finger tightening against the cold trigger of his rifle, noticed the man had a red scarf tied around his neck.

The fisherman turned to see if the others were keeping up, and that's when Dean tagged him in the back. His body jerked, and he fell into the river; the other three froze in a shocked tableau for a split-second before the whole squad, Byron included, opened up. Bullets splashed into the river like hail from a summer storm. Two more of them fell in the water, but the fourth one made it back across the river and disappeared into the tree line.

"Searchers out." Sergeant Henley pointed to Dean and Byron and they raced to the river. The fisherman lay face down in the water. Byron was surprised by how cold it was. He started to go through the fisherman's pockets, but thought he should make certain the other two were dead first.

Dean and Byron dragged their bodies to the far shore and laid them on the sand. They were toast, all right.

Byron noticed blood, a heavy trail, in the sand. He whispered, "Missing man's a stuck piggy, sarge."

"Roger that. Everybody stay in the moment."

Sergeant Hanley waved them after the wounded one in the jungle. It wouldn't be hard to follow. It must have been a gut shot. Nothing else bleeds like that.

Quiet, with only an occasional rustle blending in with the natural ambiance, the squad moved into the brush like dancers—heel, toe, heel, toe.

ABOUT FIFTY METERS IN, THE POINT MAN HELD UP after finding the enemy's rifle. He couldn't be far ahead. They picked up the pace. It didn't matter if he heard them now.

Byron signaled Dean to go off to the left while he kept on straight ahead. The heavy underbrush tangled itself around his feet, and he tumbled onto wet moss that cushioned his fall.

He lay there a moment, listening. He could hear the wounded man up ahead. It sounded as if he was dragging his leg. No mistaking it. He couldn't be twenty meters out.

Dean heard it, too. Byron got up and moved towards the sound of branches cracking. The man must have been frightened to the point of panic to be making so much noise. He knew they were right behind him. All he could do now was try to hide. Cover and concealment, that's your last defense.

Then, there he was, his back pressed into some bushes. He looked right at Byron, so he knew he had been spotted. He didn't move, but kept staring at Byron as if he were invisible and Byron couldn't see him. What must he have been thinking?

Byron stepped out into the open. Dean came up behind, keeping his rifle trained on the man. "You tell him come-on-out," mocking.

Byron tried to remember the few phrases he had learned at language school. "*Omn noi shau, da lai troung ban.*" He said it again, but the man only stared back without comprehension.

Dean took a step closer to the man. "Fuck does that mean, hombre?"

"I think it means 'give me your weapon'."

"He already dropped his iron, shit for brains. Just tell him to bring his sorry ass on out here."

Dean slid off the safety. The *CLICK* startled all three of them. The man's eyes widened, and Byron tried to think of another phrase, one that might mitigate the explosive tension now filling the air. "*Lidi malin.*"

The man cocked his head, but still didn't move.

"We ain't got all fucking night."

No, they didn't, and the man was probably going to die anyway, so what difference did it make what Byron did? He motioned with his hand for the man to come out.

Still, he didn't move, but he hadn't taken his eyes off Byron since they had first spotted him. Byron was growing tired of that insinuating stare. If things were the other way around, the son of a bitch wouldn't waste any time before killing them. That's the way it is. Do onto others before they do onto you.

Byron shot him twice in the chest; clean, well placed, center-of-mass hits. The man fell backwards, but the bushes held him up. He almost looked as if he were still alive except for the way his head had collapsed onto his chest.

It didn't feel good. Byron stood frozen to the ground, looking at a human scarecrow he'd created, the life barely gone out of the man's eyes still staring back. "Fuck me."

"Shake it off. Asshole should have learned some English." Dean searched his pockets. "*Nothing*. I'll bet those three back there had some money on them."

"If they did, Sergeant Henley's got it, now."

"True story. All's well, et cetera. C'mon."

On the way back to the river they policed up the man's iron, and as they came out onto the sand flats, they saw a stake in the ground about five meters from the river. Drying blood wound around it like a red viper—the fisherman's head was perched on the stake. His eyes remained open. They gazed out over the river.

Byron saw a hoe lying in the sand. They must have used it to cut the fisherman's head off. "Are you guys nuts?"

"None of that crybaby bullshit." Sergeant Henley walked up to Byron so there would be no doubt that he wasn't going to take any crap off him. "That motherfucker doesn't need his head any more and we do." The squad laughed behind him.

"That should make those assholes think twice about fishing here." Byron couldn't see very well in the darkness, but he thought he recognized Corporal Sykes's voice.

THREE WEEKS LATER, DEAN WENT OUT ON PATROL WITH the gun crew from first squad because their ammo humper had gotten himself blown up the week before. When they crossed a field, a sniper shot Dean in the face.

All Byron heard over the radio was that first squad had one KIA so he went up to the road to meet them when they came in. Byron wasn't superstitious, not usually, but he had a bad feeling about this. Dean was a shitbird; a magnet for bad luck. Everybody said so.

When first squad came in, they had Dean's body under a poncho, but his arm rolled out and dangled off the stretcher like a summer dog's tongue. Byron began to cry until Sergeant Henley came up and told him to knock it off, and he was right about that, too. Everyone loses friends. They get shot in the goddamn face or their legs get blown off and sometimes their dicks go flying off too. One minute you're talking to some asshole like nothings going on, and five minutes later he's toast. After a while, you learn to keep it to yourself. Better that way. Do your job and stay quiet. Byron, a short-timer, would fall back into the World in twenty-eight days.

Two days later he encountered a corporal wearing one of Dean's shirts with his name stenciled on the back. He wanted it for himself, but it was like Sergeant Henley said about the guy whose head they had cut off—Dean didn't need that shirt anymore. Nor did Byron. It would be hard enough to forget all that horror for him as it was.

$$8$$

The flight back to the real world took fourteen hours. Not long, Byron thought, to travel to another state of mind. But the distance had nothing to do with this trip. The return—the wake-up. Like traveling from one dimension to another. What ought to have been comforting, however, at first felt more wrenching and alien than like 'home.'

Walking through the airport, Byron thought he saw a familiar face, a tall man in his fifties with greying hair. At first he couldn't place him, but like some bizarre miracle, Byron realized it to be Dianne's father. That once ramrod straight posture had bent a bit and his face was thinner, but other than that, the man looked the same.

It was only when Byron walked up to him that he could see Mr. Kingsbury had been unwell. His eyes had gone watery, and the veins on the back of his hands stood out blue beneath his pale skin. It was hard to remember him as the dashing man twirling Mrs. Kingsbury around the dance floor.

"Mr. Kingsbury, how are you, sir?" Byron held out his hand. "Byron Round?"

Surprised, the man squinted and shook his head. It was clear that, for a moment at least, he had no idea who Byron was. Had he changed so much, Byron thought?

At last Martin Kingsbury held out his hand while looking intently at Byron. "Byron Round, you say?"

"That's right." Byron let go of his hand. Mr. Kingsbury's grip was so weak Byron feared he might have hurt him.

"Well, how have you been? Still in the army, I see."

"I was discharged this morning." Byron had almost forgotten he still wore the uniform. "I've been overseas."

Mr. Kingsbury put down his suitcase, so Byron guessed they were going to talk. "Well—thank goodness you've returned looking so fit."

Involuntarily, Byron fingered the thin but jagged scar that ran from below his eye to his chin. Mr. Kingsbury couldn't have missed that—hamburger meat had been hanging out of the wound, superficial as it might have been. At least he didn't stare. "Thank you."

Byron already ran out of things to say. It would be out of the question to ask about Dianne, at least directly. He didn't want to appear too eager. But he was eager. Eager to learn how she was, to see her, to collapse all those years that had passed since they had last been together. "How is your family?" Byron said this as casually as he could, but his stomach was starting to tighten.

"Mrs. Kingsbury is still painting. She took first place in a juried competition at the museum this summer."

"She must have been very pleased." Byron wished Mr. Kingsbury would mention Dianne. Maybe they were both working up to that. Carefully.

As if reading Byron's mind, Mr. Kingsbury continued, "Dianne's had some medical issues. She dropped out of school for a few semesters. You know she was at Russell-Sage."

"Yes, she told me about that before I joined the army. I always thought she'd go to a great school." What kind of medical issues? "Is she still ill?" Byron put his duffle bag on the floor. Mr. Kingsbury didn't seem in any particular hurry to leave, which was odd because he had been rather cool towards Byron the last time they had seen each other. Not that Byron could exactly blame him for that.

"The doctors don't seem to really know what it is. They keep saying her recovery will take some time."

"Well, I hope she feels better, sir." Byron picked up his bag.

"What are your plans now? I mean, have you thought about what you're going to do? Your mother was a schoolteacher wasn't she? I'll bet she'd like you to go back to school." Mr. Kingsbury offered Byron a cigarette.

"No thanks, I don't smoke anymore."

"I would have guessed that where you've been, smoking was the least of your daily concerns." Mr. Kingsbury smiled and Byron realized he had never heard him laugh. That seemed outside his emotional range. It would have detracted from his dignity, like wrinkles in a suit. Both men realized, but in different ways, that Byron having been in the army made them strangers to each other.

"It's not that. I didn't like the habit part of it."

Mr. Kingsbury nodded that he understood. Any smoker would. "Jobs are hard to come by now. You would think with the war and all that, the economy would be booming. Even at the bank we're laying people off." An edge crept into his voice when he mentioned the war. It had grown unpopular at home.

"I've applied to the state police academy." That wasn't exactly true. Until that moment Byron hadn't given any thought to a job, but once he said it, being a policeman sounded about right.

"I'd have thought you'd want to get away from guns and uniforms." Mr. Kingsbury brushed some ash from his lapel. Then, realizing how condescending that sounded, he added, "I'll bet a lot of veterans want to be policemen." The word veteran came out of his mouth like some difficult-to-pronounce word in a foreign language.

"I'd better be going. My mother is waiting for me." Byron shouldered his duffel bag.

"Why don't you give us a call sometime? Come by for dinner even."

"I certainly will, sir." Byron turned to walk away.

"Byron."

He turned back to Mr. Kingsbury. "Yes sir?"

"You haven't asked for our number." The disappointment in Mr. Kingsbury's voice was unmistakable.

Faced with the fact that he might actually see Dianne again, Byron found he wasn't sure he wanted to. He hadn't forgotten all the unanswered letters he had written her, too many of them. Maybe it was better to simply move on, but as he was thinking that he knew he would have to see her, even if only to bring their relationship to a proper end. And that was important. Until you've shoveled the last bit of dirt over such artifacts, they keep walking around like zombies.

"I'm sorry, sir. I guess I was so surprised to see you here." Byron didn't know what else to say.

"Well, here's our number." Mr. Kingsbury handed him a piece of paper and Byron took it without looking at it. He made a great deal of folding it carefully and putting it into my wallet.

"I better be off." Byron hadn't gone twenty steps when Mr. Kingsbury called after him.

"I'll tell Dianne to expect to hear from you."

Byron nodded that they could indeed expect to hear from him. He could almost feel that telephone number in his wallet. It bore the weight of all his childish and strangely resilient dreams.

As he walked along the crowded corridor to the central terminal, it dawned on him that Dianne was out there somewhere, and that he would see her again. The thought put a spring in his weary, wounded self, and he decided he would put away his resentments, along with his uniform, about the army and the war.

But he'd learned enough to suspect the troubling aspects of his service wouldn't be put to rest so easily. Did he know they'd wriggle like snakes in a bag, persistent and hissing, for years to come? Not yet. But he would.

❧

HE SPOTTED HIS MOTHER'S CAR PARKED BEHIND A BUS.

She looked smaller than he remembered her; more frail. He waved, but she didn't see him—or more likely, she didn't recognize him.

When he got nearer to the car he called out, and she finally waved back. Her smile looked more like relief than joy. He had never thought about dying during the war, but he supposed she must have thought he might, given how terrible the results of the campaign.

Byron dropped his duffel bag in the back seat and climbed into the car. His mother leaned towards him, but they had never been much of a family for affection. She squeezed his arm. It would do.

"I can't believe you still have this car." He patted the dashboard the way you would a favorite horse. "It looks great."

"The vehicle is well-tended. You can be sure of it." With that Mrs. Round put the car into gear and they headed home. She stopped at a bakery near Vernon Circle where they used to go to on the way home from church.

When she got back in the car, she held up the pink cake box. "Strawberry shortcake." Byron must have looked confused because she added, "Your favorite."

He was sure what she said must be have been true, but he didn't remember his favorite cake, or his favorite anything, for that matter. Even the idea of having a 'favorite' cake seemed preposterous. Alien. Indulgent. "Thank you."

"Wait—you don't remember, do you?"

"It's been a long time since I had any cake."

"I always used to make it for your birthday." Mrs. Round was almost pleading now. "Don't you even remember that?"

"Of course I do." Please get the hell off Memory Lane. Out of habit he felt in his shirt pocket for a cigarette. He'd decided to quit. Three tours, and a stint in the hospital, will put a man to smoking hard, and his lungs had been hurting.

"Well, I'm glad you remember your childhood with me."

"No, right," he said, faraway, lying like a rug. "It doesn't seem that long ago. Strawberry shortcake. Yeah, mom. I forgot. I mean—I remember."

His mother drove them down Route 83. They passed by Welles

Farm, Maddox Furniture and the post office where he used to go to get the suspension notices from school; there, Talcott Mills, and then 19 Elm Street. He was home. As deep into the civilian world as you could get. Byron relaxed, finally. A little.

THE HOUSE WAS THE SAME, BUT NOT. THE PAINT ON THE shutters was peeling, the grass looked as if it hadn't been cut in weeks, and there were shingles missing off the roof. He recognized the white painted brick, the red front door with the brass knocker, the large maple tree in the backyard, but everything seemed different, older, exhausted.

Byron followed his mother into the kitchen. "Why don't you go and—change?" They were like two strangers sitting next to each other on a long flight.

"Sure thing, mom."

"I'll make you a cup of tea to go with your cake."

"Sure."

He went up the narrow stairs to his room. It was as he remembered it. He looked out of the window by his bed and it was as if I'd never been to the war. All of that seemed impossible with him here in this room again, the room he had slept in as a boy. He had to wrestle into place in his mind who he now was, the past a jigsaw puzzle with unfamiliar pieces everywhere he looked.

He left the lock on his duffle bag and put it in the attic. When he opened his dresser drawer, he saw shirts belonging to someone heavier than he was now, a boy who liked bright colors.

He opened the door to his closet and there were all his old clothes hanging there in memoriam. He nearly jumped out of his skin. The closet smelt of mothballs. He found a pair of blue pants but they were too big, so he tucked his red shirt into his khaki uniform trousers.

When he saw himself in the mirror, all dressed up as the boy he used to be, he couldn't help but think of the guy wearing Dean's shirt. Wasn't Byron an imposter too now, only he was impersonating himself? He wished he had stayed in the service. They had offered him a bonus to reenlist. He'd been a fool for coming home.

Or had he—maybe seeing Dianne's father meant good times ahead. Meant Byron should have hope.

"What's taking you so long?" His mother's voice floated up the stairwell.

"I'll be right down." It was as if he was late for school or church. He took a deep breath and let the air out, slow, counting to ten. He wondered if his breath stank of war. He could still taste it at the back of his teeth.

In the kitchen he saw his mother had decorated the cake with birthday candles. He counted them. Twenty-one. Is that how old he was? Surely it wasn't his birthday. His entire body ached. He felt a hundred and twenty-one.

"I know it's not your birthday, but it feels like it is now that you're home. And by God, we're going to celebrate." Mrs. Round cut a slice of cake for each of them. She was using the china and silverware she normally reserved for guests. Well, wasn't he a guest?

"I bumped into Mr. Kingsbury at the airport." He said that knowing what his mother's response would be, but he thought it best to get it all into the open.

"I hope you're not going to start up with that girl again."

"I'm not going to start anything. I was saying I saw her father in the airport. It was weird. Maybe it means something. I dunno."

"We all still live near one another. Seeing him at that airport isn't some mystical 'happening.' I swear—that girl holds some wicked power over you."

His mother stopped speaking. They both knew she was referring to the witchcraft of sex. She characterized it that way many times. Maybe his father leaving made more sense, suddenly.

"You're right. This cake is delicious." He hoped that would be the circuit breaker that would disconnect his mother from talking about Dianne.

No such luck. "You realize she got into some kind of trouble while you were gone. Real trouble. With the law."

"Her father told me about that." Of course, Byron was lying. Mr. Kingsbury hadn't said anything about her getting into trouble. He said Dianne had been sick.

"Did he tell you what she did?"

"He said she was sick and dropped out of school for a while."

"That's not what I heard. Oh, no." Mrs. Round put one spoon of sugar in her tea and stirred, clinking the china. "Next week will be the one-year anniversary of your aunt's passing."

Oh, right—he'd been pained to get the news while overseas, but in all the 'excitement' of Dean taking one in the face and Byron himself getting shot, he had forgotten. "Sorry I couldn't make it home for the funeral."

"You were in the hospital. Nothing you could do." His mother helped herself to more tea. "Your lieutenant told us they were going to send you home after you got hurt. He said you might lose your eye."

"You know the army. All that red tape bullshit. It's still there." He checked himself. His mother hated profanity. "Once I got out of rehab, they sent me right back."

"You've lost so much weight. Your clothes are hanging off you." His mother cut him another slice of cake.

"I'll be fine."

"Eat."

"I'm good."

"I insist. You're my son, and—and I insist. Now eat another slice for mother." It went on like that until he couldn't sit still any longer. He cleared away his cup and plate and put them in the sink as he used to do.

How quiet the house was compared to his life of the last few years. His mother looked lost in the blank spaces he used to fill. And Bryon began to suffer visions of the war he'd left behind the way he had dreamed of Dianne while overseas.

9

Once home, it only took Byron five days to get his motorcycle running. He painted the tank and fender fire engine red and the tire rims marigold yellow. When the engine coughed into life for the first time in three years, he felt free again. He could go anywhere he liked, now. No orders. No officers or Sarge barking commands and cuss-words.

He found his old helmet in the tool shed behind some storm windows. Once he cleaned off the cobwebs, it looked good as new.

A sudden miracle—out on the road, he felt as he had when he got his first bicycle, the one he rode to Dianne's house years ago. He roared up and down country inclines, through dense shadowy overhangs of tree canopy, streaking across sunlit straightaways surrounded by fields and farms, the vibration of life under his guts. Free. Before he realized it, he'd ended up at the Rhode Island state line.

Giddy and half-mad, he sat at a scenic turnout overlooking a reservoir along a deserted stretched of the Hartford Pike. He remembered some racy joke his friend Dean had made one time. Laughed to himself.

Sudden, Byron began to weep, hard, into his gloves. It went on in fits and starts for almost an hour. It was for every time he had wanted to let the emotions go while in-country, which you couldn't do. Now? He had to get it out.

It felt good afterwards, like he had showered off under a clear, cold mountain waterfall. Back on the turnpike west toward Hartford, Byron wondered if he was losing his mind. But also felt better, somehow? How strange. A good cry. Surely it would take more than that to get over being in the war.

WHILE DIGGING IN HIS WALLET TO GRAB A COKE AND pay for gas at a service station, he found the note Mr. Kingsbury had given him. Gripped by urgency, he flung down a few bills and rushed outside to telephone Dianne from the payphone box.

Mrs. Kingsbury answered and said she had been expecting his call; wondered what had taken so long.

"Is she there? Is Dianne there?"

"Yes, but. Well. It's late." She said while Dianne was asleep for now, they would expect him for lunch on Sunday.

He said he'd think about it, and might have hung up without saying goodbye. He wasn't sure. He needed to talk to her. Wasn't it important enough to wake her up?

He would wait. Fine. He hoped it wouldn't rain on Sunday. Byron didn't want to arrive at their house looking like a cat that had fallen into a pond.

HE NEEDN'T HAVE WORRIED; SUNDAY DAWNED SUNNY and clear. Stayed that way.

He remembered the Kingsburys ate dinner at one o'clock, so he arrived fifteen minutes early. He didn't have any nice civilian clothes that fit, so he wore his khaki army pants with a yellow polo shirt he hoped would smell less musty after the ride over to the house. Self-consciousness about his appearance wasn't new. Dianne and her parents had always been so well-dressed.

Mr. Kingsbury answered the door and greeted him so warmly he began to wonder why their feelings towards him had changed. Dianne's father escorted him out to the pool where a table had been set for lunch, cold chicken with fruit and white wine.

Mrs. Kingsbury came out and kissed him on both cheeks in European fashion. She said Dianne was still getting dressed and then hinted that she was a bit nervous about seeing him again after so much time. They had put orange, yellow and purple flowers from their garden into the pool where they drifted in lazy circles.

Dianne, and wearing a white dress with a white ribbon in her hair, came out with a tray of cheese and crackers. Byron guessed she was playing tennis again.

She put the tray down and came over to him and held her hand out without speaking. He held her hand and the two of them stood for a moment without saying a word. All the debris and disillusionment had suddenly vanished.

"Dianne, ask Byron if he would like a drink." Mrs. Kingsbury uncorked a bottle of wine and they all laughed as Byron let Dianne's hand drop.

"Would you like a drink?"

"Yes, thank you." His knees felt weak.

Here they all were again, gathered around the pool, sipping wine as if he had only been away for a day. Dianne looked wonderful, her parents were cordial, he was dressed improperly; not much had changed.

Or had it? He couldn't help but follow Dianne with his eyes, as he had at the country club dance however many years ago. The way the Kingsburys accepted privilege as their due, how he envied and despised them at the same time. How at ease they always seemed, never caught out in the wrong clothes, never unsure which fork to use, confident that good manners would see them through anything.

When Mrs. Kingsbury came outside with a pitcher of drinks, he sprang to attention. His manners were of the rough, military kind among people who admired casual grace above everything. He must have looked like a Prussian doorman, with his short hair and too-shiny shoes.

He noticed Dianne was wearing sandals. Her toenails were painted pale pink. He tried not to swoon.

Mr. Kingsbury offered Byron a glass of wine. "I was telling Dianne's mother that you're applying to the State Police Academy."

Being a policeman might be a good way to decompress, he thought. *Come up slowly from the war so I don't get the bends.* What else would he do—sell insurance, be a security guard at Mr. Kingsbury's bank? Become a hired killer? After being in combat, he certainly had those skills. "I've already sent in my application."

"We've got a pretty good training program at the bank for returning veterans." Martin Kingsbury made it sound as though the idea had just occurred to him, but Byron suspected the Kingsburys had talked it over before he arrived.

"I think being a policeman is a good fit for me just now."

Martin frowned, but turned cordial. "Try some of this cheese. It's from France."

"Oh, yes—I can only get it this time of year. Dianne adores it." Mrs. Kingsbury's eyebrows and nodding head seemed to yearn for confirmation, and on cue, her daughter nodded that she indeed loved the cheese.

How rehearsed it all seemed. Dianne winked to let him know she knew how absurd all this was. Byron remembered how much he had liked that about her—sharing secrets kept from the grownups.

"After lunch, why don't you kids take a plunge in the pool?" Suzanne Kingsbury lit a cigarette and exhaled with a great flourish. "Martin says you've quit smoking, Byron. I wish I could. These damn things will be the death of me."

"It wasn't that hard to quit, really."

"How did you do it?"

"One day I said to myself, after midnight I'll never smoke another cigarette, and I haven't." Byron shrugged. "I became a non-smoker. I imagined it before I went to sleep that night. And the next morning, that's what I was. Or that was the first step, anyway. Telling myself what I was."

"You military men are all about discipline. We artists go with our emotions." Mrs. Kingsbury laughed and seemed to invite them to laugh with her and they did.

"I don't know about discipline." Byron's voice got faraway. "I read it in a self-help book. I can't remember what the term was. Affirming your desire. Some stuff like that."

"Well, I 'affirm' I'll have a refill on this wine," Mrs. Kingsbury said with a titter. "Martin?"

It was then that Byron noticed Dianne was the only one not having a glass of wine. She was drinking tonic water with a slice of lime. He figured it was too early in the day for her.

THEY SAT DOWN TO EAT AND ENJOYED THE AFTERNOON. The news was mostly good: Mr. Kingsbury was in line to become president of the bank, but he disliked commuting into Hartford each day. Mrs. Kingsbury was studying painting with an artist from Russia or Hungary who had won all kinds of prizes; she promised to show Byron her work after lunch. Dianne was taking a few courses at the local community college, nothing too taxing, psychology and an art class. All-American as you could want.

No one asked about the war. They were too polite for that, so Byron described all the countries he had seen as if he had been on The Grand Tour. The army had left him restless and impatient with civilian life. Byron began to wiggle his foot under the table. He admired how serene the Kingsburys appeared.

They had sorbet after lunch and Dianne helped her mother clean up. Martin Kingsbury said what a coincidence it was that he had run into Byron at the airport, because he and Mrs. Kingsbury had been talking about him. He said they thought it was charming the way Byron would ride his bicycle to their house every spring, later a motorcycle.

Byron announced how glad he was to be back, and that, indeed, it had been a happy airport coincidence. "Maybe even destiny."

"That's poetry." Martin looked Byron in the eye. "You'll find that in real life, a man makes his own destiny."

An awkwardness followed, with no mention of the unpleasant time of Dianne's life that was to follow those youthful visits from Byron. One thing he noticed was how adroitly the Kingsburys stepped around all the bits of the past that might take away from the pleasantness of the afternoon. If you don't mention those things, maybe they simply go away. That same principle probably meant they hadn't mentioned his name in years—why would they?

Byron wondered what had brought him back to life in this beautiful home with a pool on the edge of a forest. He didn't fool himself for a moment thinking a policeman's salary, a working class job, was what the Kingsburys wished for their daughter. And yet they seemed to welcome him. Strange.

AT LAST MR. AND MRS. KINGSBURY MADE A BIG production number of bustling around to go into the house to watch a golf match, leaving Dianne and Byron by the pool. A stillness descended in their absence.

He put his glass of wine down without finishing it. His head was spinning quite enough without alcohol. He looked at Dianne. Smiled.

"I'm glad you bumped into my father at the airport."

"If I hadn't, I guess we would never have seen each other again." Byron said this to let her know how tenuous he thought their meeting today was. "Right?"

"That's not so. Laura Granville told me that you'd been wounded."

"I'm in one piece. Just a scratch," pointing to the jagged scar he knew made him marked as having been in some kind of painful difficulty. More like the tough guy in the background than the handsome hero, but not too bad.

"You were the only boy in our class to join the army, so it was rather shocking to everyone. I felt responsible in a way."

"Why is that?" He knew perfectly well why she felt that way, but he wanted to hear her say it just the same.

"That night I told you about the boy I was dating. I thought that might've had an influence on you quitting school."

"School was ready for me to quit. I flunked out."

"I certainly didn't mean to hurt you. We had moved away. And at that age—"

"Enough." He stopped her from going on. "That was a long time ago. We were other people then. I'm just glad to see you again."

"I'm sure there were times when you thought we'd never be together again."

"I never thought I'd be back again. No."

But slowly, overwhelmed by the memory of how much she had once meant to him, all the resentment he had nurtured over the years started to ebb. Memories are fool's gold. That's what Dean used to say when Byron would talk about Dianne as they stood watch at night. But the false, hopeful luster began to shine with reality instead of fantasy. It wasn't then. It was now.

"My mother asked what had become of you, but I wasn't sure of that myself. 'I broke his heart'. You ask her—that's what I said." A shadow crossed her face. "I broke everyone's heart. To hear them tell it."

"That's all in the past." He said it without conviction. The past is always waiting around the next bend to become the present again. It ambushes you whenever you let your guard down. "It's ancient history. Forgotten."

"I hope so." Dianne smiled and pulled the ribbon from her hair. Her sun-streaked hair fell over one eye and he almost reached out to brush it back, but that bit of familiarity was from another life. She took his hand. He was a boy again, not a man who had been to war. It felt good.

"I thought about you so much overseas."

"Mostly during target practice, I'll bet." Dianne laughed and so did he.

"There were long stretches on patrol at night, when I'd be on guard for movement in the jungle. But my mind always found its way back to you. And here."

"You thought about holding hands with me? Like we used to?"

He asserted that it had been so. And many more warm memories.

They went for a walk in the woods behind her house. Neither of them spoke much; they strolled along the path that followed a stream through the woods. He couldn't suppress a soldier's anxiety about being there in that closed-in forest. Not so long ago, he had killed a man in a place not too different from this. But that life too now seemed even more surreal. *What a mystery my own life is to me*, he thought.

"Do you ever think of the night we went to the country club dance?" He said this without looking at her. He was speaking to himself as much as to Dianne.

"I remember you putting your arm around me." Dianne walked ahead of him, maybe so he couldn't see what she was thinking as she spoke. "I wish life could've stayed like that."

"So do I." As he watched her, he thought she wasn't much different from how she had been before.

She turned around to face him. "That was the happiest I've ever been. I didn't know it that night, but I do now."

He threw a pebble into the stream. "Well, moments like that don't last. Everybody changes. Everybody grows up."

"I'd like to think they do." She sounded none too certain. He wondered again what those unnamed medical issues were that her father had mentioned. "Maybe I will, one day."

"I didn't have any choice. Not in the war." He wanted to change the subject. "I start at the academy in three weeks, and I'd like to see you again before I go. There won't be much chance for me to get away, not once we start."

She took his hand. "I work after school at a restaurant down-town, but my weekends are free."

Did she say that so he would know there were no boyfriends lurking around? "Nice of your father to ask me to come by today."

"He always liked you. I know you think he didn't, but he did. He thought you were a bit rough, but nice. He was away when we heard that you had been hurt. I called to tell him and he said, I think that boy loved you."

"He looks a bit different than I remember. Of course, I remember him as he was years ago."

"He had a heart attack two years ago. A mild one, but serious enough." Dianne looked towards her house. "We'd better get back. Dad will think you've strangled me and left me in the woods."

"I thought of that more than a few times." He put his arm around her. Their narrow hips bumped together as they walked like in the old days.

"I know. That's why I said it."

IT WAS GETTING DARK AS THEY GOT CLOSE TO THE house. All the lights were on, even the pool lights, and the stately home looked as if it were floating among the trees. A dog barked off in the woods. The landscaping had little lights glowing beneath the shrubs. What was Byron doing here among these rich people?

When Mrs. Kingsbury saw them coming across the terrace she smiled and waved. "I thought you two had gotten lost. I was about to call the police when I remembered how you intend to become an officer yourself so I thought, how much danger could she be in? With a service member of character?"

"None, ma'am. No danger at all. I'd kill for Dianne."

"I'm sure you would, son."

Mr. Kingsbury offered Byron a crisp martini in a chilled glass with two olives. It tasted wonderful, raw and bracing. Again, no one offered Dianne a drink.

"Won't you stay for dinner? I'm making a roast." Mrs. Kingsbury opened the stove door to display the meat sizzling on a broiler pan. It smelled delicious. Of course she was an excellent cook. Byron remember they entertained a good deal, people from the bank and local artists.

"I'd better be getting back. I've put my motorcycle back together only yesterday. I'm not sure how reliable it is." He looked for his coat.

"I put your things in the guest room. I was hoping you'd stay." Mrs. Kingsbury went off and came back with his coat and helmet. "These weigh a ton."

Dianne walked him outside and watched as he stomped again and again to get the reluctant motor to turn over. The angrier he got, the more Dianne laughed. At last they were both overcome with giggles at his frustration.

When the engine finally started, she cheered and came over to say goodbye. They hadn't kissed yet, they hadn't even held hands, but everything felt as it used to. But on the long ride home, he remembered all that had gone wrong between them the first time, even if teenage romance now seemed a thousand years ago. Like his mother often said, keepsakes of the heart tucked into dim closets don't always stay hidden.

10

After graduation from the state police academy Byron asked to be assigned to D Troop in Simsbury so he could be near Dianne. He rented a carriage house apartment behind the main house on a horse farm owned by a lawyer named Robert Taylor. Mr. Taylor was glad to have a trooper on the property, so he reduced the rent by half.

Byron was surprised by how welcoming the people in the county were. These were affluent people who looked upon the police as an occasional annoyance, but understood they could be useful from time to time. In rural areas people would wave to him when he drove by in his cruiser. Being in uniform helped him ease back into civilian life.

The army had left him feeling he was still capable of doing what he had done during the war and he was glad to see that anxiety subside, if only a little. He wondered how many other men there were like him, back from the war and yet not. They were POWs same as the real ones left behind.

BYRON SETTLED IN TO A ROUTINE OF WORK AND SEEING

Dianne, and it wasn't long as a street cop before he began to develop his own stable of snitches, lowlifes who would rat out anyone in exchange for his telling the prosecutor that they were cooperating with the state. It took no time at all to get cynical and realize it was all a game, so-called 'justice', a kind of pin-the-tale-on-the-donkey where truth took a few hard knocks on the head.

He even turned up some good leads for the Bureau of Criminal Investigation. While riding down a back road he had seen a shed with its door open and in it were some tools with their handles painted red. He remembered a doctor in town who had reported tools like that being stolen from his garage.

Byron didn't need a warrant; the tools were in plain view. He turned his cruiser down the dirt road that led to a trailer off to the side of the shed. Then he turned off the motor and waited. Whoever had stolen those tools would be looking out of the window, and then? He'd know why Byron was there. He only needed to give the thief enough time to wilt.

About twenty minutes later a boy came out of the house with a woman Byron guessed was his mother. He had probably confessed to her, and she had talked him into coming out. Byron told the mother where her son was going to be locked up and then handcuffed him. When he put the boy in the back of the cruiser, he began to cry.

On the way to the jail Byron asked him who had helped him break into the doctor's house, and the boy gave him the name Lyman Schuler, an older con he had been trying to nail on something for months.

I'll get this creep in the morning, Byron thought. *No rush.*

When the accomplice learned that his friend had been collared, Lyman came looking to shut his partner up and cover tracks. Rats to the cheese. The young cop, on the hunt, felt some of the excitement he'd known during the war, but without the danger of incoming mortar rounds or stepping on landmines designed to remove a soldier's manhood, and more. Hunting crooks felt good, until it didn't. You had to be there to understand. It turned into another way for a man's soul to get poisoned. For a man to get sick of the world, and want to take action. But you couldn't. They'd put a man like that away.

⚡

HE WAS LEADING TWO LIVES NOW; AT WORK IT WAS LIKE the war in many ways, only dialed back a click or two, while off-duty he spent all his time with Dianne in the slow rhythms of civilian life. When they were together, he appeared like everyone else; they went shopping together, he picked her up at the garage when she dropped her car off, they watched movies at his place and made love when she stayed over. It was almost boring in a comfortable and comforting sort of way.

Then Dianne applied to be a substitute teacher at the elementary school near her parent's house. Their lives were maturing alongside one another. Maybe it was fate.

Byron was filing out some paperwork on a DUI arrest he had made the night before when his patrol commander called him into his office. Lieutenant Atkins didn't ask him to sit down, so he stood at attention.

The lieutenant slid a piece of paper across his desk. "Read this."

It was a report from the state police laboratory, a drug test done for the Simsbury school board. Byron could see the positive results marked in red.

"Isn't your girlfriend named Dianne Kingsbury?"

"Yes, sir. Why do you ask?"

"That's her drug screen, done by us at the request of the school board so she can be certified as a substitute teacher."

The patrol commander and Byron weren't exactly friends, but they had always gotten along so he was a bit surprised by the lieutenant's tone. "She told me she was applying for a job there."

"Did she tell you she's a drug user?"

"We spend time together almost every day. Certainly I would have noticed."

"Well, apparently you didn't. She tested positive for several pain killers—like morphine."

"Her parents told me she'd been sick. She was even in the hospital for a month last year. If she has a prescription, there shouldn't be any problem." Maybe the lieutenant didn't know all this. To him Dianne was only a name, now, and a set of statistics on a damn lab report.

Christ—they make mistakes in the lab all the time.

"She's been arrested twice for possession and once for falsifying script. She doesn't have a current, valid prescription for the drugs that showed up in her urine." The lieutenant leaned back in his chair and waited for Byron to speak. In the gap he added, "Brother, she was in drug rehab June thru July of last year, pursuant to a court order."

"I've known her since we were twelve. We were in sixth grade together."

"She's an addict and you're a trooper. The two don't go together very well. Did she tell you about the arrests, about rehab?"

"No, sir."

"See what I mean? She knows you're a trooper, and she didn't tell you about her drug problem, so that makes it your problem as well. You follow?"

Of course Byron understood what he meant. It was unfolding so fast Byron could hardly grasp what he should do next.

"Headquarters wants you to take a polygraph tomorrow morning."

"Why is that?" Did they suspect him of using drugs too? His lower back began to ache from standing at attention.

"They want to make sure you didn't know anything about her drug use." The patrol commander pulled out a sheet of paper that Byron was to sign saying he voluntarily agreed to take the polygraph exam and waived any and all legal rights he may have enjoyed before doing so.

"And if I don't sign?"

"Is there any reason why you shouldn't?"

He swallowed hard. "No."

"Good. If you refuse the test, you're fired; if you fail the test, you're fired. Sign the waiver." He handed Byron a pen.

The trooper, still wet behind the ears, did as he was told.

"Be here at zero seven hundred hours tomorrow."

"Yes, sir." No ambiguity about what Byron was expected to do. He liked that. It was what he had missed about army life. Things were clear. You knew what to do and, more importantly, what not to do.

"All right, now that I've told you that, you can sit."

"Thank you." Byron's knees were beginning to shake, perhaps from standing for so long, but more likely because everything had changed for him in a moment. Dianne and he were going along so nicely and now... what? This new infidelity, that's what. Hadn't the old one been enough?

"I want to tell you this crap because you've got decisions to make, and I want you to make the right one. We have a lot of troopers like you—guys who came back from the war and can't seem to fit in. Then they come here, and they find what they're looking for. I want that for you."

"I feel like I'm fitting in. Enjoying the work."

"Check. And you were in the top of your class at the academy, and your evaluations have all been outstanding." The patrol commander's telephone rang, and he nodded to Byron that he was dismissed before he picked it up. It was probably the polygraph examiner. "Don't throw that away because of some girl. They love a man in uniform. You can get another one."

On the drive home, Byron wondered how right his patrol commander might have been. If he cared to admit it, he had felt lost since he'd left the army, and now he'd be back in a world he understood, with a weapon resting on his hip.

But why hadn't Dianne told him about her stay in rehab, about the drug arrests? *What else is she keeping from me?*

He changed out of his uniform and drove to her house without phoning first. He'd never done that before. While the Kingsburys had made him feel as if he was one of them, it was understood that family members should also be courteous toward one another.

❧

He knocked. Mrs. Kingsbury answered.

"What an unexpected pleasure. I didn't know you were coming by this evening," a hint of a rebuke in her voice. "I'll get Dianne."

"Thank you."

Byron followed her into the living room. Martin Kingsbury sat reading the paper. On the table next to him was a glass with what looked like a whiskey sour. Mr. Kingsbury nodded when he saw Byron and gave him a guarded smile. So the news about Dianne's drug test had reached them already.

Dianne, her eyes downcast, came in and sat down next to her father. The three of them were grim faced. No one had asked him to sit, so Byron continued to stand, stiff like at the office earlier.

"Where are my manners?" Mrs. Kingsbury stepped in to the kitchen. "Would you like a drink, Byron?" Without waiting for him to answer she poured him a glass of wine and then another for herself. "And do have a seat." Suzanne was back to being the gracious hostess, her voice welcoming, her face beaming at her special guest.

Byron sat down in a chair by the window, one facing Dianne and her father. Who were these people, he thought?

Mrs. Kingsbury brought him a drink, but he put it down without tasting it. One always took a sip from the offered glass and commented favorably on the wine. This little breech of etiquette rippled across the room.

"One of our branch banks had a bit of a scare today. A man walked in and tried to hold up the teller, but two of your fellows showed up and that was it. Turns out he didn't even have a gun. Nice work by the police just the same." Dianne and her mother nodded that it was nice police work indeed.

"I hope you like that wine, Byron. It's from Argentina. An exotic new imported vintage, with a robust, complex finish."

Mrs. Kingsbury, he realized, was offering him an opportunity to make up for not having said how much he enjoyed the wine. "I'm sure it's quite nice," he said, but Byron left the glass untouched. This wasn't the same as tasting the wine and going on about how wonderful it was, but it was all he could muster. He admired how the three of them sat there, almost numb with composure. They were wonderful liars.

"Dianne is thinking about taking a vacation out west." Martin Kingsbury brightened up as he made this announcement. "I've been trying to talk her into it for some time now." He gave Dianne a little wink, as though the two of them were sharing a secret with Mrs. Kingsbury and Byron for the first time.

What surprised him most was how Dianne seemed to be absolutely beaming at the news. Was he the only one in the room alarmed that Dianne had tested positive for drugs? "I was called in by my patrol commander this afternoon to talk about Dianne's drug test."

There—now they couldn't go on chatting about nothing, as if this were just another day.

"Why on earth would they bother you about that?" Mrs. Kingsbury seemed more annoyed by the fact that Byron had been told about the drug test than by the fact of Dianne's testing positive for narcotics.

"I'm a state trooper, Mrs. Kingsbury, and my—well." He couldn't seem to find of the right words to describe his relationship with Dianne. "The woman I'm seeing tested positive for narcotics today." His mouth was so dry that he couldn't speak any longer.

"Well, I'm sorry they troubled you about that, Byron. I really am. This all seems like much ado about nothing." Suzanne Kingsbury smiled reassuringly and waited for him to return her look with one of relief now that everything had been cleared up. But, of course, nothing had been cleared up, only covered up.

"Why didn't you tell me you'd been arrested for possession, that you'd been to rehab? Why didn't any of you tell me?" Byron looked at Dianne, but she didn't say anything. The three of them seemed unpleasantly surprised at the way he was taking this. He was certainly being a poor sport.

"We did tell you, Byron. We said Dianne had been unwell and in the hospital for a month." Mrs. Kingsbury smiled, but it was obvious she was growing somewhat impatient with his stubbornness.

"You made it sound as if she had been sick." Byron felt like a man losing his footing.

"Addiction is a disease, Byron. I know for a policeman that's hard to understand, but all the doctors tell us that it is." Mrs. Kingsbury's tone was one you would use with a not particularly bright child. Byron wondered how long she would go on indulging his thickheadedness.

"It's not like I was using heroin or anything. I hurt myself playing tennis and took too many pain killers." Dianne wasn't the least bit contrite. She was parroting the party line on her drug use.

"You failed the drug test you took two weeks ago."

"You know they stay in your system for weeks. I swear I haven't used anything since then." Dianne smiled at him and looking at her sitting there in her parents' living room, he believed her. All the years they had known each other were simply too much for one possibly mistaken lab report to erase. But he couldn't quite shake the feeling that he believed her simply because he wanted to. Her parents believed her, or, at least, pretended to.

"She wouldn't even take her sinus medicine last night." Mrs. Kingsbury laughed, and they all smiled. How adroitly she had made Dianne's problem seem silly. Just a mistake that anyone might make; and isn't the law being a wee bit grumpy about what is, after all, a family matter.

"I've been ordered to take a polygraph exam tomorrow." Byron hadn't got completely onboard the departing feel-good train yet.

"What on earth for?" This was the first real concern Mrs. Kingsbury had shown since he'd arrived.

"They want to be sure I had no knowledge of Dianne's drug use."

"What happens if you refuse to take the exam?" Mr. Kingsbury lit another cigarette. He too sounded concerned. Byron wondered what had happened to their initial airy dismissal of all this business.

"Mr. Kingsbury is being considered for the presidency of the bank. Making Dianne look like some crack-head certainly wouldn't be helpful just now." Suzanne Kingsbury's tone was more strained.

"If I refuse to take the exam, I'll be fired."

"Maybe that would be good. I don't mean you being fired, I mean if you were to resign. I'd love to have you join us here at the bank. We're looking for NCO's with combat experience. They make great managers." Mr. Kingsbury looked around the room and everyone shook their heads in agreement, everyone except Byron. Dianne's father said, "The bank needs someone like you—a man who can think clearly in a crisis."

"I like my job, sir."

"There's no money in it. You and Dianne will want to get married one day, have a family and a home. That takes money." That was the first time anyone had mentioned Dianne and he might get married. Byron was surprised that it was Mr. Kingsbury who had brought it up.

"You know dad is right, Byron." Dianne came over and sat on his lap with a familiarity she had never shown before in front of her parents.

Now that he thought about it, he did want to marry her. This dope business was like she said—blown way out of proportion. As a boy, he'd imagined being with Dianne forever. Maybe that dream was the right one to hold after all.

He had been afraid to let himself think so seriously before, because he was certain her parents would object. Byron was flattered by how eager they seemed to accept the idea. Suddenly things had changed around yet again. Before coming here he thought Dianne and he might be through, but now? Now they were talking about tying the knot. Byron's head felt funny, like that space between waking and dreaming. He supposed this was real. Not much had felt that way, not after shipping out.

IN THE MORNING BYRON PUT ON YET ANOTHER uniform, this one with its new trooper first class chevron, the one he had been so proud of only a few months earlier, and drove to the D Troop barracks.

His patrol commander and the polygraph examiner were there waiting for him. He handed them his hand-written letter of resignation. Then he went downstairs to supply and turned in his uniform and weapon. Everyone looked at one another, said little. He overheard some vulgar remarks, presumably about Dianne.

He was no longer a trooper. Who was he now?

On Monday Byron began his first day at the bank as a manager trainee. At nine o'clock he began all-day seminar on gender and race awareness. His life at the bank, a new life, was now officially underway.

All during the dull seminar, however, his mind wandered onto night-slick wet streets filled by hustlers on the make, thieves, bad guys. Byron wondered about his snitches. He already felt bored.

11

Byron and Dianne celebrated their first anniversary at the Kingsbury's house. Most of the people there were from the bank. Byron had wanted to invite some troopers he knew, but Dianne said they made her uncomfortable because they all knew about her having been arrested. He couldn't fault her for that.

At the party, Mr. Kingsbury announced his anniversary gift to the newlyweds—a house on Lake Hampstead. When the architect uncovered his drawings, everyone gasped. The house was designed to look like a hotel Dianne and her parents had once stayed at on Lake Tahoe.

Byron never dreamed he'd live in such a home. He had seen the vacation photographs of them standing in front of that lodge many times. They always spoke of that visit as one of their happiest times together.

Byron wondered how he would pay the mortgage on an eight-thousand square foot house on his junior manager's salary. He needn't have worried. The bank was negotiating to buy a mortgage company on the west coast, and apparently part of those negotiations included giving the bank president's son-in-law a mortgage with a low interest rate.

They drank a toast of champagne, even Dianne, and the party

went on until late into the evening. Byron was ready to leave by midnight, but his wife, relaxed and happy, was enjoying herself. Life seemed a happy dream.

When they finally got home to their more modest rental house, he helped her out of her dress and couldn't help but marvel at how beautiful she was. They kissed by the bedroom window while the half moon lit her body with a faint glow. He guided her to the bed, but she said she didn't feel well—the champagne, and all.

As she fell asleep almost immediately, he tried not to feel resentment. After all, sex had always worked well between them. One night seemed a small matter to fret about, but it disturbed him nonetheless. Maybe it was her drinking—that made him uneasy. And unlike his teenage self, he had learned to trust his intuition.

BYRON GOT UP EARLY AND WENT DOWNSTAIRS TO MAKE breakfast. All the noise he made woke Dianne, and she joined him in the kitchen before he had her omelet ready.

"You're up very early for a banker." She kissed him on the cheek. "Are we pouting this morning?"

"What? No." He poured her a cup of coffee. "Maybe a little."

"Sorry about last night. Really, I am." She seemed amused by his petulance. "I'll make it up to you tonight, I promise."

He had to smile at how silly he was being, but some inner voice whispered that he wasn't being silly at all. Still, Dianne looked cheerful and sunny in her yellow nightgown, and he thought of the day that lay ahead, the two of them doing whatever they liked.

"Let's go sailing." Byron had bought a little sunfish and was teaching himself how to sail. Dianne was uncomfortable out on the water, but she always joined him when he asked her. He was surprised at how happy he was, how happy they both were. Marriage didn't seem like work at all. They enjoyed being together and sex was a kind of bonus, like discovering that your best friend is also a talented pianist. He missed her when he was at work and looked forward to getting home each night. The American Dream seemed to be unfolding before his eyes.

ONLY MONTHS LATER, MARTIN PROMOTED HIS SON-IN-law to Senior Mortgage Compliance Officer. Byron tried to make an amusing acronym of his job title, but to his ears it came out sounding like *schmuck*.

This role at the bank was considered a back office function, but one that was increasingly important as the mortgage business grew. He was to make sure the bank's mortgage lending practices were in compliance with all applicable state and federal regulations. Mr. Kingsbury thought his background as a trooper made this a perfect fit for Byron and the bank.

With a great deal for him to learn, he started spending more time at work. The bank paid his tuition at the local community college so he could begin work on his degree. Dianne helped him study for his examinations, and for the first time in his life he was a straight "A" student. She quipped that her name should rest alongside his on the gilded degree. She wasn't wrong. Was this the best time of his life? You might think so.

ONE DAY BYRON REALIZED HE HAD NEVER MET ANY OF Dianne's friends. Oh, occasionally she might mention someone's name, and he'd ask who he or she was. And Dianne would say, "Just a friend." He was so busy with work and studying at night that he never gave it much thought, but looking back he could see he should have paid more attention. Their social life, what little there was, usually included her parents.

When his mother caught the flu, Dianne drove to her house every day until she was well. She even fixed up a guest room on the north side of their house for her. They talked about having Byron's mom move in with them. It would be good to have her there when the children came. Byron squirmed at the thought, but didn't make a fuss. He was glad he had Dianne to help out with his mother and her issues.

They decided they would like to start a family right away, but couldn't quite seem to conceive. They both thought that might be because they were so anxious about having a baby that it was interfering with their sex life.

They went away for a weekend to the shore to be alone. They had a wonderful time, doing nothing but walking on the beach, having late dinners, making love whenever the felt the urge, and sleeping in until they felt like getting up. A lovely vacation.

They returned home feeling confident Dianne had become pregnant. It would be one of Byron's happiest memories of their marriage.

But like so much, it was a false dream. After another six months of disappointment they went back to her doctor. It turned out Dianne had scar tissue on her fallopian tubes that was preventing her from getting pregnant. The gynecologist told them the scars had been caused by gonorrhea.

At first Byron thought there must be some mistake, and asked the doctor to examine her again, but he said it was no mistake—she had been treated for it well before their marriage. By him, seemed the intimation.

While Dianne was getting dressed, Byron asked the doctor if the gonorrhea was related to her drug use. He said yes, many female users turn to prostitution to support their drug habit and end up with STD's.

His heart pounding in his throat, Byron felt as if he were about to collapse. They drove home without speaking.

They had soup for dinner since neither of them was hungry. Dianne said she was tired and went up to bed. Byron tried to watch television, but all he could think about was how she had not told him about having had gonorrhea. He had the same feeling in the pit of his stomach as he had when he first saw her drug test, the same feeling he had when, years ago, it was obvious she had a new boyfriend.

Who the hell was she? He thought of her sleeping upstairs in their bed. And where do we go from here? Could we ever have sex again? Could he ever trust her again? The house didn't feel like their house now. It felt like her house, the house her father had bought them.

Did her parents know she couldn't have children? Of course, they must have. Everyone knew but him, the husband of last resort.

He couldn't bring himself to go upstairs, so Byron slept on the couch. He left for work before Dianne woke up. As he backed out of the driveway, he realized they might never sleep together again. His disappointment that night of the party seemed insignificant indeed, now.

THEY FELL INTO A ROUTINE WHERE BYRON WOULD GO TO bed before Dianne, saying he had to get up early for work. She would say she wanted to watch the late news. When Dianne came to bed, Byron would pretend to be asleep. In the morning it was Dianne who would pretend to be asleep while Byron dressed for work. At dinner they would talk about day-to-day details that neither of them cared much about. He suspected Dianne was using again. Her moods swung from irrational happiness to sullen silence.

Byron spent more time at work. They came to dislike each other precisely because they had once cared so much for each other. Their marriage staggered on in this way for weeks and months that became a year. The Dream had evaporated.

MEANWHILE AT WORK, A COLLEAGUE FROM BYRON'S department got sent to California to audit Sunwest for mortgage compliance. Byron would normally have sent one of his staff, but it gave him a good excuse to get away for a bit. He had his admin assistant book a room at his favorite hotel in San Francisco.

When he told Dianne that he'd be away for a few days, she said that was fine, and went off shopping with her mother. She didn't ask where he was going.

As he sat in longterm parking at the airport contemplating his suit-bag, however, he realized it was the first time in their marriage he had gone on a trip without leaving a note for Dianne under her pillow. Angry with himself for breaking that tradition, he beat out a pulse against the steering wheel with the heel of his hand until it started to hurt.

But then, it seemed hypocritical to write words he was no longer sure he truly felt. That was the hard truth, the kernel lurking in the bucket of popcorn that cracks a tooth. The walk through the airport felt long and lonely, a different sort from his arrival home. Before he ran into Dianne's father that day. Everything changed after that. Hadn't it?

ONCE SETTLED IN SAN FRANCISCO, WITH A BRACING, stiff breeze coming off the unsettled bay, he treated himself to a wonderful dinner at a little restaurant Dianne discovered on an earlier visit. The faces on the streets looked back at him either aggressive, it seemed, or pitiful among the homeless and addicted sprawling in alleyways. Even the faces of the people like him, in suits and with means, seemed empty and cold. Byron himself felt dead inside, like a mannequin wearing a suit strolling along Market. The world answered him back with stark indifference.

He wasn't afraid. Merely lonely.

Once seated, everything about their favorite spot only made him angrier. Why the hell hadn't she told him before they went to the see the doctor she couldn't have children? Why pretend she was trying to get pregnant?

Christ—was everything an act?

Do I know my own wife?

At times, the teen girl he loved still lived in her eyes and her smile, her rare touches of affection. But mostly a stranger.

Shaking, he ordered a drink, vodka. Tried to read the menu. Tried to choose. The choices seemed a blur.

His patrol commander's warning that you can't have a relationship with an addict because they're already in love with drugs, and three's a crowd, rang in his ears. But Dianne had been sober for years.

Or had she? That was the trouble with getting involved with someone with a drug habit, you could never be quite sure of anything. It wouldn't be very hard to fool him if she was using again. She had fooled him once and so had her parents. How they must despise him. The thought of them mocking him behind his back was more than he could bear.

On top of his cocktail Byron ordered a stupidly-expensive bottle of wine and drank it all, even though he knew he would feel awful in the morning. On the walk back to the hotel, he tripped over a chipped curb and tore the knee of his suit and the skin underneath. Feeling foolish, he'd nearly vomited from the wine sloshing in his gut. This was not behavior befitting a grown man.

When he got back to his room, no message from Dianne. He called the house, but she didn't answer. He hung up without leaving a message.

When he turned out the light, he felt as if the room began to spin. At last the meal, and most of the wine, began to come back up. Afterwards he lay against the tiles, cold against his hot face. He stayed there until realizing with revulsion how much bacteria likely lurked on the average hotel room bathroom floor.

A DRIVER FROM SUNWEST MORTGAGE PICKED HIM UP AT eight o'clock. Everyone there seemed pleasant, and why wouldn't they be—his father-in-law ran the parent company of Sunwest.

After the usual pleasantries, he got down to work examining a random selection of mortgages for compliance with state and federal law. It didn't take long for Byron to discover a great many of the mortgages were out of compliance. By noon he was able to estimate that twenty-five to thirty percent of those mortgages were illegal. Since they did over thirty thousand mortgages a month, the problem was huge.

He ate lunch by myself so he'd have time to think over how he should handle what he had discovered. He could run it by the Sunwest people, or report it directly to Mr. Kingsbury and let him decide how he wanted to handle this potentially damaging crisis.

He decided to meet with the Sunwest people and see if they could explain what was going on. Then he'd have more information under his belt before approaching his father-in-law.

Helen Stone ran Sunwest for the bank. He met with her after lunch. Mr. Kingsbury had picked her for the job, so Byron had to be careful not to appear too abrasive. She was only a few years older than Byron, self-assured, attractive, with pale, intelligent eyes that pierced. He immediately saw why Mr. Kingsbury had picked her.

Ms. Stone offered him a seat and had tea brought. "I hope you found everything in order on the compliance side." She poured tea for them both and offered him a scone. "If I had known you were coming in last night, I would have met you for dinner."

"Well, we didn't want to put you out. I didn't get in till late." Byron nibbled a scone. Set it down. Made a show of wiping his mouth with a small paper napkin stamped with a SunWest logo. "But, I did find problems."

"How many?"

"Well—some. One or two."

Her nostrils flared, but otherwise her face stayed the same. "Shall I call in Ken Roberts?"

Byron felt out of his depth, suddenly. "Sorry. Who?"

She narrowed her eyes. "He's our compliance officer."

"Right. Roberts. No, I think it would be better if we went over it alone, first."

"All right, then. Tell me what's troubling you." The earlier welcoming tone had been replaced by let's-get-to-it.

"Statistically, about one-third of your mortgages are not in compliance." Byron waited to see how she took that news.

"How big's your sample?" No hiding how annoyed she was.

"I reviewed, well, let's see: maybe a hundred-fifty mortgages. Give or take."

"We did over forty-three thousand mortgages last month. Your sample is too small."

"Ms. Stone—Helen—I can order a team of people from my department to review a much bigger sample if you like. I thought it would be better if you and I spoke before I do that."

"I don't think there's any reason for a full-blown audit." Helen Stone leaned back in her chair. The earlier, smiling Helen had returned. "Do you?"

"Depends in large part on my conversation with you today." There, he was pleasant, but firm. He had to tread carefully but still do his job.

"I'll have my compliance people look into it. What time is your flight back?"

He admired how nimble she was, shifting focus from her problems to his travel schedule. "I'm afraid that won't do. I'd like to send some of my people back here to sit second chair with your compliance people."

Helen Stone laughed with no sense of humor. "Don't you trust us?"

"Of course. We're colleagues. It's simply bank policy to verify that compliance issues meet our standards."

"You're married to Martin Kingsbury's daughter, aren't you?"

Trying to make him out to be the incompetent son-in-law breezing in on the wings of nepotism. "That's immaterial to the issues at hand."

"She's pretty. I met her once when he came here before the bank bought us out. I heard she was taken sick some time ago. I hope she's better."

"She is. Thank you for asking." What the hell did that mean? Was she signaling that she could make trouble for him and Mr.

Kingsbury if he pushed too hard? Was that a threat to reveal Dianne's problems with drugs?

"That's good to hear. Sometimes people can have a relapse with a serious illness."

"She's quite recovered, thank you."

"Recovered—oh, I see."

So Helen did know about Dianne's drug problem. How well informed Helen Stone was. Byron wondered how she had learned so much about his family.

"And how is Mrs. Kingsbury? I think she 'paints,' doesn't she?" Helen made painting sound like an avocation no intelligent, ambitious woman should deign to pursue.

"Suzanne is fine. She's still at it. I think she's begun working in oils."

"That's quite a change from watercolors."

"It's possible I misunderstood."

"Yes."

Byron stood to signal Helen that the topic was no longer up for discussion. "I'm sorry to have to insist, but a team from my office should assist in any compliance audit you might conduct. And I suggest you do."

Helen came around her desk. He hadn't noticed how tall she was. She was only an inch or two shorter than he was. "I think Martin has to approve any audit."

"He usually accepts my recommendations. You understand I'll have to alert the board about what I've found here."

"You might want to talk to him before saying anything to the board." Helen held out her hand. She certainly seemed confident. "Have a good trip back."

But he didn't; she had stonewalled, or so it felt. Suspicious, and confusing. Byron was an uneducated grunt compared to most of these people. He tried not to feel in over his head, but the numbers didn't lie.

Byron went straight to the office from the airport. He rode the elevator up sixteen floors to Mr. Kingsbury's office. His assistant waived Byron in.

"How was the trip?" Mr. Kingsbury put his arm around Byron's shoulder and ushered him to the couch that sat in the middle of his office. "I see you met Helen. Quite a woman, wouldn't you say?"

"She's quite cool to the idea of a thorough compliance audit. That's all I can tell you." Byron thought it best to get down to business right away.

"She's been bending my ear on the phone all afternoon. Said you were rude to her. 'Pushy,' she said."

"That's a lie."

Martin Kingsbury laughed as if he were trying to settle a squabble between two children. He offered Byron a drink of brandy, and after pouring they both had a sip and sat back, staring for an awkward moment. "Flight home all right?"

"Martin, don't change the subject. You must know they're way out of compliance, and I suspect Helen knows but is hiding it from me. She didn't seem too surprised when I told her what I'd found." Byron took another sip of brandy. His hand was shaking.

"I think you may be exaggerating, but I'm going to look into this myself." Mr. Kingsbury poured more brandy into Byron's glass. "I take you very seriously, son."

"Well. All right."

"There, see? Now. Suzanne wants you to have dinner with us tonight. She says our Dianne is upset about some damn thing or other."

"Yes. We've had our disagreements."

"That's part of being married, son."

Here it was again, the Kingsbury trick of diverting attention away from anything unpleasant with reference to social trivia. "I'm the compliance officer, Martin, and I think I'm obligated to report these issues directly to the board. It could be very serious for the bank. Also, I want to order a full audit tomorrow."

"Slow down, Byron. You just got home. Let's think about this in the morning. If word got out that we were auditing our own mortgage company, it could hurt our stock. I have to think of our shareholders."

"I've seen enough out there to support a full audit by us. There's no reason to wait on this." Byron put his drink down. "There's something else. Helen seems very well informed about you and your family, and I got the impression she would use that information to block an audit."

Martin Kingsbury tossed back his brandy and grimaced. He dropped his voice and leaned over. Byron could smell the liquor, hot. "All right. Man talk. Some time back, when we were looking to buy Sunwest, I made a mistake and got 'involved' with Helen. It was stupid, I know, but it happened, I've atoned, it's history. But if I press her on this audit business, our affair will almost certainly become weaponized."

Byron tried to sound menacing. "I don't want to see Suzanne get hurt."

"The embarrassment would kill her. Don't you see, son? Humiliation. Get what I'm saying?" Martin Kingsbury said all this in an almost jocular, man-to-man tone. They could have been two chums in a country club locker room talking about shaving strokes off their golf scores. "We mustn't do it to her."

"You must see Helen would only threaten you like that if she had something to hide. That means we have to do the audit. We have to call her bluff, Martin." Byron looked at Mr. Kingsbury and tried to imagine him romancing Helen Stone. It seemed impossible. "It will come out anyway, at least once the compliance irregularities are discovered."

"Who's going to discover them?"

"If I was able to, someone else will."

"Yes yes, and you've reported it. Bravo, my boy. I'll take it from here." Mr. Kingsbury raised his now empty tumbler in a kind of faux toast. "We're expecting you and Dianne around eight. Suzanne is doing Cornish game hens. That's Dianne's favorite."

This reminded Byron of his first conversation with the Kingsburys about Dianne's drug use. They talked around him until the problem seemed to go away, at least until it got lost in the noise of all that chatter.

He went down to the parking garage to get his car and drove home. Dianne and he hadn't spoken in three days. And while they went to dinner later that night, they never got around to discussing the pregnancy issues. Next? She disappeared, this time never to return. And in an instant, Byron Round went from whistleblower to murder suspect.

12

The initial newspaper story about the police's interest in Byron—as good as a public conviction for Dianne's murder, even before the trial—ran a week before Christmas.

Later that same morning Lieutenant Atkins reappeared, this time with two uniformed troopers. When Byron answered the door, the cop fluttered a warrant. He ordered the troopers to handcuff Byron while he rattled off the Miranda bullet-points in a voice free of emotion.

Byron caught the eye of the one of the troopers, who quickly looked away. He kept his arms folded. "This is preposterous. You all know I didn't do it."

"Not for me to determine. Just doing my job." Atkins rested two fists on his substantial hips. "You aiming to give us a problem?"

"*I was a good cop.*"

That shut the Lieutenant up, but only for so long. "Don't make trouble, pal. All I'm asking."

"I'm innocent; I'm cooperating; I'm ex-LEO." Byron had wondered when they would come, but one is never prepared for the reality of being arrested—the formality, the rigmarole; the loss of agency, often of dignity itself. "No need for the irons."

One of the uniforms said, impatient, "As a former officer, you know we can't transport a detainee without the restraints. Now turn around, please."

Byron recognized the aggressive trooper as the one who had come by to collect the missing person report. He offered his wrists. "It's really not necessary."

"Protocol is what it is," Atkins said. "So just relax, ex-good cop. We're at least as civilized as you are. Right?"

"Sure," Byron said, sarcastic. "Better safe than sorry." The cuffs pinched into the tender skin around his wrist.

Glancing across the street he saw his neighbor, Ed Kosecki, staring over at the scene. Ed waved, embarrassed, when he saw Byron, who tried to return the gesture but couldn't because of the strong arms holding him on either side.

The whole neighborhood must have been wondering why the police hadn't arrested the murderer at 1422 Willow Lane sooner. The newspapers had been full of stories suggesting Byron had a motive. Such notoriety could only hurt the value of everyone's property.

"What's next?"

"We're going to lodge you in the county jail for tonight. They'll set bail tomorrow morning. You can call your lawyer when we get there." Lieutenant Atkins smiled, a little cruel. "You know the drill, Round."

Byron thought of all the people he had arrested when he was a trooper without giving a moment's thought to the disruption to their lives. Now the system had him like it had gotten hold of his collars, some of whom disappeared like a ring dropped down a drainpipe. He shuddered at thoughts of his bleak future.

The lieutenant put his hand on the top of Byron's head as he bent to get into the rear seat of the police car. When the lieutenant shut the door, Byron looked through the rear window at his house. It already looked like a home that had lain unoccupied for a long time.

Byron got shoved into a holding cell with about thirty other inmates. He settled in, tucked into a cold corner against the farthest end of a bench supporting two drunks and a tweaker twitching with withdrawal. That's what he was for now—an inmate, one expected to use the one toilet exposed in the center of the cell. He hoped to God he wouldn't have to squat upon it anytime soon.

AFTER AN HOUR, A GUARD CALLED HIS NAME. BYRON WAS told him to sit in the waiting room until he was called for fingerprinting. When the cop asked what he was in for, Byron said he wasn't sure.

The guard glanced over Byron's sheet. "Murder in the first." He whistled. "You the guy killed his wife?"

Byron said he was, then he realized it might be considered an admission that could be used against him. "I mean—I'm the guy you people *think* killed his wife."

The guard laughed and tucked the warrant back into Byron's shirt pocket. "Respect. Hey, every swinging dick in here's innocent. True story."

After fingerprinting, he was photographed and sent back to the holding cell, the lock-up montage in a movie, except for the stripping down part.

Byron sighed—only a small space left on the bench along the wall. When he went to sit down in his shoes without their laces, a hard-eyed tattooed man in his late forties with deep acne and wound scars, a street veteran who stunk of alcohol and mildew, told him to get scarce, "or else."

Another prisoner, a young black man trembling from withdrawal symptoms, said through a snotty nose, "You best watch your ass, Cruz."

"Why's that?"

"That mo-fo done killed his old lady. Seen it in the paper."

"Whoa—no shit?" A respect for violence prompted the previously unfriendly Cruz to move aside and allow Byron to sit. "Make way, then."

Cruz, an apparent veteran of the lockup, now became gregarious to pass the time. The clock on the wall showed three in the morning, but inside, the minutes and hours ceased to flow like normal. Not without exterior light. It might have been anytime.

He advised with anticipation that breakfast would be served promptly at six. "You looking at a peanut butter sandwich with orange juice. Ain't much. But it sticks to the ribs after a sleepless night here in the county honeymoon suite."

"Thanks."

"Hey, no." Cruz leaned over. "Don't kill me, bro. If I fall asleep first, I mean."

"Ha-ha."

He held out his hands, rough, covered in gang symbols. "Brother, I got a good woman on the outside. *Don't shiv me.*"

All Byron could think was that prison would be a constant negotiation for survival, not unlike being in combat. He shuddered and held himself against the chill. A nightmare, but real. But he had the truth on his side. It would be all right. No prison. A bump in the road, this night in jail, the kind an experienced motorcyclist handles with ease.

AT LAST HE MUST HAVE FALLEN ASLEEP, BECAUSE NEXT thing he knew, Cruz, smiling and giving this crazy thumb's up, nudged him that it was time to go for chow. It all seemed oddly familiar—like being back in the army.

After breakfast seven of the inmates were handcuffed and chained to each other around the waist and led off to a bus that would take them to the courthouse. With a start, he realized he hadn't called Robert. Byron, cursing himself—what had he been thinking. Shock. That was his excuse.

The prisoners were led off the bus and told to sit in the back of the courtroom until their names were called. He hadn't been there five minutes when a guard came up and asked if he was Byron Round. When he said that he was, the guard took off the cuffs and told him to sit on the front row of the hearing room.

Byron rubbed his wrists. "Front row? My lucky morning."

"That's right. Says here you're represented by Mr. Taylor, and that y'all get to go first. Looks like he knows how to make things happen down here."

He nodded his gratitude and went to the front of the courtroom. Before he could sit down, the judge's clerk came over and also told him his case would be heard first. Byron thanked her and sat down, pulling up his khakis, which needed the belt that had also been taken along with his shoelaces.

How did Robert Taylor even know he had been arrested? Well, thank God he had found out somehow. A stroke of luck already.

ROBERT APPEARED AT ABOUT EIGHT-THIRTY. HE LOOKED every inch the successful criminal defense lawyer: expensive dark blue suit, gold cufflinks, a starched white shirt, slick haircut and manicured nails, all of it half a head taller than anyone for several miles. He chatted downward with the other lawyers and guards milling around waiting for court to begin. It was obvious Byron's attorney was in his element.

Taylor finally made eye contact, winking across the room, and for the first time since Byron had been arrested, he thought he might actually go home again soon.

After the judge took the bench, Robert came over. "First. Do not say a word. That's why I'm here."

"Can you get me out of here?"

"We'll see. The prosecutor's set to ask bail be set at eight hundred. Thousand, that is."

"I can't get my hands on the deposit for that much."

"It's just grandstanding by the state. "

As Robert laughed, Byron wondered how he could take the prosecution's demand with such obvious lightheartedness. As if in answer Robert said with a scoff, "Everything's negotiable," looking faraway for a moment with a distasteful set to his mouth. He had been practicing for a long time now. Who knew the depths of the moral compromises a lawyer like Robert Taylor had either witnessed, or perhaps perpetuated on his own?

"From the docket I see another one of Mr. Taylor's dramatic bail reduction episodes is brewing first this morning." The Judge's sarcasm wasn't entirely unfriendly. You could see from a wry twinkle in his eye he liked Robert; they were probably colleagues outside this context, peers out on the golf course, but here needing to appear impartial. "So we start right out of the gate today with front page, above-the-fold excitement. Lucky us."

No one chuckled, least of all Byron. Robert said simply, "Thank you, your honor."

"State versus Byron Round." And then? The charge. Murder.

At the mention of the crime, Byron realized the dream had turned real. He would be tried for murder. He wanted to gasp in Robert's ear to explain how it couldn't be so, all was a mistake, but remembered he had been told to stay quiet.

A woman in a black suit stood, shooting a hard glance at Byron. "Your honor, if it pleases the court, I am Joann Kerns with the prosecutor's office, and we are requesting this bail hearing for Mr. Round." She looked at papers and over at Byron. "Because of the especially heinous nature of this crime, the state requests bond be set at eight hundred-thousand dollars."

It looked as if Ms. Kerns had more to say, but the immense bulk of Robert Taylor rose like a new mountain and stepped in front of the judge. "Your honor? If it may please this court, I'd like to first say—"

"An attorney of your provenance is well known here, Mr. Taylor. You are entering an appearance on behalf of Mr. Round?"

"I am, your honor."

"Proceed."

Taylor beamed with confidence, a quick glance at his client, and then licked his lips before beginning. "Very good. Now, let's get into some facts here: Mr. Round is employed by the largest bank in the state, in an important oversight role; he owns a home in this county, and is prepared to turn over his passport to the court. Therefore, he poses no flight risk whatsoever."

"Mr. Round is accused of murder in the first degree, your honor. The charge alone indicates he poses a threat to public safety." Ms. Kerns turned a withering glance in Byron's direction. "How many more women have to be murdered before Mr. Round is *kept* behind bars?"

Curiously, Robert looked as if he had received a particularly timely bit of good news. "Your honor, Mr. Round stands here accused of killing his wife, not going on a Hollywood-style slasher film rampage. The state's case does not in any way match its rhetoric here. The state has offered *no evidence* that her killing was part of a larger rampage against women generally. Mr. Round has *no prior* arrests. Why would he? This citizen is a former police officer, one who departed the force not under a cloud but simply to pursue a more lucrative line of work, a sentiment I suspect even his arresting officers would find agreement with. Ex-cop. A good cop. Just a small tidbit Ms. Kerns forgot— neglected, rather, perhaps in incompetence or haste—to mention."

"From the files of 'enough already' comes the tale of an innocent man wrongly accused." The impatient judge's twinkle had vanished. But after scanning over a document or two in silence, he shot an odd look at the prosecutor and slapped the case file closed.

The judge sighed and rubbed his temples during a pregnant pause that left the courtroom shuffling its feet. Finally: "What do you propose for bail, Mr. Taylor?"

"As not only counsel but friend to Mr. Round, a personal recognizance bond sounds right to me."

Ms. Kerns snorted. The judge shook his head. "Three hundred-thousand. Best I can do."

"Very well, your honor."

"It is so ordered." The judge shuffled the folders onto the next case from his clerk as a small, brief bustle enveloped the courtroom. On the way out, Cruz leaned over and said, cheerful, "PR bond would've been sweet, bro. Next time."

It was over, but Byron had no idea what had happened. Was he going back to the lockup? "I can't make that bail either, Robert."

"Mr. Round, I suggest you 'chill' as the kids say. Your bail's all arranged." Robert snapped his briefcase shut with a satisfied click. "I have a check for thirty grand right here."

So much had happened since his arrest last night that Byron couldn't seem to come to grips with events as they unfolded. *"What are you talking about?"*

"Your mother's posting bond for you. She called me this morning when she heard on the news that you'd been arrested."

Byron had to sit down again. "My mother doesn't have that kind of money either." He hadn't seen his mother since the funeral.

"She put her house up as collateral."

Byron felt something inside of him shake. After so many years, the distance between himself and his mother had closed in an instant. He wasn't sure he'd ever felt gratitude to her like this, which inspired some guilt, too, as he was taken back to jail, given his belongings and released.

The air and sunlight on the sidewalk had never seemed more beautiful—and that had only been one night in jail. Suppose he went away forever?

WHEN BYRON STEPPED OUT OF THE CAB IN FRONT OF HIS house, he was surprised to see Suzanne Kingsbury waiting for him.

Humiliated, he stepped past her and went inside without speaking. He mixed a dry vodka martini even though it was only eleven in the morning. He needed a bracer, even before lunch. "I'm surprised to see you here."

"I certainly understand that. I'm sure you're furious with all of us now that you know everything." Suzanne lit a cigarette and looked around for an ashtray. With none at hand, Byron gave her a teacup saucer. The use of the fine china for such an uncouth purpose seemed to trouble her.

"I wouldn't say I know everything. I know you all lied to me, and have been lying to me for years. That's rather hard to take."

"I can tell you this. Dianne loved you very much. That wasn't a lie."

"Well, it's hard to know what's true and what isn't at this point." Byron tried not to sound too sarcastic. "And now I'm accused of killing her."

"I can't say that I blame you for feeling upset with us."

"I'm not sure exactly how I feel. Other than grieving for her."

She hung her head. Sniffled and blew her nose. "While you were in the army, Dianne got involved with drugs. You already know that, but it wasn't only painkillers. She was using heroin, and the doctors tell me once that happens, it is difficult to get well. It wasn't long after she was arrested for prostitution. When we found out, I thought Martin was going to have a heart attack. And the second time she was arrested? He did." She took a contemplative drag on her cigarette. "And then you showed up."

"Yes. There I was."

"That's exactly how Martin put it that day after the airport." She smiled for the first time. "We'd known you since you were a little boy, and we thought since you were going to be a policeman? You'd be able to help her stay sober."

"Being a policeman has nothing to do with helping anyone kick a habit."

"I know it was stupid and selfish of us, but by then we'd become desperate. And when Dianne was with you, she seemed like her old self again. She told me you had given her a chance to get her life back. For the first time in years, I could see she wanted to be sober."

"Why didn't you tell me all that before we were married?" Byron downed his drink, mixed another.

"Martin and I talked about that, but we were afraid you'd leave Dianne. Leave us too, I guess. The three of us were simply worn out, and you seemed so sure of yourself. You were a war hero, and we were at war. When Martin bumped into you he was coming back from a visit with Dianne at a rehab center in Nevada. He told me that when he saw you standing there in your uniform, with all those medals, he just knew you had been sent to help us."

"What made you all feel that way?"

"Martin said it couldn't be a coincidence that you showed up when you did, and I believed it too. We both thought it was the miracle we had prayed for. We had been through so much by then. Too much." Suzanne Kingsbury was talking as much to herself as much as she was to Byron.

"You forgot to mention my other virtue. Because I was overseas, I had no idea about what Dianne had been up to. I only knew the girl she was before I left."

"Yes, that too." Suzanne snubbed out her cigarette and immediately lit another. "But she was still that girl too. She was still the girl you remembered, and the longer you were in her life, the more she became like the girl she had been." Suzanne began to cry at the thought of her daughter, before heroin, before becoming a prostitute, out on the lawn of the country club on a summer's night with her beau.

Byron had lived with that false dream for too long himself. He felt like crying too, but for different reasons. How could the three of them have used him in that way? How could they have lied to him for so many years?

Byron thought it time to bring this romanticized twaddle back down to earth. "And Martin was being considered for the top spot at the bank."

"Yes, he was. And Dianne's behavior certainly was not helping." Suzanne took a handkerchief from her purse and dried her eyes. His rebuke had hit home.

More than a little hypocritical, it all seemed: These were, after all, the people who had put him in the position he was in now, facing the death penalty. That reality kept slapping him in the face.

"I'm sure you think Martin and I were just thinking of ourselves, of his position, but that's not true. I know it must look like that to you."

"I have to admit it does look a bit like that. The two of you watched me step into your trap and, presto, here I am facing a murder charge. That's quite a miracle." Try as he might, Byron couldn't hide how angry as he was.

"That's why I told your lawyer I'd pay his fee. Martin and I owe you that."

"Does Martin think I did it?"

"He thinks you may have had something to do with Dianne's death. Yes. But I told him Dianne just went back to drugs. It's not that much of a mystery."

"No—she was murdered. The police say she didn't die in her car. Somebody put her there after she was already dead." Byron was amazed at how clinically they were discussing Dianne's death. "It's not always the easiest answer."

"Yes, Martin said the police told him that." Suzanne brushed ash from her black skirt. "She may have died from an overdose and her dealer got frightened and put her in the car."

"They must think I hired someone to kill her with what they call a speedball. It's a lethal mix of drugs that dealers use on junkies who don't pay their bills." He was thinking like a cop now.

Suzanne stood to go. "I know you had nothing to do with her death. Martin knows that too, but he's too hurt to admit it just now. You're our son-in-law, and nothing is going to change that."

Byron walked Mrs. Kingsbury to her car. "I hope you can forgive us." She held out her hand. "Not only me and Martin, but Dianne, too."

As he clasped her slender hand, he noticed how frail Mrs. Kingsbury had become. Dianne would kill all of them, even from beyond the grave.

13

Martin Kingsbury slid what Byron guessed was his resignation letter across the desk, along with a fountain pen. Byron picked it up—heavy, the kind you use to seal a deal.

"Son, the board met last night in executive session. They've instructed me to ask for your resignation."

"Not unexpected."

"You're to receive a generous severance package. Very generous." Martin repeated that last part to underscore how fairly Byron was being treated. All handled in the best possible taste.

Byron took up the pen and made to sign when, in mid-air, he stopped. "What about the Sunwest audit?"

"What about it?" Martin pursed his lips as though biting into something bitter. Byron could see how disappointed Martin was that he didn't understand how these matters were to go.

"Are you going forward with the audit?"

"Well, you don't have to concern yourself with that any longer. You've got other things on your mind."

"One way of putting it."

"Given our unusual circumstances, the board agreed that a senior vice president in HR should handle this today. But I wanted to tell you myself."

Of course, why have someone else fire me when you can take the pleasure yourself?

"That's so kind of you." Byron hoped Martin got the sarcasm, but picking up on nuance wasn't exactly Martin's strong suit. "Lucky day."

He thought about asking Martin if he had told the board about his fling with Helen Stone, but thought better of it. What the hell good would that do, anyway?

"We've had our differences, but I thought it best to keep this in the family, so to speak." Martin managed a weak smile.

"I'd like to sign this letter for you, Martin, but I was the chief compliance officer when I discovered how out of compliance Sunwest was, so I have some continuing obligation to the board to make sure they understand the magnitude of the problem out there."

"And you've done that by telling me about it." Martin's impatience was starting to show through those lovely manners.

"Will you put that in writing?" There it was, out in the open for both of them to see.

"What are you talking about?"

"Before I sign this, I want a letter from you saying I've advised you of the compliance issues at Sunwest, and you have taken my concerns to the board."

"You're in no position to ask for anything. I could fire you right now." Anger was peeking through the carefully cultivated veneer of control Martin prized so much. Byron hadn't seen him shed even one tear at Dianne's funeral.

"What would be the grounds for firing me?"

His voice trembled. "You've been charged with the murder of my daughter. That should be enough 'grounds'."

"If you were to fire me and I'm found not guilty, I'll have one hell of a lawsuit against the bank." Byron had no idea if what he was saying was true or not. Grasping at straws, he made the next threat that popped into his mind. "And maybe you, personally."

"And me, too?"

"Yes. As much as it hurts to say that."

A modicum of sentiment filled the air in the room. The old family ties rendered both men silent for a time.

How strange it all seemed. It wasn't simply Martin's asking him to resign; he'd expected that. No, it was the fact that Byron's father-in-law insisted on feigning graciousness about the process even as he was booting sentencing Byron to destitution.

"If I discharge you, you'll lose your severance package. And you'll need that money to pay your legal fees."

What a practical fellow Martin was turning out to be, too practical for someone whose daughter had been murdered. Suzanne must not have mentioned her offer to cover the costs of the defense.

Something was wrong, but Byron had no idea what. Perhaps Martin was having second thoughts about treating his son-in-law so badly. Maybe Suzanne had softened him up. "I do need that money, but not enough to turn my back on the Sunwest business. If those mortgages all go south, I could be held liable—and so could you." Byron fabricated that business about his possible liability. He was stalling for time to figure out why Martin Kingsbury was so eager for him to sign.

"I think you have more to worry about than civil liability just now." Byron was a bit taken aback by how snide that sounded. Martin certainly had taken the gloves off. "You're a mid-level officer with this bank, or you were until today and, as such, you are bound to follow my instructions. I suggest you reconsider the board's offer and sign that letter."

"I'm afraid I can't do that." For the first time since this whole nightmare had begun, Byron felt as if he were pushing back against all the forces lined up against him.

"Then I have no choice but to terminate your employment immediately. Suzanne will be very disappointed in you." Martin was pulling no punches, now. The old heave-ho.

Byron thought about asking Martin if Suzanne would be disappointed in her husband if she ever learned of his affair with Helen Stone, but that was too far below the belt.

"I'm sorry, Martin." Byron held out his hand.

Martin buzzed his assistant. "Please have accounting draft Mr. Round's final check." When he turned back towards Byron, Mr. Kingsbury's face held its usual impassive mask. "I think you've made a very serious mistake today. No bank in the country will hire you now."

"I never did think I was cut out for banking."

"Well, I don't think there's much left to say, do you?" Byron was being dismissed.

"No, I suppose not. Except—good luck with Sunwest."

When Byron got back to his office, a bank security guard was already there to escort him to the parking lot.

The guard and Byron had said good morning to each other for eight years, so this was awkward for both of them. "Mr. Kingsbury says you are not to take any bank documents with you."

"I understand. I just want to get some personal things. You can search my briefcase if you like." Byron held his briefcase out. Frank took it.

"I'm sorry, Mr. Round, but those are my orders." After he finished searching Byron's briefcase, Frank escorted him to the first floor and shook his hand goodbye.

BYRON DIDN'T REMEMBER DRIVING HOME OR MUCH OF what happened over the next few days. He wanted to leave the house but with nowhere to go, he instead sat watching television all day and most of the night.

He drove to the liquor store a few times. He thought about how it would look if he got picked up for DUI. He chewed a few breath mints as he drove.

Watching television for so many hours each day, he saw the news cycle dominated by such topics as the best way to get wrinkles out of your trousers when you're traveling, and how to make a waffle your whole family would enjoy; that the new leader of China was progressive by totalitarian standards; and watched the mother of a missing sixteen-year-old tearfully plead with the abductors to bring the girl home.

Two days later, a performance by a new talent show singing sensation was interrupted by the news that a body believed to be the missing girl had been found. As news helicopters gave dizzying views of the scene, an attractive female reporter named Sidney Biddle asked the girl's mother if she felt closure now that the body had been located. The woman broke down on camera, with the smug, artificial reporter all but winking to the camera with satisfaction.

Disgusted, each program worse than the last, Byron found himself having conversations with the television, along with the walls holding portraits of Dianne at various points in her life. His topic kept coming back to forgiveness, as though he had been the criminal of the family needing redemption. Weeping. Begging.

Nude and covered with mysterious cuts and bruises, he woke up the next morning in the back yard. Sitting on the grass trying not to get sick, he decided he had better get the drinking under control.

On Monday, he telephoned Robert's office and made an appointment. The high-powered lawyer hadn't taken his case Pro Bono and, if Byron didn't find a way to pay, he'd soon be without a lawyer. So much was going against him that he felt almost numb.

"You look like shit." Robert laughed and waved Byron into the office. "Would you like coffee?"

"Tea, remember?"

"Right, right. But, looks more like you could use a blood transfusion."

Byron shrugged. "I got fired. I have no money to pay you. I've put my car up for sale, at least, so that will be something."

"Your father-in-law fired you?"

"The board did actually. He just passed on the message." For some reason Byron couldn't bring himself to tell Robert the truth. And in a way, what he had said was true enough, if not wholly factual.

"I don't believe that. Tell me what happened."

Byron explained how he had been fired, with Mr. Kingsbury refusing to give him a letter saying he had been advised about the Sunwest compliance issues. Byron didn't go into Mr. Kingsbury's affair with Helen Stone. He doubted this side issue had much to do with his being fired.

"My friend, I think you've just given me an answer to most of your problems."

"How's that?" Byron was growing mistrustful of Robert's indefatigable optimism. Perhaps so much success at such a young age had taken the edge off his judgment. In the meantime, Byron's judgment was being sharpened like an axe, first by Dianne's death, then his arrest and now his being penniless.

"You need a job and a way to make money to pay your very pricy lawyer, and I need a way to discover why the president of a bank would be reluctant to expose regulatory violations that happened right under his nose." Robert pushed his chair back and put his feet up on his desk.

"I'm afraid I'm still a bit lost."

But not Taylor. He snapped his fingers, sat back up. "You'll start tomorrow as my law clerk. If you're right, there is a Whistleblower suit waiting to be filed against your bank and Sunwest. I'll need your help in drafting the complaint and making my way through all those banking regulations."

"Even if I could be of some help to you, how would that pay my bill?" Byron could see that no amount of law clerk hours could help him pay the fees of an eight-hundred-dollar an hour lawyer.

"If you're right, there may be as many as one million mortgages originated by Sunwest and sold to Fannie and Freddie Mac that are damn near worthless. Tomorrow you will research what those claims look like from our perspective. You can expect to work twelve-hour days. I'll teach you about the law, and you teach me about banking."

"What about my criminal case?"

"I can't very well have my senior law clerk sitting in jail, can I?"

"Robert, I'd be lying if I said I wasn't scared to death. Who wouldn't be in my shoes?"

"I always promise my clients a great trial, and I always deliver more than I promise. You're going to have to rely on that. You have no other choice, really. It'll help you to sleep better until this is over."

"It isn't that I don't have confidence in you, it's that—"

"Let me tell you why I think we're in good shape." Robert didn't wait for him to finish. Byron had begun to learn the attorney did this with everyone—once he knew what you were going to say, he jumped in with both feet. People who knew him accepted it; opposing counsel endured it. "Have you noticed the odd way incriminating evidence keeps tumbling out and falling into the lap of the police? Someone's rolling those boulders down the mountain, and they're all aimed at you."

"It does feel that way. Like I'm about to be crushed."

"No question. Tough, tough situation. But, the other thing that's in our favor is the way the state brought charges against you so quickly. There's no statute of limitations on murder—why rush to charge you, not when they've got such a weak case?"

"Seems strange to me."

"I'll tell you why: because the prosecutor's feeling pressure from the press. And that's good for us. I have friends with sympathies to my worldview."

"I won't pretend I entirely understand what you're saying, since the papers have been so rough one me."

"Don't sweat it. Let me tell you what a first-degree murder trial's really about. It is most definitely not about who did what, because in a circumstantial case like this, where no one witnessed the murder? It's about who the accused is, and who the victim was. That's what the jury wants to know: is the would-be villain in our little tale capable of murdering his wife? Was she a ne'er-do-well? Who lived a life that put her in danger?"

"You're going after Dianne to save me?"

"Relax. I'm going to show the jury the real Dianne Kingsbury Round, not who you imagined her to be or wished her to be. Some illusions are difficult to let go. People find they need them even after they know they are just illusions."

Byron had to admit, if only to himself, that he never had been sure he knew who Dianne was. That's how it is with addicts. Robert didn't appear to be someone who relied upon prayer for his brand of miracles. "Understood."

"Good, because your life depends on it. Another mistake the state made is thinking the horrible way she died will help them convict you. Actually, it's the opposite. The jury will find it difficult to believe that even the angriest husband would kill in that way, watching his wife flopping around on the floor of a restroom. I'm sorry to be so blunt, but that is our case."

"Robert, I'm thoroughly confused. Everything seems the opposite of what it appears to be."

"Let's hope the state is as confused as you are. I want you to concentrate on our case against the bank and you leave it to me to keep you out of prison." Robert stood and extended his massive hand. "We begin work at eight tomorrow morning. Don't be late."

"I won't."

As Byron drove home, he thought how good it felt to have a job again. Of course, he was still facing the death penalty, but now he felt certain he had the best lawyer representing him.

He would concentrate on the lawsuit against the bank and Sunwest. He couldn't deny a certain pleasure in that. Martin Kingsbury would get what was coming to him when everything about Sunwest came out in the whistleblower suit. And Suzanne would learn about his affair with Helen Stone. It would be interesting to see if their marriage could withstand that, as Byron's own union with their daughter had also been undermined, even profaned, by such lies.

14

After the flurry of tension and activity surrounding the dreaded criminal charges nothing happened for a time, as if the state forgot about the case. Once enough quiet days went by, Byron thought he might have imagined the nightmarish affair. Only the occasional letter from the prosecutor's office jolted him out of that pleasant denial and back to reality.

Not to mention Dianne's ghost. Byron noticed her occasionally sitting in a chair by the front window where she used to read. A glimpse of her, barefoot, her shoes placed side by side on the carpet below. But only a flash-frame.

Byron's choices: he could stay at home and worry or keep busy, so he went each morning, coffee in hand and a tie around his neck, to the Taylor Law Firm to cobble together the case against the bank and Sunwest Mortgage Company. He'd never seen anyone as confident as his old landlord and friend Robert. His faith in victory was the only aspect of the case that let Byron sleep at night.

Robert's wife, Maryann, had been Robert's paralegal before their marriage, and she came in days each week to teach Byron about legal research. It didn't take him long to get the hang of it. Maryann was the exact opposite of Robert—where he was intense and bursting with confidence, she sat quiet and almost shy. Byron liked them both with genuine affection. In their presence, he almost felt safe. Almost.

ON APRIL 8TH, THE BANK MOVED TO FORECLOSE ON Byron's house. Not unexpected. After all, he hadn't paid his mortgage in months, not after being unemployed by that same financial institution.

Robert, as usual, scoffed and blustered as though losing one's home were a minor blip. He advised not to contest the foreclosure; they had bigger fish to fry. Byron was given thirty days to clear out of the house.

Really, he didn't want any of the furniture—it reminded him of Dianne, and their ambiguous life together. That reading chair of hers in particular. Her clothes and shoes, slowly coated with a fine layer of dust. He began to store his own clothes in a closet at the office. Dianne's parents came one day and took all her clothes and keepsakes they wished to have. It was a big help.

ONE DAY MARYANN CAUGHT BYRON LOOKING FOR A PAIR of shoes in a battered cardboard box kept underneath his desk.

"You can't go on living out of that box."

He stood up, flustered and red-faced. Maryann laughed at his embarrassment.

"This is only until I find a sturdy perch."

"Our guesthouse?"

"I couldn't. But thank you for asking."

"You'd have to babysit Nicole on the odd night when Bob and I go out, and you and he could ride to work together." Maryann, leaning in, seemed aware of how much Byron wanted to accept. "You liked it there, once. You might again."

"That's so kind." Byron cleared the emotion from his throat

and slid the cardboard box out of sight. "But Bob's been good enough to me already."

"He thinks that way he can get you to work nights and weekends the way he does."

"You're both invested in me. No question. It's comforting."

"He's excited about your bank case. 'This thing could be tremendous,' he keeps saying. Besides—we know you."

After months of living alone, Bryon found Maryann's easy banter and generosity wonderful. On the verge of tears: "Thank you. I'd like that."

He was always prepared for cruelty—the war had seen to that—so sudden kindness never failed to unnerve him. Maryann seemed to understand, leaving him alone.

That night after work he took a last load from the house to a storage shed, loaded his essential possessions into his car and followed Robert and Maryann home.

Their large stucco house, on twenty-five wooded acres of what had once been farmland, included an old barn converted into the beautiful, familiar guesthouse where he had lived. The moment Byron stepped inside, he felt at home. Everything looked as he remembered it from his days living there.

What a different life, almost as if he had been someone else entirely. With few details in the guesthouse unfamiliar, he unloaded and collapsed onto the bed, awash in sense memories from over a decade ago.

THEY INVITED HIM UP FOR DINNER. HE HAD FORGOTTEN what it was like to sit down with a family for a meal. The food settled into his gut with a weight that felt comforting.

Nicole ran around the kitchen chasing their Labrador retriever, Polly, who kept a well-chewed tennis ball in her mouth. Robert cooked salmon on the grill and Maryann mixed a salad in a large wooden bowl. Byron made drinks for everyone. Conversation remained light. You'd have thought nothing in the world wrong.

After dinner Maryann asked if he would take Nicole into the living room and read to her while they cleaned up. Byron sat on the couch by the fireplace as Nicole took up a position on his left and Polly settled in on his right. He had only been reading for a few minutes when he noticed both Nicole and Polly were asleep. He didn't dare move for fear of waking them. He hadn't been this happy in a long time.

When Robert and Maryann came in they took Nicole upstairs to bed. Byron was exhausted himself and after saying good night he walked down the long gravel driveway to the guesthouse. Polly followed after him. For the first time in months, he slept with the lights off.

It was a relief when he got the court order awarding the bank title to the house on Willow Lane. Now all that had happened there lay behind him—all, that is, except his trial for murder.

Byron still couldn't make himself believe this was real. He had read the indictment and spent a night in jail and seen all the work Robert was doing on his case, but it all seemed to be happening to someone else. It was the way he had felt during the war. People were being killed around him and he knew he could be, too, but it seemed surreal somehow, as if he might wake up in the morning and remember the war as a bad dream. Except that every morning, there it was again.

But really, what are nightmares once they're in the past but dreams only half-remembered? His trial would be that way as well, one day.

In May, the prosecutor's office called Robert for a meeting about Byron's case. When he returned, the normally garrulous attorney seemed quiet.

"Just tell me what happened."

"A plea bargain, it seems, is now on the table."

"And this is positive, or not?"

Robert shut the door to his office. When he sat down again,

heavy, he didn't immediately elaborate on the offer. Byron assumed it wasn't good. A cold rock settled in his gut.

"You don't seem pleased." Byron felt sweat popping out of the palms of his hands.

Byron had never seen Robert look so serious, not glum exactly, but concerned. "Not pleased. No question."

Byron managed a weak smile. "I can take it."

"Here's the drill-down: They're filing a notice with the court that the state intends to ask for the death penalty if no plea deal is reached. They'll allow you to plead murder in the second, with a recommendation for life in prison without the possibility of parole."

"So death, or life."

"One way of putting it. Either way, we have to let them know by Friday."

Instinctively, Byron looked at his watch as if that would tell him how much time he had left to live. Death penalty. The words alone were bad enough, but Robert's concern was contagious. *So, after defending this country overseas, back home the state will now try to kill me. Won't that be murder too?*

He recoiled from memories of terrible images he'd suffered, and caused. The friends he cared about, his buddies, the ones didn't come back from the field except in a bag; sometimes the enemy himself, if the results of the unit's work were glimpsed up close. The acts men like Byron must do to survive, at times, under conditions of combat. These are not normal conditions that most people understand. They are lucky. He shuddered and closed his eyes.

"What do you think I should do?" He wanted someone to make these decisions for him, because he was too confused to think clearly.

"I can tell you this much—even if you were convicted, it typically takes about seventeen years to carry out the sentence in a death penalty case." Robert meant this as reassuring.

"So I have that going for me?" Here they were discussing the logistics of when Byron might be put to death as if we were talking about buying a new car. "Not much different from a life sentence."

"Yes it is, Byron. It's very different. You have to let me know what you decide by Friday. Take a few days off from work so you can think about it."

"Honestly, I can't seem to think straight." Byron hated to sound so pathetic, but he was being honest. "Maybe I should take some time off."

"Do that." Robert stood.

"Do you think we can win?"

"I always think I can win, but you have to consider what happens if we lose."

Byron tried to stand up too, but his legs had gone weak on him. He sat back down. Hearing Robert say he must consider what happens if they lost had frightened him more than learning the state was going to ask for the death penalty. Unflappable, confident Robert had to be considering that too. Byron thought of how unbearable that responsibility must be for him.

"We won't lose, Robert." Byron stood up and clasped Robert's hand. "I have every confidence in you."

Robert gripped Byron's hand like someone saying a last good-bye. "You know I'll do my best."

"Your best is good enough for me."

Byron went back to his office and put some research he had done on bank regulations into his briefcase. He thought he might work from home, but as he drove along he found himself headed towards Dianne's old house. Wallowing.

THE ROAD THAT HAD LED THROUGH HAY FIELDS WAS now four lanes wide and wound its way through one housing development after another. He turned right on Sunnyview Drive and up the hill he had pedaled on his bicycle so many years before.

He found her house. The new owners had painted the house yellow and added a room on the side. A plastic blue wading pool sat on the green lawn of the front yard. The people who lived there now must have small children. Whatever it was that he was hoping to find was no longer there. He turned around and headed to his mother's house.

When Byron pulled into her driveway, he saw his mother working in her garden. The iris were in full bloom. She always had a way with plants. She got on with them more than people, he thought.

He got out and watched as she pulled at stubborn weeds, throwing them behind her once they finally surrendered to her furious tugging.

When she saw him, she stood and brushed the dirt from her gloves. "I didn't hear you drive in."

"I was watching you give those weeds hell." Byron tried to sound upbeat. "The Iris look beautiful."

"We've had a lot of rain." She put her hands on her lower back and stretched. "I'm too old for this kind of work."

"Can I give you a hand?" They both knew he was making conversation. He wouldn't know a hoe from a hammer.

"You and your father never were much help in the garden, so I guess it's too late now." Suddenly she looked aghast at what she had said. She must have read in the papers that the state was asking for the death penalty. "I just meant—well."

"I know what you meant, mother." They both smiled, strained as could be. "Awkward, sure. But you know I didn't do it."

She took off her gardening gloves and laid them in the wicker basket that held her tools. "Let's go in and I'll make you some tea."

Byron followed her into the kitchen and sat down at the round table were they argued for so many years. Now they were left with a silence that they each wore like a suit of armor. Perhaps whatever she'd planned to say had been deflected by his preemptive suggestion of innocence.

"Got anything to eat? I'm starved."

"I made a peach cobbler. That used to be one of your favorites." His mother took it out of the refrigerator and set the dish on the kitchen counter. "Would you like some ice cream with it? I've got vanilla."

"Yes, I would. I'd like that very much." As if by magic, they galloped over all the fences that had divided them for years. The difficulties he faced made past trouble seem insignificant.

"I think I'll have some with you."

His mother served two large helpings of the dessert and set them on the table. After she made tea, she joined her son.

"I'm glad you stopped by." She reached across and patted his hand.

"I was thinking I hadn't seen you in some time, and that I'd take a chance you were in."

"Were else would I be?"

Why the hell hadn't they been like this before? "The cobbler is delicious."

Mrs. Round stood up. "I forgot the ice cream."

"I don't need any, really."

"You always liked ice cream with peach cobbler."

They seemed to be floating along on a tide of pleasant memories and he had to admit, he was glad to see her again.

Byron held his plate out and his mother set a generous scoop of vanilla ice cream on top. Reverent, he set his plate down and stared down at it. He was a boy again, but only for a fleeting instant.

Fighting to keep his voice steady: "Aren't you having any?"

His mother rejoined him at the table. "That's the last of it."

"Take some."

"No. I'm getting too fat, anyway."

"You look wonderful."

Next they ran out of small talk they needed to avoid what was on both their minds. He didn't want to let on how frightened he was, but such an emotion is hard to hide from your mother.

She saw you scared too many times as a kid. She knows.

His mother set her plate aside. "I read in the papers about your case."

Byron took another bite of cobbler. He scoffed and said through his food, "You can't believe what you read. They're just trying to sell papers."

"They say you were offered a plea bargain."

He took a long drink of coffee. "They're trying to scare me into pleading guilty to a crime I didn't commit. That's all. My lawyer says we can't lose." Byron wondered how Robert would feel about his lying like that.

"They're going to make you out to be a monster and her to be an angel so they can kill you." His mother spoke without lifting her head. In those few words she had made him see exactly what was waiting for him and more clearly than all of the legal explanations Robert had offered.

"Of course they are. That's how these cases go, mother. Even my lawyer admits that. It's not what you did but what they make the jury think you are. It's a kind of popularity contest in reverse."

Even Byron had to laugh at that. His mother tried to laugh too, but without success.

After that they talked about gardening and the weather and how Mrs. Crawford's roses had got rust from all the rain. Her grandson had been accepted at Yale, and Phyllis Smith was pregnant and her husband had been overseas for a year, so everyone was trying to guess whom the father was—it all sounded like inconsequential noise.

Around four Byron said he'd better be going, and his mother walked him out to the car.

"I'll be back soon." That wasn't true, but he thought his mother was glad he had said it anyway.

"Come back when you can, son." The finality in her words hung like a storm-cloud.

She kissed him on the cheek. Lingering in the hug, he felt her tears against his neck. That was when Byron knew his mother thought he was guilty. Then, and when she failed to look him in the eye before going back inside. Now that hurt.

15

I n response to the Brady Motion Robert filed, the prosecution turned over what modest evidence they had compiled against Byron, which the seasoned defense attorney characterized with mocking disdain. The state was supposed to include any exculpatory evidence as well, but there didn't appear to be much of that, either.

But both Byron and Robert noticed the state hadn't requested the videotape from the security cameras at the store where Dianne's body had been found. That seemed a rather curious oversight, even to Byron.

"It looks like they're not trying very hard to locate whoever it was who gave her those drugs."

Robert didn't seem surprised by this apparent lapse on the part of the police. "If it had been distribution weight, they'd dig around. Anything that doesn't allow the cops to seize money or property is beneath their notice."

"Do they think I gave her the junk?" Byron still had no idea what the state's theory of the case was. Since the time of his indictment he hadn't been able to think straight. "Is that it?"

"No. Best guess? They think you might have paid some dealer to give her an overdose."

"Somebody's seen too many TV shows."

"Granted. But it won't be hard for them to get some junkie to say you hired him to kill your wife. You knew about her drug problems and your marriage was in trouble. You'd had enough, and didn't think anyone would care enough to give a rip about another dead doper. That's the narrative I'm sensing."

"Our marriage wasn't always in trouble." Byron wondered why Robert had to hear it anew. With a sigh: "Well—only for the last ten years."

"Yeah. No question." The attorney made a sound as though sucking a cough drop. "They produced all the emails between you and your assistant. Remember those?"

A chill in the air. "I wrote them."

Robert's hard gaze pierced into Byron. "I wouldn't be so dismissive if I were you."

"Whose side are you on?"

"Byron: I've read them. And there seems to be a modicum of flirting going on."

"I explained that to you. We were—are—good friends. We had dinner together last night, in fact. But it's never been more than collegial."

With his substantial jowls shaking, Robert scribbled onto his notepad and sighed. "Brother—no more dinners with her until this is over."

"I don't understand."

He put down the pencil. "Are you serious? What time did the turnip truck drop you off?"

He wanted to protest the insinuation behind Robert's remarks, but the kernel of truth in what the lawyer said finally landed home. Byron had been attracted to Martha Temple from the first time they'd met and he was quite sure she felt the same way, but they had never done anything inappropriate. Yes, that was exactly the right word. There had been innocent flirting, but nothing that close to sexual behavior. They had prided themselves on that. Byron was employed by his own father-in-law, for one thing.

But emotionally, they had been cheating on their spouses while pretending otherwise simply because they weren't sleeping together. What perfect hypocrites. It would have been more honest all around if they had made love once or twice. At least that would have taken the self-righteous halo off their heads.

"Let's stop playing, shall we? They have all your credit card receipts and, guess what? You and your assistant stayed at an awful lot of hotels together."

Byron felt himself shifting from irritation to alarm. His mind ran through all that could be used against him. "She traveled with me when I gave speeches to branch bank managers."

"I know what you told me, but how do you think a jury will look at such evidence?" Robert leaned back in his enormous chair. The expensive leather creaked under his bulk. He pursed his fleshy lips and waited for a reply.

"I hadn't thought about that. But, I didn't have an affair, nor did I kill Dianne." Was he in a madhouse where facts didn't matter? "The truth must count for something."

The ice broke. Robert burst into brief laughter. "Oh mercy, my boy. Not as much as you might think. I told you this case will be about who the jury thinks you are. What they are led to believe you're capable of doing. Some of it may come first in the form of sympathy—'the victim put everyone through hell,' which becomes motivation, after a fashion."

"I get it. But, you mean the state can get some junkie to say I paid him to kill Dianne, and that's enough to convict me?" Sweat moistened Byron's forehead. This couldn't be true. "That's not evidence."

"Here's wisdom I suspect you already know: cops are working-class joes who do what they're told. Unless they have orders to dig for the truth, they won't; and prosecutors like to win cases so they get nice headlines in the papers. It's not an ancient mystery."

Byron tried not to sound naïve, but it was hard not to. He couldn't imagine that the assertions Robert were making were true, or that he could accept them so matter-of-factly. "Seems criminal not to look for the real murderer."

"Once they began to focus on you, well, then they quit looking for anyone else. That's how these cases go."

"That's insane."

Suspicion crept back into Robert's tone. "Sometimes I forget you were a cop, the way you act as though you don't know how this world works. No authority figure will ever admit publicly they were wrong on a screw-up like this. Not even after losing a case; not even caught red-handed. Too much insulation thanks to 'the club,' and too much liability."

"I wasn't on the force long enough to get initiated, I guess."

Robert shook his head. "It always comes down to money, connections. But it's class, after a certain point, to get into the 'big' club."

Exhausted, Byron slumped in his chair. He felt like a man with a bad case of the flu, too weak to care for himself. "I just can't believe this has happened to me."

Robert took a cigar out of the cherry wood box that sat on his desk. He rolled it between his thick, powerful fingers and snipped off the end before lighting it. The rich aroma of expensive tobacco filled the room and seemed to soothe them both. "Care for one?"

Robert held the cigar box out to Byron, but he waived it away. He didn't feel worthy. "Doesn't it bother you that no one seems interested in the fact that I'm innocent?"

"I'm not a philosopher, Byron. I'm a lawyer." Robert puffed on his cigar and confident clouds of blue smoke billowed up over his head. "And you ought to be glad I know the difference."

"Of course I'm glad. It's that it all seems so—I don't know."

"Callous? Inhuman?"

"The cops do their job, the prosecutor does hers and you do yours, while I stand by watching as if all of this is happening to someone else." Byron was close to collapse. *"I'm a dead man."*

"High stakes. No question. But pull yourself together. Back to strategy." Robert became enveloped by blue smoke. "I'm gonna subpoena the videotapes from the store's security cameras. I want you to look at them and tell me if you see anyone you know with your wife. There are four main entrances and, who knows? Fifteen hundred people went in there during the time your wife was in there? That's a lot of suspects. But I want you to look at every face you can make out. Every bit of body language."

The mere thought of a task at hand helped. Somewhat. "Let me know when you get the videotapes. I'll get right to it."

"One more thing—own any stock in Sunwest Mortgage Company?"

Byron had started to stand up to leave. He sank back down into the chair. "Of course not."

"Well—the police found records of you owning two hundred shares."

"It's news to me."

"I looked up the price per share at close yesterday. Three-oh-five." He whistled. "That's thousands of dollars' worth of stock."

"I swear to you I have no idea where that came from."

Robert's tone was neither incredulous nor accusatory. "Why would 'someone' put so much stock in your account?"

"I can't answer that. You know I don't have the kind of money it would take to buy it."

"Apparently you do. Those shares are in your name."

Byron thought he detected the slightest hint of skepticism in Robert's voice. "My God—what do the police think?"

"That you've been embezzling. They just haven't figured out how, yet."

Sheer panic. Byron gripped the back of the chair as if holding on for life. "Someone's making it look as though I did all these things—can't you see that?"

Then it occurred to him, "Wait—Helen Stone and Martin Kingsbury could very well have transferred those shares to me. If the transfer was discovered, it would look as though I had embezzled them. Or if not, it would be a kind of warning shot to keep me quiet about the Sunwest business." He was surprised by how bold they had been and how far they were willing to go. "They could expose me any time they liked."

Robert set his cigar on the edge of his desk. "Think what that would do for our whistleblower case. If we could prove that."

"I thought the state had to prove I'm guilty."

"In the criminal case, yes. But I think they've done that already, Byron."

"Even to you?"

"What I think doesn't matter, but if any more incriminating evidence drips out, we're gonna think hard about that plea deal. That's my truest advice for a man in your position."

A plea deal? Byron had forgotten that tomorrow was the last day for him to accept the offer of life in prison.

Life in prison. That sounded ridiculous even to him. What life could there be in prison?

Yet Robert said people took those deals all the time to avoid the death penalty. How do they kill you in Connecticut? Lethal injection, he thought. He'd have to ask Robert about that. He had always hated needles.

"What you think does matter to me."

"Then, I think you didn't do it. Zealously so, my boy. But, again, there's a one-more-thing. The police forensic report shows they found traces of Dianne's blood in your car. In the trunk."

The words 'in the trunk' sounded dreadful, and Byron could almost hear the prosecutor using them in her opening statement to the jury. They would be imaging Dianne in his trunk for the rest of the trial. "She often used my car. Maybe she cut herself on a sharp edge in the car trunk. Taking out the groceries, for instance."

"Well, we'll just have to pitch that to the jury." Robert's enthusiasm about the prospect of doing so with success seemed modest.

"Can they introduce that into evidence?" It was absurd that every innocuous detail of his life could now be construed as evidence of guilt.

"Yes, of course they can. If the judge finds it relevant to your case, it goes to the jury," a hint of exasperation in Robert's voice. Maybe all those unpaid hours he was spending on Byron's case were beginning to wear on him a bit.

"What determines if evidence is relevant or not?"

Robert's cigar lay smoldering, its ash growing longer. "If the judge thinks the evidence tends to prove you killed Dianne, then it comes in."

"That seems rather a vague standard."

"It is. My job is to persuade her to not let those facts in." Robert reached for the neglected cigar and puffed it back to life. "I wanted to tell you all this so you can see what we're up against. You have to consider that when you make your decision about whether to take the plea deal or not. They also found hair belonging to your assistant."

"Naturally they would. We drove all over the state together."

"Did she sit in the back seat?"

Byron tried to remember if Martha had ever been in the back seat of the car, a difficult task. "Maybe when I took her and Mr. Kingsbury to a banking conference in New Haven."

"You can see how this all looks, the girlfriend is in the back seat while the wife is in the trunk. Just sayin'."

"I'll keep all that in mind."

A DEJECTED BYRON TRUDGED BACK TO HIS OFFICE, BUT he couldn't concentrate. He drove home.

As he turned up Ashley Drive, he was startled by flashing blue lights in his rearview mirror. *My God, am I going back to jail?* Had they revoked his bond? He thought of the hundred small details he needed to address—change the sheets on his bed, pay the phone bill, have the tires on his car rotated, all ordinary day-to-day duties.

He pulled over and waited. When the door of the unmarked cruiser opened, he saw it was Lieutenant Atkins.

"I saw you go by, so I pulled you over so's we could talk."

Byron fumbled for his driver's license, but the lieutenant indicated he didn't want to see it with a wave of his hand.

"Now what?"

"Look, brother: I persuaded the prosecutor to offer you a plea deal because I think you got in over your head with the Kingsburys."

"What would you know about them?"

"Take the deal. We've got more than enough evidence to convict you."

Byron sat shaking as he sat behind the steering wheel. *"I didn't do it,* you son of a bitch."

"Relax. I'm trying to help you. I know you find that hard to believe. But after tomorrow? It'll be too late. Just trying to clear the air." The lieutenant went back to his car.

Byron sat for he didn't know how long, his head against the cool vinyl of the steering wheel. A neighborhood resident, a middle-aged woman with tense body language, knocked on the window to ask if he was ill. Startled, he snapped at her to go the hell away, and she scurried back across the street with the devil at her heels.

At home finally, he stared at all the familiar objects in the guesthouse—the chairs, his books, the curtains—as though for the last time. A hollow silence like death filled the air.

He tried to concentrate on the plea deal he was being offered: life in prison, or possibly the death house. Here he was sitting in this comfortable living room, listening to music, thinking of what to have for dinner and whether he would go to jail for the rest of my life, or die. It was all too incongruous.

Maybe if he were to lie down and close his eyes, it would all be gone when he awoke. Perhaps Dianne would come and wake him for dinner. He could hear her voice, smell her perfume, see her face as she sat in the reading chair, her long legs slung over the arm. They would have grilled chicken with asparagus, and he'd say he had forgotten to pick up some white wine on the way home from the bank.

Only, he no longer worked at the bank; and Dianne was dead. No waking up from that cold fact.

He watched the news and picked at a salad, but couldn't eat. After dinner, he showered and went to bed. Byron stared at the ceiling. Ideas spun like a runaway carousel. *Take the deal. Don't. Life in prison. The Death Penalty.* Round and round.

When the sun came up, he still had no idea what to do. The mere act of deciding, one way or the other, seemed a kind of surrender. The system and all its gears like sharp teeth grinding approached from behind him, whirring louder and closer.

16

O nce at the office the next day, Byron was too nervous to operate machinery, so Robert drove them over to Ms. Kern's office to discuss the plea.

When they arrived, her assistant announced that Ms. Kerns was on the telephone and that they should be seated.

"Probably busy reading tarot cards." Robert, fuming, paced the reception area as staff and lawyers bearing file folders scurried around. "I hear the DA's relying on divination rather than hard evidence these days," loud enough for the assistant to hear and later report to her boss.

Byron, suspecting the only card a mystic would turn for him would be Death, sat in morose silence. Robert, meanwhile, took out a cigar and thrust it between clenched teeth.

The admin assistant frowned. "You know there's no smoking in this building, sir."

"It's not lit, as you can see." Robert—the old confident version —held the unlit cigar aloft for her inspection. "I'm saving it for when this adjudication is dispatched to our satisfaction."

Her line buzzed. The assistant pursed her lips and picked up the phone. "Yes—the death penalty case is here about the plea offer." She said this as you might announce that lunch had arrived. "That's right. Okay."

At that exact moment Byron knew what he would do. He was as frightened as anyone facing execution, but for the first time in weeks, he could think with clarity. He stood to follow Robert, the flaps of his suit coat billowing in his wake, into the office.

Ms. Kerns enjoyed a wonderful view of the park from her office window. A young girl walked her dog twelve stories below them. She threw what looked like a tennis ball. The dog chased after it, returned the item to its master.

Life goes on, Byron thought, and somehow that made his predicament seem less serious. All those people walking by below had no idea of what was happening to him above them, and why should they? They all had bills to pay, exams to take, dental appointments to keep—in a word, lives of their own. Before this, he hadn't taken much notice of other people's problems, so why should they care about his? At best, he would make for a few minutes of entertainment on the nightly news.

"Mr. Round—do care for coffee?"

It was Kerns. Byron realized he hadn't heard her at first. Declining with a curt "I'm fine," he realized he *was* fine. Now that he had a plan, he felt better. His position hadn't improved, but at least he wasn't being pricked by fearful uncertainty. Now it was only garden-variety, baseline survival-instinct fear.

"Let's get down to business." The district attorney looked over the tissue-thin paper of the plea offer through glasses perched on the tip of her nose. "Well. In some ways you're a lucky man, Mr. Round."

"That's hard for me to feel—lucky." He looked to Robert, but his face was a blank. Byron supposed years of these negotiations had taught the defense lawyer to mask any emotion.

"I only meant that Lieutenant Atkins has persuaded this office to offer you a plea agreement."

"I hardly think that qualifies as good luck, maybe less-awful luck would be more accurate." Byron smiled at Kerns, but his sarcasm seemed to annoy her. In her mind he was supposed to be grateful for any kindness she showed him. The fact that he might be innocent didn't seem to have occurred to her. He almost had to laugh at the earnest prosecutor telling the innocent-until-proven guilty man the state might not kill him, if only he'd deign to confess.

"I hardly think you're in a position to make jokes, Mr. Round." Ms. Kerns laid down her papers. Now the gloves were off. "The evidence against you appears overwhelming, if largely circumstantial. I can review it point-by-point for you and counsel if you choose, but I think we all know the facts by now." There beneath her long fingers lay all the forensic reports, photographs, interviews and charts that condemned him. She tapped them with a gentle rhythm.

"Joann, there is one rather troubling omission in that bonfire of evidence." Robert Taylor's unlit cigar jumped about as he spoke. "Why weren't the tapes from the store's security cameras obtained?"

"In light of the amount of evidence against Mr. Round, we simply didn't feel any need to spend more resources on this case. Of course, if he doesn't accept our plea agreement, we will lay out additional evidence."

"While I appreciate your concern for the taxpayers of our state, I'm a bit confused about why the police didn't request those videos." Robert scratched his head in a pantomime of confusion. "It couldn't be that when the police get around to convincing some junkie to confess to killing Mrs. Round because my client asked him to, that the videos will then suddenly appear as evidence, could it?"

"I resent the implication of what you're suggesting."

"Imagine how much Mr. Round resents being falsely charged with murder."

Ms. Kerns tapped her pile of evidence yet again. "You've tried enough of these cases to know your client will be convicted if we go to trial."

"I know you don't have an eye witnesses that can finger Mr. Round, I know you have no idea who actually killed his wife or even where she died."

"We know something better—where she *didn't* die, and it wasn't in her car. Someone put her there, and that proves she was murdered." Ms. Kerns was speaking only to Robert now, two lawyers playing chess while Byron sat watching.

"It might only prove that some dealer got frightened when she overdosed and carried her back to the car to make it look like she was alone when she died."

"Except for one thing; how did the dealer know which car was hers?"

"Maybe he'd seen her in it before."

"Or maybe Mr. Round told him what car she's be driving."

"Such guessing is unbecoming of an officeholder such as yourself." Robert made no attempt to hide his contempt for the state's case against his client, and for a moment Byron almost believed the evidence against him was as weak as Robert made it out. But, of course, he was the one who would suffer the consequences if Robert were wrong. And Robert's face was now as much a mask to Byron as it was to Ms. Kerns.

"The grand jury didn't think we were guessing when they indicted Mr. Round." It was hard to argue with the logic of the argument.

"The grand jury would indict the pope if you asked them to." Robert laid his unlit cigar on top of his briefcase. "I'd like some time alone with my client, if you don't mind."

"Of course, take all the time you need." Ms. Kerns seemed positively delighted to grant them these few moments of privacy. After all, there was no doubt as to how this would all end. Mission accomplished; another trial avoided, another killer put away for life.

As soon as the prosecutor closed the door behind her, Byron stood up and went to the window. The sun was shining outside, and office workers filed into the park to enjoy their brief lunch breaks sitting on grass and breathing fresh air. The early days of spring were always the most wonderful, the chill of winter in the morning, glorious warmth in the afternoon.

He wondered where the girl with the dog had gone; maybe to meet her boyfriend, perhaps for a glass of wine in a sidewalk cafe, somewhere. And later, to make love in the afternoon. What a nice way to spend the day, much more than sitting in Ms. Kerns' too-air conditioned office. Plus, now that the DA had left, Robert didn't seem quite so confident.

"A lot of what she said?" Pulling each word from deep inside. "It's true."

"Yes, I know that."

Off in the far corner of the park, Byron again saw the blond girl and her dog. The dog was eating a sandwich out of her hand. He thought how lucky they were to have found each other and decided if he got ever out of this, he would get a dog of his own—a big one.

"Is there anything you want to ask me?" Robert's powerful hands were busy fighting with each other in his lap. Byron felt sorry for him. He seemed so distraught.

"I don't think so." Byron turned away from the window. "You've told me everything I should know."

"Well, this is the time to ask me any questions you have. She'll be back in a few minutes."

"I do have a question." Byron turned back to the window. A light breeze was making the new leaves dance.

"I thought you might."

"What is the name of that park?"

"Finley Park, I believe." After a long silence, Robert stood up. "Lots of people facing such choices can't think clearly." He put his heavy hand on Byron's shoulder.

"I've never seen things more clearly in my life." Byron smiled in an effort to reassure that he hadn't gone mad.

"You have to decide about the deal she's offering you." Robert had lowered his voice in the way that one does in church. He was doing his best to bring Byron around to the unpleasant business at hand without appearing brusque.

Sensitivity seemed foreign to Robert. "I'm quite aware of that."

Robert's booming voice had dropped to a whisper. "Shall I call her back in?"

"Yes, I think so." Byron straightened his tie. One needed to look ship-shape in front of the firing squad.

Robert disappeared for a few minutes and Byron could hear him talking to Ms. Kerns. They appeared to be arguing, but when they came back into the room, they were both somber-faced.

"Ms. Kern would like to ask you a few questions. If you have any questions you would like to ask, either of Ms. Kerns or me, please feel free to do so."

With the preliminaries out of the way, the bloodletting couldn't be far off. Ms. Kerns took a sip of water from a bottle labeled *Fresh Springs*. "Have you been advised by counsel of the terms of the plea agreement the state has offered you?" She was all business now.

Byron felt as if he were at the motor vehicle department applying for a new license. "I have."

"And have you had an opportunity to consult with counsel about the terms of the plea agreement?"

"I have." Should he stand to attention and salute as Ms. Kerns went on?

"Have you reached a decision to accept or reject the offer the state has made to you?"

He wanted to say 'I do' for some reason, but restrained himself. "I have."

After a moment of silence, Byron realized they were waiting for his decision. He had become so used to other people telling him what to do since his arrest that he'd gotten out of the habit of calling the shots. Maybe time for him to turn the tables, dodge and weave in an unexpected feint to throw off his opponent in the legal ring, the state, and even his own counsel:

"I do *not* accept the state's offer."

Robert looked startled. Ms. Kerns' disappointment in his lack of judgment was so strong she couldn't resist another go at getting him to plead guilty. "The defendant understands the state will be asking for the death penalty in his case."

"'The defendant understands." Byron was unable to keep the sarcasm out of his voice.

"If you're found guilty, you may be executed."

"You've been quite clear on that point." He felt Robert's hand, huge but gentle, on his shoulder.

The prosecutor said with a breezy air of professional nonchalance, "All-right then. Let's peek at the trial calendar, such as it can accommodate a capital crime of this magnitude."

So that was that. After the indictment and the endless conferences and plea discussions, Byron would stand trial for murder in the first degree. But his strategic feint, it seemed the best chance to air the whole truth about the bank, Dianne's father, all of it.

This real-world process of jurisprudence in Byron's case seemed medieval compared to sanitized TV versions. Where were those forensic investigators one saw on television who produced scientific evidence either proving, or otherwise, the innocence of the accused? These wizards seemed in short supply here in Connecticut, with speculation and expediency in the place of hard evidence. That alone gave him hope.

With that, Robert and Ms. Kerns got down to the business of scheduling Byron's trial. Ms. Kerns wanted to go to trial immediately, Robert wanted time to assess the so-called evidence. They began to squabble about who was the busier.

Finally they both agreed a trial was a waste of time and money, Robert because Byron was innocent, Ms. Kerns because he was so obviously guilty. Could two experienced lawyers actually see his case so differently? Or was this the usual posturing the adversarial system invited to each trial?

He tuned them both out and looked through the window to the park below. A young man had joined the girl with the dog. They kissed as the dog barked and jumped around for attention. Byron wanted to shout to the young lovers, but of course they wouldn't have heard him.

For a moment he thought the two of them had forgotten he was still in the room because they talked about him in the third person. He'll want a speedy trial. He better have a psychiatric exam. If he's convicted, there'll be an automatic appeal. That could take years. On and on. He could hear what they were saying, but it was like eaves-dropping on a French couple next to you in a Parisian café—Byron heard them, but had no idea what the words meant.

"I think that about does it." Ms. Kerns held her hand out and Byron shook it. Why not? You have to be a good sport about these things. After all, she was only doing her job. Isn't that what people say in times like this, when some mindless bureaucrat is grinding you into the dust?

Yes, I'm sure that's the proper thing to say. Shows good sportsmanship on my part. Don't want to be a sore loser.

Byron managed to return Ms. Kerns's smile. She was pretty. He hadn't noticed that before. As he went to leave, he even felt a gentle hand on his shoulder guiding him out. Odd and invasive.

Byron looked at his watch. It was nearly one. Ms. Kerns must be late for lunch somewhere. Perhaps even in the park, to meet a friend or lover. To live her life of freedom.

THEY RODE BACK TO THE OFFICE IN SILENCE. ROBERT tried to be cheerful, and once or twice even assured Byron the state had no case against him.

He tried to mimic Robert's optimism, but everything he said seemed to fall flat. He was terrified now that the clock was running. He could hear it ticking away inside his head. He tried not to imagine the jury foreman announcing the verdict, but he had seen that movie too many times to be able to block it out, not when he was poised for a starring role in this drama.

But despite his role as the main character, Byron had almost no part to play at all. He was supposed to show up and listen to the lies people said about him. If the state had designed a torture machine for the sole purpose of driving defendants mad, they couldn't have done a better job.

If you were guilty, it all made a kind of sense—the delays, the expert witnesses, the endless testimony for and against. It was an endless wait in the doctor's office while he read your chart before announcing if the tumor was fatal or benign. It was hell. But Byron wasn't guilty, and that made it all the worse.

17

Working on the Sunwest case helped Byron think about something, anything, other than his approaching trial. He spent his days—and most of his sleepless nights—assembling evidence that Sunwest had packaged thousands of substandard mortgages together and sold them to Freddie Mac and Fannie Mae without disclosing how out-of-compliance they were with federal loan regulations.

Immediately after Robert filed his whistleblower suit against the bank and Sunwest, the bank filed a motion to dismiss the complaint. They had found an obliging judge who set a hearing date for August 3rd. That gave them only three weeks to prepare. Some nights he worked so late he started sleeping on the couch in the lobby of Robert's office, when rest would come.

THE BANK HAD RETAINED THE LARGEST DEFENSE FIRM in Hartford and they would spare no expense in trying to get their motion granted. Robert learned the judge had been a member of that firm before being appointed to the bench. It was all quite cozy, and Byron could see Robert was concerned.

The bank had attached an affidavit from Mr. Kingsbury to their motion. In it he described Byron as a disgruntled former employee who had been fired for cause. Martin Kingsbury also mentioned that Byron was his son-in-law and had been indicted for murder. The bank wasn't afraid to throw a punch below the belt.

The thrust of Martin's affidavit was that Sunwest was an independent, if wholly owned, subsidiary of the bank, and therefore its actions could not create internal liability in the manner here alleged.

"Throwing them to the wolves, I see." Robert put down Martin's affidavit. "They're trying to distance themselves from Sunwest, their own company."

"That's crazy."

Robert laughed. "No, it's typical."

It sounded like Martin, the cat who always landed on his feet, to pull a clever feint like this. Of course, as the chief architect of the Sunwest deal, mud would splatter Martin Kingsbury's fine leather loafers, too, if the bank lost the case. Which he wouldn't let happen. Not Martin. Every time Byron thought about running into him at the airport that day, the hair on the back of his neck stood on end.

ON THE DAY OF THE HEARING AND WITH STEADIER nerves, this time he drove his attorney to the courthouse. After all the work, both held an air of confidence bordering on cheerful nonchalance, joking and chatting with the young woman who served them crullers and coffee through a drive-through window.

Inside the august courtroom, Byron's mood settled and the true stakes crept back into his troubled mind. Robert had attached affidavits from various homeowners who had been foreclosed on by Sunwest to his Reply brief. Two lawyers who represented the bank introduced themselves to Robert and ignored Byron. He didn't see his father-in-law anywhere.

A few minutes later the judge entered and took his position

above them all. He was a man in his late sixties, with coiffed grey hair that crowned his thin face so perfectly that Byron guessed he must have it styled.

The judge smiled at the lawyers representing the bank, greeting the various actors. His honor peered over reading glasses at Robert. "And who have we here?"

"Robert Taylor, your honor."

"Oh, my. I know of your criminal defense work." A little smile. "But I don't believe you have appeared before this court. Not your typical area of expertise."

Robert seethed but remained cordial. "I can assure his honor that the case is well prepared."

The judge raised a skeptical eyebrow. "The court will hear from Mr. Boswell on the bank's Motion to Dismiss. But, before you begin, I should tell you I have read all the pleadings submitted by the parties, and while my impartiality in all such matters remains quite unimpeachable, the court already sits persuaded that the motion should be granted."

"Then why the hell are we here?" Robert whispered.

"May it please the court, I am—"

The judge cut the lawyer off with a wave of his hand and snapped, "You're well known to this court, Mr. Boswell. Get on with your argument."

Chastened, Boswell shifted in his loafers and stammered into his discourse. "Yes. Well. Now, let's see here—since the court has read the bank's motion and the attached affidavit of its CEO, Mr. Kingsbury, I can be brief. Mr. Kingsbury is not only the bank's CEO, he is also a man active in community affairs. He has twice been awarded the governor's legion of honor for service to the state. He is a veteran who served eight years as a major in the National Guard, winning three commendations for revising the Guard's procurement practices. In his affidavit, Mr. Kingsbury swears under oath that Sunwest, while wholly owned by the bank, is an independent entity that controls its own affairs. In their complaint the plaintiff's do not allege any wrongdoing by the bank, other than its failure to supervise Sunwest. In light of Mr. Kingsbury's affidavit, we ask that the Complaint be dismissed as to the Bank." Mr. Boswell, having quickly regained his groove, remained standing like an actor waiting for applause before leaving the stage.

That applause wasn't long in coming: "The court finds the affiant to be a credible witness. Additionally, the court notes that the plaintiffs have offered no affidavit to counter the assertions made by Mr. Kingsbury. Therefore, the court is prepared to grant the motion to dismiss as to the bank."

"Perhaps the court would like to hear from the plaintiff before making its ruling?" Robert leapt to his feet. "While it's true that the affidavits of the homeowners do not respond to the issues raised by the bank, we have brought with us today another witness who is both credible, knowledgeable, and prepared to testify. Today."

Byron turned around in his seat to look towards the back of the courtroom to see who the surprise witness was when he heard his name called.

"Your honor, the plaintiffs call Byron Round to the stand."

Byron thought there must be some mistake. Was he to be the surprise witness on whose testimony the whole case depended? He made his way to the front of the courtroom.

Robert smiled his most reassuring smile and began his questions. "Mr. Round, the bank has told us a good deal about Mr. Kingsbury's background, so I have no doubt the court would be interested in hearing about yours as well." By this little maneuver Robert had cut off all objections the bank might have to this line of questions.

The judge appeared pained he would suffer so much irrelevant testimony, but now powerless to cut it short, he flicked his fingers at Robert to proceed.

"Are you too a veteran, Mr. Round?"

"Yes," Byron said in a soft whisper. What did this have to do with the lawsuit against the bank?

"Please speak up so the court can hear you." Robert seemed to be enjoying himself.

"Yes, I was in the army."

"And what rank did you hold?"

"Staff sergeant."

"Did you serve overseas at any time?"

"I did two tours overseas."

"Did you see combat during those tours?" Robert had turned his back to Byron, like a bandleader smiling at his audience.

"Yes."

"And were you, in fact, wounded in combat?"

Where the hell was this going? Robert must have known that he was embarrassing Byron. "Yes," Byron said as quietly as possible.

"And that scar on your face, Mr. Round—is that a result of your wounds?"

Byron reached up to his scar. "Yes, it is."

"Were you hospitalized for your wounds?"

"I was in the hospital for three months, and rehab for two months after that."

"One last thing—did you receive any medals for your service?" Robert faced Byron again, now with a smile wide enough to be seen outside the courtroom.

"I received a Purple Heart, a Bronze Star and a Silver Star."

"All awards for heroism and courage under fire. I see. Mr. Round, I'm sure the court and the defendants join me in thanking you for your gallant service to your country." Here Robert swept eyes to the judge, opposing counsel and few others in the courtroom, giving them all an opportunity to nod that yes, indeed, they too were grateful for Byron's service.

Byron marveled at how adroit Robert had been in the courtroom that within five minutes of his taking the stand, there could now be no question about his client's credibility. "You were employed by the defendant bank shortly after you were honorably discharged, is that correct?" He held up a finger to delay Byron's reply. "By Mr. Kingsbury, I might add?"

"I started in what we call back office operations. That's where we do all the clerical and regulatory work for the bank." Byron was starting to get a feel for what Robert wanted him to say. "I was later promoted to chief compliance officer for the bank. My duties were to insure all bank operations were in compliance with state and federal regulations."

"And in your capacity as chief compliance officer did you have occasion to review the operations of the Defendant Sunwest?"

"I did. The bank purchased Sunwest, and shortly after that purchase, I started to notice some irregularities in their residential mortgages."

Robert had turned to the judge once again, holding his gaze while asking Byron the question. "What sorts of irregularities?"

"Chiefly in the supporting documentation used to verify the income for mortgage applicants."

"And what problems did you perceive with this?"

"Income documentation was either incomplete or, in some cases, missing altogether. In other cases the documentation looked as if it had been altered to meet the loan criteria."

"Do you mean income statements had been falsified?" Robert pretended to look aghast. The judge, for the first time since Byron had been sworn in, leaned forward in his chair.

Byron, having now grown to understand how much of all this was actually theater, slipped on his reading glasses so he would appear every inch the credible professional. "To my eyes, yes. They appeared to be falsified."

"And did you share your concerns with anyone at the bank?"

"Not at that time, no."

"And why not?"

"Because they were only concerns. I wasn't sure a real problem existed at Sunwest." He cleared his throat and prepared a zinger regarding his other case. "Not with only circumstantial evidence."

"But that would change into hard evidence."

"That's right."

"Did you take any steps to confirm or dispel your concerns about Sunwest?" The two lawyers from the bank were scribbling notes now.

"Yes; I flew to San Francisco and did what we call a windshield audit."

"What does that term refer to?"

"It means you take a small, but statistically meaningful sample of documents to examine for regulatory compliance. The term gets its name from the idea that you're doing a kind of drive-by audit."

"And what, if anything, did this audit uncover?" Robert was fairly lounging against the podium, now, like a man without a problem.

"I found an unacceptably high rate of regulatory noncompliance with Sunwest's residential mortgages." Byron could almost hear the judge draw in his breath.

"Did you reveal your findings to anyone at Sunwest?"

"I did. I met with Sunwest's chief executive, Helen Stone. I told her what I had discovered in my audit."

"And what was her response?"

"Objection, hearsay." Mr. Boswell had come to life.

"It is not hearsay because it is offered to show the state of mind of this witness. It will help the court to understand Mr. Round's actions following this meeting." Robert said this with the authority of a Moses.

"Overruled." It was clear the judge wanted to hear what Byron had to say.

"She became angry and challenged my methodology and fitness to conduct an audit."

"Your response?"

"To ask for a full audit of Sunwest's books."

"And what did she say to that?"

"The same objection, your honor." Mr. Boswell's voice was noticeably lower now.

"Overruled, counsel." He glared at Boswell, seemed to restrain himself from further comment by pressing his lips together. "Go on, Mr. Round."

"She said I didn't have the authority to order an audit."

"And is that correct?"

"It is. But as soon as I returned to the office I met with Martin —Mr. Kingsbury—to report what I had discovered. And so he could order the audit."

"And how, if at all, did he respond to your report?"

Mr. Boswell again found his voice. "Your honor, we must object to this piling on. It's hearsay upon hearsay."

"If one simple word—'overruled'—isn't sufficient this time: In addition to the exception cited by plaintiff's counsel, I believe the residual exception to the hearsay rule applies, and therefore your objection is overruled."

Boswell, red-faced and huffing, eased back down into his chair. It was starting to look at though Robert had struck a nerve with the court.

"Kingsbury said he would take my concerns under advisement. I then told him that as chief compliance officer, I intended to notify the board of my initial findings."

"And how did Mr. Kingsbury respond to *that*?"

"He absolutely forbade me from going to the board."

"And to your knowledge has the board to this day ever learned of your concerns about Sunwest?"

"They have not. Not to my knowledge. No."

"No further questions, your honor."

The judge blew out his lips. "Do you have questions for the witness, Mr. Boswell?"

"We most certainly do, your honor." Mr. Boswell, as though spring-wound, leapt from his seat to grab the podium with both hands. "Fact: the purpose of your testimony today, Mr. Round, is to persuade the court that the math was amiss with the books at Sunwest. Is that correct?"

"I hadn't thought of it that way, but, I suppose so." He looked to Robert, but he was wearing his poker face. Yes or no, the judge reminded Byron. "Yes, I mean."

"And when you were telling this court about your background, did you omit anything?"

"I answered the questions counsel asked me."

"And did counsel ask if you have been indicted for first degree murder?"

Now it was Byron's turn to feel his face flush crimson. "No, he did not."

"Speak up, Mr. Round. You weren't shy when you were telling us about all the medals you had won during the war." Instantly Mr. Boswell had made Byron look like a loud-mouthed braggart. "Well, I'll ask you then. Have you been indicted for the first degree murder of your wife, Mr. Round?"

"Yes, I have." Byron forced himself to speak in a normal tone although he couldn't stop feeling ashamed for some reason.

"And prior to meeting your now deceased wife, weren't you yourself a state trooper?"

"I was."

"And didn't you often tell your people about how thorough a state police investigation was?"

"I suppose I did."

"And didn't the Connecticut State Police conduct the investigation into your wife's murder?"

"Yes."

"Was that investigation thorough, Mr. Round?"

"Objection. Mr. Round invokes his Fifth Amendment privilege against self-incrimination."

"Sustained."

"Mr. Round, is it true that Mr. Kingsbury fired you from your job at the bank?"

"Yes."

"Isn't it equally true that after you were fired the bank foreclosed on your home?"

"Yes, that's true."

"And lastly, Mr. Round, Mr. Kingsbury is also the father of the woman you are charged with killing—isn't that correct too?"

"It is." Byron couldn't look at anyone as he answered these last questions.

"We have no further questions for this witness, your honor. We believe his testimony is neither credible nor unbiased, but in fact has a deep-seated hatred for the defendant bank, and Mr. Kingsbury in particular."

"Have you any rebuttal questions for the witness, Mr. Taylor?" The judge didn't seem particularly interested in hearing any more from Byron. Now his war record, far from seeming to demonstrate his patriotism, seemed like the history of an unstable murderer.

"Just a few, your honor." Robert adjusted the cuffs on his shirt, which featured the symbol of one of the many clubs and societies to which men of the law belong. "Did the state offer you a plea bargain if you would plead guilty to killing your wife?"

"They did."

"And did you accept that offer?"

"I did not."

"Why not?"

"Because I didn't kill my wife."

"Thank you. I have no further questions for this witness, your honor." Robert turned on his heel with a grace that would have done a flamenco dancer proud. There could be no doubt about it now, in the eyes of the court Byron was innocent at least until proven guilty.

"Thank you, gentlemen. The court is ready to rule. After hearing arguments from the parties and reviewing the evidence presented here today, the court finds as follows: The affidavit offered by the defendant bank in support of its motion to dismiss under Rule Twelve demonstrates that the affiant Kingsbury is certainly credible, but offers little in the way of evidence to meet the plaintiffs' claim that the defendant failed to supervise Sunwest properly. Indeed, the affiant's statement that Sunwest operates as an independent entity is purely conclusory, and not supported by the evidence.

"On the other hand," he continued, "the testimony of the plaintiffs' witness, Byron Round, demonstrates that the witness was both credible and knowledgeable. Mr. Round was the bank's chief compliance officer, and was sent by the bank to investigate compliance issues at Sunwest. This fact alone contradicts the bank's assertion that Sunwest operated independent of the defendant bank. Therefore, the bank's Motion to Dismiss is hereby denied."

The judge stood, with the assembled courtroom also bustling to its feet. "Good day, gentlemen."

It all happened fast. Byron, his head spinning, said, "I've no idea how I should feel."

Robert shoved papers into his briefcase and said, "We accomplished two important steps on our journey."

"You mean defeating their motion?"

"No. One: we taught the bank how to lose." Robert snapped his briefcase closed. "And, two? We demonstrated to the judge that we're the truthful party in this case."

The lawyers from the bank left without shaking hands, as is customary. Apparently the one lesson Robert hadn't taught them was professional collegiality. To him, though, it was only 'another good sign,' and Byron left the courthouse in a state of wary, relative grace.

18

The videotapes from the store's security cameras arrived. Robert viewed every frame, but found nothing terribly helpful to the prosecution. He said the state police laboratory had examined them as well to find that the person who entered the women's restroom after Dianne was approximately the same height and weight as Byron. The theory emerged that it was a man disguised as a woman.

"Well, that narrows it down to the hundred-thousand people in Connecticut who match your size." Robert laughed, but it was difficult for Byron to see how the same evidence that could be used by the police to arrest him, was viewed by Robert as meaningless. "Brilliant detective work by our Lieutenant Atkins. Now he knows the size and weight of the killer. Hell—he doesn't even know the sex of the person in the video."

"He claims it's me wearing clothes that belonged to one of the cleaning women at the store."

"The woman in the video has red hair." Robert looked again at the grainy video. "Shoulder length red hair."

"They say it's a wig."

"Why don't they charge you with being a drag queen, too, while these feckless bastards are at it." Robert looked over at Byron.

"Besides, with a scar like that? You'd make a downright hideous woman."

"Appreciated."

A jovial wink. "Hey–you got it."

One of the videotapes featured Dianne going into the ladies room in the basement of the store. About seven minutes later, a store employee—or someone dressed as one, anyway—trundled a cleaning cart into the same ladies room. Twelve minutes passed until the 'cleaning woman' left. The tape never showed Dianne leaving.

"It's obvious, in theory, that Dianne's body was in that cart, and that's how it got moved to her car." Byron noticed that Robert had winced when Byron referred to Dianne's body as 'it.' He made a mental note not to repeat that mistake again.

"Have the police talked to the cleaning ladies at the store?" Byron asked this with reluctance. It seemed an obvious part of the investigation.

"No, they haven't. They're certain it was you, so they're not looking for anyone else."

"What if the cleaning lady was the one selling drugs to Dianne? Maybe she went in the bathroom to see what was taking Dianne so long, found her dead and decided to move the body."

"You think the cleaning lady moved her body?" Robert sounded incredulous. "That would have to be a very strong cleaning lady."

"I do. There's no other explanation. The cleaning lady goes in and comes out, Dianne goes in and never comes out."

"You mean Dianne killed herself?"

"Yes. That's the only thing that makes any sense."

"The prosecutor will never buy it. Especially not coming from us." Robert lit a cigar. When he was especially puzzled, he would reach for his expensive cigars. This might be a two-cigar problem.

Byron tried to keep the anger he felt out of his voice. "We could ask the store who the woman was. Maybe she'll tell us something useful."

"That can't hurt." Robert puffed smoke into the air. It floated above them like blue cotton candy. "I'll call the store tomorrow and find out who that woman was. She can't be too hard to identify. She looks about six feet tall. And that red hair. There can't be two like that working over there."

Byron couldn't be certain if Robert was humoring him, or if he really thought Byron was onto a lead. He had to make Robert believe him. Even Robert couldn't ignore the inescapable logic of those videos. The last time Dianne was seen alive was when she had entered that ladies room. She must have been died there. The cleaning lady must have been involved. She was the only other person to go in after Dianne.

Once they found the cleaning woman, they would see the connection. Perhaps the dealer had delivered bad drugs to Dianne. When she found her customer dead, she panicked and came up with an idea to get rid of the body. That sounded like a theory.

God, here he was referring to Dianne as 'the body' again. This is where he was, now. But he had no time for sentimentality. Dianne was dead, he was accused, and the justice system would decide his fate. If he wanted to live, he had to play the cards in his hand.

Byron tried to disguise the sense of urgency he felt. Robert wasn't one to be pushed into anything. "Think you could call the store today?"

"Of course." Robert put his cigar in the ashtray and looked up. "You bet."

Byron could see Robert expected him to leave while he made the call, which might be awkward with him standing there. After all, he had a great deal riding on what was said. He took the hint and went back to wait in 'his' office.

An hour later, Robert's assistant buzzed to summon Byron to the big office upstairs.

With concern on his face, the small mountain of attorney motioned Byron to sit. He relit the recently abandoned cigar while the defendant—or whistleblower, depending on the time of day—waited as he puffed it back to life.

"The only person fitting the description of the woman in the video is a black man who works on the housekeeping staff at the store." Robert leaned back in his chair and exhaled a swirl of smoke.

Byron's voice trembled. "What does that mean?"

"I'm not exactly sure. But that was no black man in that video."

"How can you be so sure? You never see his face. The wig covers up the back of his head, and he always has his back to the camera. Even the police think it was a man."

"Look at his hands. They're white."

"The cleaning crew wears white rubber gloves when they're working."

"You seem to have given this a lot of thought." Taylor seemed impressed.

"I have every reason to, don't you think?"

"I guess that's true enough. At the very least we have enough to go to the prosecutor with. At trial, this would be devastating to the state's case. It will show the police quit looking for the real killer the moment they focused on you."

Robert wasn't saying this proved Byron couldn't have done it, merely that they now had enough evidence to raise a reasonable doubt in juror minds that he might not have done it. Byron grew frustrated by Robert's endless pessimism, but he ascribed it to the lawyer's years as a trial attorney, years when he must have heard every lie imaginable uttered under oath. That would make anyone cynical.

"I know that has to be what happened."

"You don't 'know' that, you merely think it. You couldn't 'know' it. Not unless you were there."

"I mean, I think that," Byron corrected. "It seems so obvious."

"What's obvious to you may not be quite so obvious to the police." Robert drew another mouthful of smoke and let it rise to the ceiling in three perfect lazy rings. Insinuating, his manner, in a way Byron didn't care for, but he thought he might be imagining that. A man accused of murder can become paranoid.

Indignation crept into Byron's tone. "Well, they've been so eager to prove I killed Dianne they haven't even considered that someone else might have done it."

"Don't be too hard on them. You know how it goes. You were a policeman yourself, once. They get a solid lead, a reasonable theory, in their pointed little heads, and that's that. You remember the constant drumbeat from the brass to clear cases."

"I wouldn't be so hard on them, as you put it, if they weren't trying to put me away."

"Understood." Robert stood and stretched. "I think we should go over and visit with Atkins. Play a card. See if he squirms."

"I'll get my coat." Byron went back to his office and, for the first time in months, he felt as if he might have a chance to prove his innocence.

Still, he remained concerned about Robert's attitude. He seemed to take every opportunity to remind Byron that a verdict of not guilty was not the same as being found innocent. Perhaps it was a lawyer's way of being precise about legal terms, but Byron found it irritating. He thought about expressing his displeasure to Robert, but thought better of it. He needed his lawyer too much.

THEY ARRIVED AT THE STATE POLICE BARRACKS. THE dispatcher buzzed them through the locked door into the office of Lt. Atkins.

The police officer stood when he saw them and held out his hand to the attorney. "I've been expecting this visit."

Robert ignored the outstretched hand and sat without waiting to be asked. "Why's that?"

"I reviewed the store videotapes, and I guessed you would want to talk to me about them."

"Then I won't beat around the bush. We believe the tapes show

Dianne's body was moved by the cleaning person who went into the restroom after her."

"I thought you might say that." The lieutenant sat down. He didn't seem too troubled by what Robert had said. "And what would your evidence be—the fact that a cleaning woman was in the bathroom? There's nothing very unusual about that."

"The fact that Dianne never came out of that bathroom after the cleaning lady went in." Robert sounded surprisingly confident, not at all like the Doubting Thomas back at the office. "That's pretty strong circumstantial evidence."

"Of what—that a cleaning lady who probably had never even met Dianne decided on the spur of the moment to kill her? For what reason?" The lieutenant tried not to smirk.

"The cleaning lady didn't kill Dianne. Dianne overdosed and the cleaning lady found the body and panicked. Then she moved the body back to Dianne's car to make it look like she died there."

"There's only one little problem with your theory. Why would she put on a disguise if she didn't know Dianne was dead when she went in the bathroom?" Lieutenant Atkins sat back in his chair and smiled.

"Because she was running a drug operation out of the basement of that store, and she knew there are security cameras all over the place." Now it was Robert's turn to smile. "When she was making a sale, she put on one of the cleaning ladies' dusters, along with that obvious wig."

"The store manager reports that nobody who works there quite fits the description of the person in the video."

Robert took out a cigar and stuck it in his mouth unlit. Its presence gave his voice a growl. "Did you check the men on the cleaning crew, or only the women?"

Lieutenant Atkins paused to collect his thoughts, pulling at an earlobe. "Just the women."

"In the affidavit supporting your arrest warrant, you state that Byron disguised himself as a woman to gain entry to the restroom and administered a fatal injection to his wife, who was passed out in a stall. If you believe Byron disguised himself as a woman to go into the restroom, then why didn't you check to see if any of the men on the cleaning crew were his size?"

The lieutenant's face betrayed annoyance; there could be no good answer to Robert's question.

"Could it be that you were so eager to prove Byron did it that you don't care what the evidence shows?"

"You know better than that." Lieutenant Peter Atkins was growing visibly uncomfortable. "We know your client did it."

"That's the problem, lieutenant. Since the very beginning you've assumed you knew who killed Mrs. Round, instead of letting the evidence lead you to the killer."

"We'll check out the men on the cleaning crew. I'll let you know if we find anything." This grudging capitulation only left the lieutenant even more certain he had the right man. He had jumped through these hoops before set up by lawyers every bit as clever as Robert Taylor.

Robert chewed energetically on his cigar. "One of them might even be your killer. Something you apparently never even considered."

"All the evidence pointed to Mr. Round." Both Byron and Robert noticed the lieutenant had used the past tense. An almost plaintive air had crept into the lieutenant's words. "I mean—the affair, the money problems, the troubles in their marriage?"

"Didn't it seem odd to you the way that evidence came tumbling out? It was almost as if someone wanted you to have it. Wanted you to think Byron had killed his wife." Robert looked for some place to spit out the chewed end of his cigar and finally settled on the lieutenant's trashcan. "You're going to put away an innocent man to keep from looking wrong."

"The evidence came together because your client is not a very smart criminal."

"The chief compliance officer of a large bank, a decorated war hero with two combat tours, and he's not clever enough to plan something like killing his wife in a public bathroom?"

"I'm not inside anybody else's head."

"Come on, Lieutenant—you don't believe this story for one

moment. Nor will a jury." Robert grinned. "Not once I paint the picture for them. If you're not careful, they'll never believe another cop in this lousy town again."

"I've seen stranger things." The lieutenant paused to scribble a note as he spoke. "Than some supposed good guy turning out to be a killer."

"That's all you can say? This is a damn death penalty case."

The lieutenant continued scribbling. "The grand jury indicted him."

"The grand jury indicts everyone. At the least I can prove you quit looking for the real killer the moment you settled on Byron."

"That's not true." Now it was the lieutenant's turn to sound indignant.

Robert's skepticism spewed across the room. "Then tell me who else you looked at in this case."

"Some junkies she used to hang out with. Two of my detectives pressed them hard on this and came up short."

"Well, I look forward to examining your detectives on the stand. And by the way, you better supplement your Brady responses to include the names of those detectives, or I'll have the case tossed for prosecutorial misconduct."

Atkins held up the pen he'd been using. "I've already made a note on that."

"I think you might want to find out who that red-haired person in the bathroom was before you go any further with this case. You should have done that before you charged my client, and I'm sure the jury will want to know why you didn't."

"If your defense is that someone else killed Mrs. Round, you're taking an awful big chance, counselor. You might want to focus on the evidence that incriminates your client."

"Thank you for the advice, Lieutenant, but I think we'll continue to look for the real killer since it seems the police aren't very interested in doing that." Robert stood up and dropped his cigar into the trashcan. It landed with a wet thud that perfectly punctuated his words.

"We've already got him." The lieutenant shook Robert's hand. He didn't offer to shake Byron's.

"Aren't you a little curious about the person in that video?"

"I think we both know who it was." The lieutenant managed a weak smile as he held the door open for them. "See you citizens in court."

From his days as a state trooper, Byron knew this much about Lieutenant Peter Atkins: the man was no fool. And that worried him about his case now worse than ever.

19

A reporter with the local television station telephoned to say they were going to do a piece on Byron on the Sunday news show. It seemed they had received a tip about alleged improprieties at the bank. Was he willing to talk, either off or on the record?

At first he was reluctant, but after she explained how it would be a good way to get his side of the story heard, he finally gave in and promised to meet her at a local restaurant. Byron knew Robert would object if he learned about the interview, so he kept it to himself.

WHEN HE GOT TO THE RESTAURANT, BYRON OBSERVED an attractive woman about his age sitting alone at a corner table. As soon as he entered the dining room, she had stood and motioned him over.

"I'm sorry. When they said on the phone that a Sidney Biddle wanted to meet with me, I expected someone taller."

"You thought Sidney was a man? And that I was his assistant?"

Embarrassed, Byron unfurled his napkin and laid it in his lap. "This is certainly awkward."

"Think nothing of it. It happens all the time. I think that's why my mother named me Sidney." Ms. Biddle gave a hearty laugh. "You know—to confuse people."

He nodded that he understood, even though he didn't have the slightest idea what she was talking about. Byron looked at the menu with feigned interest. "Well, it certainly worked in my case."

"Thank you for meeting me. I thought your lawyer might not let you."

"I haven't mentioned it to him. I'm sure he would object."

Sidney looked at him over the tortoise shell rim of her glasses. "Do you think that's wise?"

"I don't know. But once the police focused on me, they never looked for the real killer."

"There's a mountain of evidence against you." Ms. Biddle took a sheaf of papers out of the oversized leather bag she had hung on the chair next to her. "But it's all just 'circ,' as we say on the crime beat."

"I'm quite familiar with what they call evidence. Our marriage was troubled, and I was good friends with my assistant. And we were in debt. That could describe a million couples." Byron dabbed at his forehead with his napkin. "And if I'm such a killer, why would an attractive woman like you want to meet?"

"For one, I was surprised myself at how little forensics evidence my sources told me they'd seen on this case." Biddle took out her pad and began to make notes. "How long has it been since your wife, since they, since she..." She paused to find the right word. "Since her passing."

He counted back the months and answered.

"Why do you think the police didn't request the store videotapes sooner?"

"My lawyer says it's because they were trying to find some junkie to confess that I hired him to kill Dianne."

"That probably wouldn't take five minutes."

"Right. We can't prove that, but we can show they didn't request the videotapes right away. You tell me why they waited."

"An oversight?" Byron could see Ms. Biddle was playing devil's advocate here. She couldn't possibly believe what she was saying. "You know cops."

"In a capital murder case?"

"I take your point. It certainly looks like the cops focused on you without bothering to look at anybody else."

"Exactly." In his excitement, Byron almost grabbed her hand. At last, here was someone who believed him, or at least didn't believe the police. "She was my childhood sweetheart. I wouldn't kill her."

"All that will be tough to explain to a jury." Ms. Biddle raised a finger for the waiter. She ordered a Cobb salad and a glass of the house white wine.

"I'll have an iced tea."

"No lunch, Mr. Round?"

"I'm not hungry." A diet of high anxiety was what Byron was living on these days. He'd lost almost thirty pounds in the last year. His clothing hung loose on his shrinking frame. "I'll have two iced teas, if my stomach growls."

Ms. Biddle slid a grainy picture across the table to Byron. "Can you tell me who the people are in this photograph?"

Byron studied it for a moment, but it wasn't as though he needed to search his memory. "The woman to my right is my assistant, Martha Temple. That's me, of course, and then there's Martin Kingsbury and Helen Stone, the CEO of Sunwest." He handed the photograph back.

"Your assistant? She's attractive." Ms. Biddle spoke as she was putting the photograph back into her bag, as though the question an afterthought. "No mistaking that piece of evidence."

"I had probably noticed that in passing." Byron tried to sound equally casual in his reply, even though he knew where this was headed.

"Have you seen Martha since your wife's death?" The reporter again took up her notepad.

"Why, yes. Once or twice," he lied.

"My sources tell me you've seen her a good deal more than that."

"I may have, now that you mention it." He could almost feel

Ms. Biddle's excitement across the table. Her reporter's instincts were on high alert.

"Now that I've mentioned it, exactly how many times have you seen her?"

"I'm not sure exactly, quite often. Lunch mainly." Byron toyed with his silverware.

"Dinner?"

"Oh, yes, I'm sure we've had dinner together a few times." He answered the questions as if they were talking about the weather instead of the motive for his killing his wife.

"And when was the last time you saw her?"

"Three, four weeks ago, I would guess."

"Not ten days ago at The Avon Old Farms restaurant?"

"You're unusually well informed. Yes, we were there."

Sidney tried to repress a slight smile. "Are you sleeping with Martha, Mr. Round? Search your memory hard."

There it was, the high inside curve ball, the gotcha, slid in underneath all the over-the-plate pitches. Byron tried to sound indignant, but he had already answered this question so many times that he was merely reciting his lines now. "No. We were colleagues. And friends."

"Does that mean, no, I'm not sleeping with her now, or no, I've never slept with her?"

"That latter."

"I'm rather surprised to hear that."

"And why is that?" It was Byron's turn to be sarcastic.

"Well, let's see. You admit your marriage was troubled, your assistant is attractive, and she was quite fond of you. That's sounding like math to me."

"We were good friends."

"Your co-workers thought it was more."

"People do love to gossip."

"They do, but there has to be something to gossip about." Biddle scribbled notes as she spoke. "Surely an untenable place to be in at such a job as yours."

"In this case, there was nothing to it."

"Ms. Temple got divorced two years after she went to work for you. Just a coincidence?" The sarcasm made its way back into Ms. Biddle's questions.

"If you like."

"And when you got promoted to chief compliance officer, she transferred with you."

"Yes, that's right. We enjoyed working together."

"And you worked long hours?"

"Very long."

"Two of your colleagues will testify they saw you hugging Ms. Temple."

"That's quite a bit short of having an affair, isn't it?"

"A jury might not think so."

Their meal arrived and Byron took a sip of tea. His throat was so dry he could hardly speak. "I thought you wanted to talk about Sunwest."

"I do. Did Mr. Kingsbury work closely with Ms. Stone?"

"Yes, he arranged the merger. She was the CEO out there and Martin kept her on after the bank bought Sunwest."

"Well, oddly enough, Ms. Stone was in Simsbury on the day your wife was killed. She was here for a meeting with Martin Kingsbury… and you."

"My wife was killed on a Sunday."

"I know. Ms. Stone came in early because the meeting was set for eight o'clock on Monday. Your assistant made the travel arrangements. The hotel Ms. Stone stayed at was a ten minute drive from where your wife was killed."

"That doesn't prove anything. She had no reason to kill Dianne. She barely knew her."

"Oh, I wasn't implying that, but it is interesting that you should bring it up. Ms. Stone did know Dianne, didn't she?" Ms. Biddle put her pen down and leaned across the table."

"Yes, she knew her." Byron recalled what Helen had said to him about Dianne. He didn't want to say anything about Martin's affair with Helen. It would look like he was stabbing his father-in-law in the back.

"Did she know about her drug problem?"

Byron grew tired of this interview. "Yes, but what has that got to do with anything?"

"Do you know what's really odd? One of the bellboys at the hotel where Ms. Stone stayed said Martin Kingsbury went up to her room around eight, and didn't leave until two in the morning."

"They were probably getting ready for our meeting." Byron marveled at how well informed Ms. Biddle was.

"Please don't pull my leg, Mr. Round. Two adults in a hotel room at that hour spells sex to me."

"I think you have a lively imagination, Ms. Biddle. I'm sure that's a great asset for a reporter."

"What was the meeting about on Monday?"

"Irregularities in the documentation Sunwest was using to support some mortgages. You must promise me you won't print that. It could harm the bank enormously." Byron knew Ms. Biddle would break her promise. His request was pro forma, what one said to keep up the appearance of playing fair.

"I'll do as you ask. How widespread were the irregularities, and how serious where they?"

"They were fairly widespread, and they were rather serious."

"Who uncovered them?"

"I did."

They sat in silence for an interim, broken only by the soft babble of conversations at other tables and the sounds of a busy diner at mid-day. "Byron: don't you think that presented a pretty big problem for Ms. Stone?"

"I hadn't thought about it in personal terms. It was a compliance issue that had to be dealt with." Frustration threatened to bubble up. "It was my job."

"Here's a curious detail, Mr. Round. I've spent the better part of the last hour suggesting Ms. Stone might have a connection to with your wife's death, and you've done nothing but argue that I'm mistaken. Now wouldn't you think a man accused of murder would be glad to hear that there's evidence out there that someone else might have committed the crime?"

"I've been accused of a crime I didn't commit, and it's damn near ruined my life. I'm not going to start accusing other people without knowing some facts first." Byron dropped his napkin on the table and stood to leave. "That's the kind of thing the police seem particularly good at."

Ms. Biddle, used to getting attention, shouted after him. *"Has it occurred to you that people at the bank may have framed you to stop your investigation into those compliance irregularities?"*

The other diners hushed and looked up from their meals. Byron felt their eyes burning into him.

Chastened, he returned to the table. "It's possible I hadn't considered that. This has been a confusing time."

At last, the real interview finally began. "So, then: let's explore that angle. Shall we?"

ON SUNDAY NIGHT BYRON SAT WATCHING AS SIDNEY Biddle devoted the entire hour of her broadcast to a series of 'stunning revelations' about the Dianne Round murder case. She held up the photograph from lunch, only now a red circle had been drawn around Helen Stone's face. Naturally, Ms. Biddle detailed all that Byron had told her about the irregularities at Sunwest. He had counted on her doing so. A crucial step.

Watching it unfold, he was almost disappointed, in a way, by how predictable people behaved—Lieutenant Atkins, Ms. Biddle, even Helen Stone with her clumsy attempt to gin up the numbers at Sunwest. All the world's a stage, and its men and women merely players. But who is the author of this mystery? All Byron knew was that if he couldn't prove his innocence, he would have plenty of time in jail to ponder philosophy.

20

As Byron entered his office on Monday, Robert, huge by anyone's measure, rose from behind his desk like an angry god about to deliver fiery wrath. *"Don't you realize what you've done?"*

"I think so. But you'll tell me. So go ahead."

As Robert paced circles around him, plumes of bluish cigar smoke following after as he puffed with fury like a steam engine struggling up a steep hill, Byron sat cowering in his customary chair. "The bank's already moved for a restraining order to stop you from giving further interviews, and to have me sanctioned as well." Robert stopped in mid-stride but only long enough to glare down before continuing his course around the room that, large as it was, seemed barely able to contain his ire. "Mercy, son. What were you thinking?"

Byron spoke quietly so as not to antagonize Robert even further. "That we've been on the defensive ever since my arrest, and perhaps it was time to go on the offense."

"You thought it was time to go on the offense? Who the hell are you to decide that? Did you go to law school when I wasn't looking?"

It seemed to Byron that everyone connected with the law had a penchant for clumsy sarcasm. "No, I haven't gone to law school, but I am the one charged with murder. If you lose my case, you go home to dinner, and me? I get lethal injection. The stakes are a bit different for us."

The smoke circling Robert's head began to clear as he calmed down. "And that's exactly why you shouldn't be making decisions like this. You're under enormous strain, and that can affect your thinking."

"I'll certainly discuss my ideas with you in the future."

"Oh, *yes*," Robert said in a voice filled with false gratitude. "By all means. Please do that."

They both laughed at Byron's audacity. It was obvious Robert secretly admired what he had done, even if it wasn't an action the attorney would have recommended. "Now: we must handle the bank's motion for a restraining order."

"That shouldn't be too difficult."

"And are you going to share your ideas on that topic with me as well?" Robert's anger was creeping back. He sat down behind his desk and crushed out the cigar.

"Banks hold deposits in trust. I doubt the court will think the bank has a right to conceal its violation of regulations from those same depositors." Byron offered this cautiously, as Robert could sometimes be put off by advice from a layperson.

A fresh cigar came out of his drawer. A good sign. "That might work."

Byron tried not to sound overly confident, which was rather difficult since he felt certain the bank's motion would fail. "The newspapers will almost certainly oppose any restraining order as a violation of the Freedom of the Press. And no judge wants to be on the wrong side of the press."

"And where did you get that idea from? Sidney Biddle?"

"She did mention it, yes."

"She's using you to get a story, for god's sake."

Byron was not backing down, not now when the tide might be turning. "That may be true, but she still has a point."

"You know, things can't be manipulated as easily as you seem to think they can."

"I didn't mean to imply that," Byron lied.

"Well you did, my boy."

It was too late in the game to antagonize Robert. Where would he get another lawyer now? And besides, Robert was in no real hurry to abandon the case against Sunwest, because it meant millions of dollars. No, they were stuck with each other, Robert and Byron, despite their mutual misgivings.

But, Byron had been told that often happens in long and difficult cases like his. It's like a marriage in some ways, and everyone agrees those can be difficult even in the best of times. It's the intense closeness: it can be claustrophobic.

"I thought the court might find the interest of the depositors in disclosure outweighs the bank's interest in secrecy."

Robert rolled his pen between thick fingers. The idea seemed to intrigue him. "I hadn't thought of it in exactly that way. I mean, the public's interest in this."

"Perhaps you could get an affidavit from the Treasury Department stating that violation of department regulations by a bank is a public and not a private matter." Byron was guessing now, but the idea sounded reasonable to him.

"Maybe you should go to law school after all."

"I intend to, once this is all over."

"It was certainly a bit of good timing on this Biddle story hinting that you were framed."

"See? I thought you might like that."

"It said her station received a photograph of you and some other bank officers in the mail from some anonymous source with a note suggesting irregularities at the bank. That source wouldn't be you, would it?"

Byron tried not to sound too pleased with himself. "I thought that picture might get Ms. Biddle to do a little digging on her own. And it worked, too."

"You're playing with fire. If the police find out it was you that sent that photograph, it could be used against us." Ever the lawyer, Robert thought it appropriate to sound a cautionary note even if he didn't believe a word he was saying.

"I thought it worth the risk. After all, you yourself said all the evidence was against me."

"That's true, but that doesn't entitle you to manufacture evidence."

"I haven't done that. I merely sent Ms. Biddle a photograph I thought she ought to see."

"I suppose that's true." Robert sounded doubtful. "So, when you told her you didn't think Helen Stone was involved in your wife's death, you were leading her on?"

"I wasn't leading her on. I wanted her to reach her own conclusions. What I think doesn't matter. The police and everyone else have made that abundantly clear."

"I understand why you feel that way, but you must promise me you won't do anything like that again."

"Of course." Byron said this knowing he didn't mean a word of it, and he was quite sure Robert knew that as well—the lawyer seemed satisfied that he had done his duty as an officer of the court.

"I must admit that sideshow has changed things. Now the state has to be thinking they may have botched their investigation. I'm sure they'll be looking at Helen Stone as a suspect now. It certainly complicates matters. They're damned if they investigate her, and damned if they don't. That was rather clever."

"Didn't Johnson say the prospect of being hanged focuses the mind wonderfully?"

"In your case, it certainly has." Robert stood up and brushed cigar ash from the swell of his huge stomach where it tended to collect. "I better get to shuffling briefs."

Byron stood as well. "We understand each other, then?"

"I think we do." A guarded reply. It seemed they didn't understand each other at all, and both of them knew it. But they needed to pretend all was well, at least for now. No other choice.

※

WHEN BYRON GOT BACK TO HIS OFFICE, HE FOUND A

note that Sidney Biddle had called and wanted to meet at the Blue Heron after work for a drink.

When he arrived, he found her surrounded by young men whom he took for reporters with her television program. They were all clearly infatuated with Ms. Biddle, whom they called 'Sid' in a kind of palsy slang that did nothing to conceal the real allure she exerted over them.

When she saw Byron, she motioned for him to a join her in a corner booth.

Byron eased into the booth. He was rather surprised when Sidney Biddle slid over next to him.

"You certainly have a throng of admirers."

"They're summer interns. College boys with hot pants who want to sleep with an older woman." Sidney laughed loud enough to draw the attention of the circle of young men she had just left. They frowned when they saw her close to Byron. He couldn't help feeling flattered.

"You said you wanted to talk about my case."

"Down to business, are we?"

Sidney signaled to a waiter who reappeared with two mysterious, dark cocktails. She slid one glass in front of him. "You like Black Russians? If not, I'll drink them both."

"I like them well enough." Byron took a sip of his drink as if to prove how much he liked it. "Yum."

Sidney Biddle's eyes glowed over the rim of her drink. "Did you know your father-in-law was having an affair with Helen Stone?"

"Is that some kind of reporter's trick? Where you lead off with a shocking question to catch the subject off-guard?"

"It's nothing they taught me in journalism school."

Byron could feel Sidney's shoulder against his. He wondered if charm was one of her reporter's tools. "I had heard they had once been involved."

"I like the way you say that. It's so—Victorian. Quaint, even."

"I'm glad that pleases you." Byron took another sip of his drink. It was obvious Sidney was a good two drinks ahead of him, or at least pretending to be.

"My investigation since our last meeting shows they never broke off that affair."

"I think you're mistaken. Martin admitted it all to me, but said it had been over for some time."

"And you believed him?"

Byron had never actually believed Martin, but he wanted to be accurate in what he told Sidney. He could smell Sidney's perfume. *Chloe*, he thought. Dianne also liked that one. "I had no reason not to."

"Let's not kid each other. You and I both know affairs unwind slowly. And they never ever end simply because a husband is feeling guilty."

"I see what you mean. I suppose I didn't really believe the affair was over."

"Did you know about the relationship before he admitted it?"

"When I met Helen, she knew so many private details about Martin and Suzanne, and Dianne, too." Byron shrugged. "It seemed obvious."

"Understood. What kinds of things about Dianne?"

"About the difficulties in our marriage."

"Did she know Dianne had a drug problem?"

"That's what made me suspect that she and Martin were having an affair. I mean, how else could she have leaned those private matters? The Kingsburys were humiliated by their own daughter."

Sidney shook her head. Laughed. "Don't you get it? The police thought an affair was the motive for Dianne's murder, and they were right. They just have the wrong people having the affair."

The Black Russian and Sidney's perfume were making it hard for Byron to think straight. "I'm afraid I don't follow."

"A theory: Helen knew Martin would never leave his wife while their daughter was struggling with a drug habit, so she had Dianne killed."

Byron sobered up. "Wait—even you can't believe that."

"It's far more plausible than you killing your wife over an affair with your assistant—an affair you never had."

That might have been someone's motivation in an old movie. But real life isn't like *Double Indemnity*, he thought.

"Listen, the police jumped on you the minute they thought you were getting some on the side. Let's see what they do when they have evidence of a tryst that's also hip-deep in the looming Sunwest scandal."

Sidney was even more ambitious than Byron had dared hope. "What are you going to do?"

"I'm going to break the whole story. How every paper and TV station in the state got it wrong. How the police arrested an innocent man. And how the justice system is railroading a capital murder case." She pointed. "That's you, Byron."

"You're the first person to believe I'm innocent." Byron checked the time, nearly ten. "But I'm about to fall over with fatigue."

"Come on to my place. I'll make us dinner, and you can fill me in on Helen Stone."

"I'm afraid I'll have to take a rain check on that dinner. I'm exhausted."

"Did you think I was trying to seduce you?" Sidney said this as though the idea was absurd.

Byron blushed at his presumption. "I did think it possible."

"That's not a proper presumption to make towards a girl who's asked you to her place. Not for a gentleman. Nor for a reporter who's invested in helping you prove your innocence."

"Thank you."

Before they said goodnight Byron added, "By the way—I think you've forgotten one possibility."

"And what is that?"

"Helen and Martin Kingsbury may take a big risk and present an ironclad alibi—I'm almost certain the two of them were in bed together at the time of the murder."

21

Robert telephoned Byron to let him know the state police had done a background check on all the men working on the cleaning crew at the store the day Dianne had been murdered. One, Lyman Schuler, had a long criminal record involving petty drug offenses.

But, more interestingly, he had done a year in prison for criminal domestic violence, second offense. It seems he had beaten up his then-girlfriend.

When Byron arrived, he saw Robert's assistant beaming with pleasure. "I always believed in you. We all did."

"Well, thank you, Jean." Puzzled by this unexpected outburst of support, Byron went in to Robert's office.

"They found the red wig. It was up on one of the heating ducts near the bathroom where Dianne was murdered."

Byron felt for the chair behind him and sat down because he suddenly felt weak. He almost didn't dare to let himself believe this long nightmare might be coming to an end. "What does it mean?"

"That the police were so sure you killed your wife they never even looked for evidence linking someone else to the crime."

All Byron's fears came rushing back. "How can you be so sure he's the one who did it? Maybe he wasn't even at work that day."

"He was there. The police are testing the wig for DNA to connect Schuler to it. The results will be back in a few days."

Byron shook his head in disbelief. "I can't imagine they overlooked evidence like this."

"The lieutenant has some egg on his face today, boy." Robert offered Byron a theatrical smile. "You have every right to be upset after what you've been through."

Byron smiled best he could. "I'm fine. It's just so overwhelming."

"I imagine Atkins is feeling a bit overwhelmed right now, too."

Robert laughed, and that reassured Byron the end drew near. "I want this over, before there are two victims."

"When that DNA test comes back, it will be."

Byron made his way back to his office. He had a great deal of work to do on the Sunwest case, and keeping busy took his mind off thinking about the DNA results that would surely force the state to drop the charges against him. Try as he might, Byron couldn't stop thinking about the red wig the police had found. Surely this must be the end of the case against him.

THE NEXT EIGHT DAYS WENT BY SLOWLY, BUT AS THEY passed Byron became more and more confident the charges against him would be dropped. Even the dogged Lieutenant Atkins had to see Byron was innocent. He finally got a good night's sleep, found an appetite again. It all might work out.

On Wednesday Lieutenant Atkins telephoned Robert and invited them back to his office to discuss the DNA tests.

When they got to the state police headquarters, Byron felt a confidence Robert didn't seem to share.

"Not a word in there," he cautioned. "Not a whisper."

Lieutenant Atkins stood as they entered his office. He looked cheerful for a man about to admit a serious mistake. Byron's confidence began to desert him.

Terse pleasantries. When Robert asked how everyone at police headquarters was feeling today, Atkins replied, "Actually, we're a little puzzled."

"And why is that?"

"The DNA test came back, and Lyman Schuler's DNA is all over that wig."

"What's so puzzling about that?"

"Because there wasn't a single hair fiber from Schuler in that wig. That's pretty curious, don't you think?"

"Maybe Schuler wore a shower cap under the wig."

"Maybe he did, but then how did the DNA get transferred? It is a bit odd. Even you have to admit that."

"What was the wig made of?"

"It was made in China from synthetic fibers. They're sold all over in costume shops all over the place."

"Since Schuler worked in the store where Dianne was killed and the wig was found there with his DNA on it, I'd say the only thing puzzling about this case is why you haven't arrested Mr. Schuler." Robert's cigar bounced as he spoke.

"We have a search warrant for Schuler's car." A hint of sarcasm. "I'm half expecting to find the cart used to move the body in the truck of his car."

"Then the case will be closed."

"Not exactly." Lieutenant Atkins slide the DNA test results across his desk to Robert. They both acted as though Byron was not in the room. "You see, Schuler has an alibi."

"And what would that be?"

"Three of the women on the cleaning staff swear they saw him at work during the time of the murder."

"Really?" Skeptical as ever, Robert took the cigar from his mouth and appeared to be admiring it. "And will they swear they saw him for every minute of the day?"

"Of course not." The lieutenant was getting a taste of how good

Robert was at his job. "But they did see him during the time of the murder."

"Never looked away for a minute? Didn't take a smoke break? Didn't have to work in another part of the store?"

"You can save your cross examination for the trial, Robert."

"You've got the wrong man, and you know it. This Schuler character killed her. You said yourself he had a long record of drug arrests and violence against women."

"I did say that. And do you know what? One of the troopers who arrested Schuler for beating up his girlfriend was a young officer by the name of Byron Round." The lieutenant handed a sheaf of arrest records to Robert.

He peered at the documents with his huge lower lip rolled outward. Finally he said, "So what does that prove?"

"It proves your client knew Schuler, and that he had a record for drugs and beating up women."

"I'm afraid you've lost me."

"Pretty big coincidence, don't you think?

"Byron probably arrested hundreds of people when he was a trooper."

Robert looked at his client. Byron nodded that, yes, he had arrested a good many people. "I was a cop."

"Indeed you were. But how many of them worked at the very store where his wife was murdered? Only Mr. Schuler. And if your client was in that store, say, shopping with his wife, he might have seen Schuler. He might even have said, why, I have the perfect fall guy right here."

"I think you're forgetting the bottom line: the jury will hear that the wig has Schuler's DNA on it."

"Yes, but there's a theory: We think there were two wigs. One your client wore when he killed his wife, and the one he left on the air duct for us to find." The lieutenant looked like a man who had finished a difficult jigsaw puzzle. "The one covered in planted DNA."

"Can Kerns prove any of that?"

"Not yet. But she will."

"It looks to me like you're holding your theory together with bubble gum, lieutenant. And it'll look that way to a jury as well."

Lieutenant Atkins seemed unconcerned about Robert's low opinion of his case. "I thought you might say that."

"Because it's so obvious you don't have one bit of evidence that places Byron in that bathroom. Is that a coincidence, too?" The old sarcastic Robert was in full display.

"Not a coincidence at all. You see, our Mr. Round here is far more clever than either you or I gave him credit for. I remember you once said how all that evidence against him seemed to just tumble into our laps, and that was true. And we were like coonhounds with our noses on that trail that led right to your client. Of course, it never occurred to me that Mr. Round might be deliberately putting us on his own trail."

"Why would anyone do that?"

"I thought he was merely another angry, stupid husband who had killed his wife in a fit of rage. All the pieces were there: the troubled marriage, the relationship with the adoring assistant, the money problems, the big life insurance policy. All false leads."

Byron tried to interject. "This is preposterous."

Robert told Byron to hush. He turned contemptuous at this latest theory. *"And why on earth would he do something that would surely result in his arrest for the crime?"*

"So we would do just that. He wanted us to suspect only him. He was like a man playing poker, and Schuler was his ace in the hole. We would arrest your client and then, presto, he lays Lyman Schuler on the table. And that trumps our too-quickly put together case, as he had planned all along."

"You're giving Mr. Round a great deal of credit. You make him sound like some master criminal."

"That's what he is. My mistake was in not recognizing this fact earlier. When he found out that Sunwest was committing fraud and Kingsbury was slapping the ham with Helen Stone, he knew he could not only get rid of his junkie wife but ruin Kingsbury's career and his marriage as well—like he had a vendetta against the whole family."

Byron twisted in his seat as though he had stomach cramps. He pressed his lips together and his pulse beat in his temples.

A smirking Atkins continued. "When Kingsbury refused to tell the board about what your client had learned, Round knew he had him cornered. All that was left was to deal with Dianne, and he did that, too. That settled things up with the three people who had hidden Dianne's problems from him." He finally looked at Byron. "And got rid of a longterm problem for himself. Once they start injecting, it's tough to get them back. Even childhood sweethearts."

"You go to hell."

Atkins snorted. "See you there, Round."

Robert all but put his huge hand over Byron's mouth. "I think you're trying to find a way to repair a crumbling case. No jury will believe this contrived foolishness. Hell, I sure don't."

"There's a million and one little ways to blow a complex plan like his. We'll find enough of the mistakes eventually."

"There's another problem with this theory gripping you right now. How could my client be sure you would pursue Schuler?"

"He knew he could always point you in that direction if the trial was close, and we hadn't stumbled onto Schuler yet. And, isn't that what happened? It was you who told us to look at the men on the cleaning crew. And I'll bet it was Mr. Round here who suggested that to you. Now, I'll admit I should have looked at Schuler early on, but you see Mr. Round had put blinders on us by making himself look so guilty. Brilliant in a way."

"Don't you find it curious that you're willing to accept the leaky alibi Schuler is offering, and yet you didn't believe Mr. Round's own solid alibi?"

"You mean that nonsense from the neighbors that said they saw him doing 'yard work' at the time of the murder?" He added, "Was he digging? With a shovel? Rectangular hole, about four feet deep?"

Robert seemed set off by the sarcasm. His booming baritone peeled the paint in the cop's office. "*Why are you calling eyewitness testimony nonsense?*"

"Because they said they were busy all day, in and out. And that they only recalled glimpses of him working in the yard 'somewhere around that time.' It's flimsy as tissue."

"Like the testimony you got from the women on the cleaning crew about seeing Schuler that day?"

"All right. I'll have to give you that. But both alibis are thin."

"One of the neighbors swore he saw Byron's car in the driveway all afternoon. You don't suppose he flapped his wings and flew to the mall, do you?"

"No, I don't think he flew to the mall, but I do know how he got there. From his house you can walk out the backyard to a jogging trial that leads to a bus stop on Higgins Avenue. The mall is a mere three stops from there. It would've taken him no more than fifteen minutes."

"Did anyone see him on the bus?"

"No. No one."

"And I assume you've questioned the driver?"

"We did. He didn't remember seeing your client."

"Well, I'm sure the jury will find your speculation lacks a certain basis in fact. Perhaps the reason you're so determined to persecute Mr. Round is because you're humiliated about your own blatant incompetence."

Byron could see this would be the theme of his defense. He could also see that the lieutenant understood how powerful a defense that would be: bungling cops trying to frame an innocent man to cover-up their own mistakes.

"That's where his plan is so clever. No matter we do now, it makes his case look better."

"Then you'll have the charges against him dropped?" Robert stood, and Byron did as well.

"No, I don't think so. He's been indicted, and I know he did it. We'll let a jury sort it out."

"That's foolish, lieutenant. When these monkeyshines are finally dispatched, I'll to sue the state for malicious prosecution, and when I win, the best you'll hope for is a demotion back to sergeant and ride out until that pension." Robert snapped his briefcase closed. "Now, you go find some better evidence to tie my client to this murder before you end up wasting valuable tax dollars on a frivolous prosecution."

"Good advice, counselor. I think I *will* get me some more evidence against him. That second wig, maybe."

Robert tossed Lyman Schuler's arrest record onto the lieutenant's desk. "You got an indictment only because you withheld evidence from the grand jury. If there had been a proper investigation, it would have uncovered the evidence against Mr. Schuler, and then, of course, the grand jury would have had the opportunity to hear your theory about Mr. Round planting evidence against himself so he could frame Schuler later on. But your judgment has been clouded by this fanciful theory of yours that Mr. Round is some master criminal, banker by day and Dr. Moriarty by night. It would be funny if it weren't for the fact that you've almost ruined an innocent man's life, while damn near letting a guilty man roam free. It's Lyman Schuler who's laughing at all of us, not Mr. Round. He's crying. But not for much longer." He grabbed Byron by the upper arm. "Now, let's get out of here. It stinks."

Lieutenant Atkins held out his hand. "I'm sorry you feel that way."

Robert refused to shake. "And I'm more sorry you're not capable of seeing what you've done. It's remarkable. No question."

"We haven't done our best job until now, but that was before I knew how clever Mr. Round was. But now that I know his game, I'm pretty sure we have him cornered. We've stopped chasing the clues he's been feeding us, and now we're looking for the real ones."

"You'd better hurry, because you're going to be off this case soon."

"I don't think so, Mr. Taylor."

"Trust me, lieutenant, the state is going to run away from you as fast as they can once they hear terms like 'malicious prosecution' and 'criminal malfeasance' about themselves on the evening news."

Atkins shrugged. "Do your worst."

On the ride home, Byron and Robert barely spoke. They were both thinking about what the lieutenant had said about Byron being the one to suggest to Robert that one of the cleaning crew must have killed his wife. Perhaps it was a good guess on the lieutenant's part, but no getting around the fact that he had been right. And Byron's mood did a one-eighty from the morning's optimism.

22

Judge Allyson Wright allowed cameras into the courtroom over the prosecution's objection that this would turn the trial into a media spectacle, but it was too late; the circus had already pulled into the town square.

A bustling throng of reporters, Sidney Biddle included, who was bathed in light while doing a breathless standup next to the curb, crowded the street in front of the courthouse to scream questions at Byron as he made his way to court. Following the broad back of Robert, Bryon kept stopping as the gregarious and confident attorney barked into every microphone to protest Byron's innocence, and to declare that he intended to put an out-of-control government on trial for its own misdeeds.

The reporters, most of whom had covered Robert's trials for years, shouted back at him with familiarity such questions as, "Bob, you lose any weight to get ready for the trial?"

"This is gonna be one heavyweight trial—and I weighed in this morning at three hundred and five." Robert unbuttoned his suit jacket so the reporters could see for themselves. He slapped the hard gut beneath his pressed shirt. The report echoed in the tall granite courthouse entrance like a gunshot. "Here's hoping the DA got to the gym over the weekend."

"You giving up sex for as long as the trial lasts, Bob? Like DeNiro in *Raging Bull?*"

His voice boomed loud enough for the fringes of the crowd to hear. "I serve at the pleasure of Mrs. Taylor, so y'all will have to seek comment on that from her."

Laughter rolled like a wave through the throng of press. Byron thought, everyone's awfully jovial.

In the laughter's wake a tenacious reporter called out, "But if your guy didn't kill his wife, who did?"

"Stay tuned. I'll show that the police not only focused on an innocent man, they ignored the most obvious perpetrator of this heinous crime against my client's wife."

Sidney Biddle shouted, *"Robert Tayler: Will you name the real killer in court?"*

"We will, and we'll show how the police ignored evidence of that man's guilt." Here Robert held up his huge hand and swept it around in a half-circle. "Now, enough. There'll be plenty of time to voice our takeaways about this miscarriage of justice after the exoneration."

Robert grabbed Byron and pushed him through the bustling knot of journalists into the courthouse. The lawyer's size-fifteen Italian leather footwear accidentally crushed a TV cameraman's toes, his howl of pain echoing after them into the lobby.

As he made his way to the defense table, the table nearest the jurors, Byron could feel everyone staring at him:

The accused.

Meanwhile, he mulled Sidney's advice: she had persuaded Robert during a strategy session the night before that the perfect juror for Byron's case was a single female between the ages of twenty-seven and thirty-four. These women, she reported, made up the majority of the *Sidney Says* television audience, and they had shown a pronounced willingness to believe Byron was innocent.

Meanwhile married women, on the other hand, started out thinking he was guilty and nothing seemed to change their minds. Men of all ages were about evenly divided in their opinion of Byron.

"Curiously our polling shows successful, older men think you're innocent, or at least not guilty. Ya know," she had said with wink while ordering another Black Russian. "Wonder why."

With all this mind, Byron sat watching as Robert used all his challenges to pack the jury with young women, a game of chess between the opposing sides.

The defense, as expected, tried for older, married white women, for the obvious reason that they were the most invested in protecting marriage and punishing husbands like Byron. Two such candidates had actually scowled at him as he took his seat. Byron smiled in their direction as Robert had told him to, but they quickly looked away. This wouldn't be easy.

When Sidney entered the courtroom and took a seat behind Byron, the entire courtroom grew quiet. She was wearing her blond wig and a white fur coat. Hollywood had come to the courthouse. The two jurors who had scowled at Byron brightened when they saw Sidney. One of them even gave her a surreptitious wave. *Ah-ha*, Byron thought.

Sidney nodded royally to the left and the right before taking her seat and letting that white fur coat fall around her. A slight gasp rippled as the audience saw how short her dress was, Sidney's trademark on her show. Looks for the men, substance and feminism for the women.

Byron found himself ever more cynical about the press. It seemed more like show business.

The judge didn't care for being upstaged by a TV reporter. She brought the court to attention by rapping her gavel with force. "Today we hear the State of Connecticut versus Byron Round on a charge of the first degree murder of his wife, Dianne Round, by a fatal overdose injection of heroin. Counsel, are you ready to present your case?"

"That state is ready, your honor." Joann Kerns was dressed in a brown wool suit and pale, no-nonsense makeup. She looked quite formidable, a shark on the scent of chum.

Robert's deep bass voice seemed capable of parting the Red Sea. Every face not already watching snapped in his direction: "The defense sits not only ready, your honor, but suffers undue enthusiasm at engaging with the process."

"So I hear. Well: suffer no more, counsel." To the prosecutor: "Proceed with your opening remarks."

Ms. Kerns began a long recitation of the facts of the case, or, at least, the facts that she thought proved Byron had murdered his wife. It was the usual: insinuation of the affair with his assistant, money problems, a troubled marriage, the two million life insurance policy on Dianne, a soldier who had killed in battle finding it easy to kill at home, troubles with his father-in-law at work, getting fired and losing the house his in-laws had bought as a gift for the newlyweds. It was all right out of the playbook the unimaginative Lieutenant Peter Atkins had given her. Had he not been so frightened, Byron would have laughed.

Then, Kerns went over the murder scene in minute detail, leaving out none of the gore. Dramatic. Breathless. Like the back of a torrid crime novel, her points underscored by grunts and sighs from Robert, who filled up page after page of a legal pad with notes, a fever of nonstop pencil-scratching that often drew the attention of the jury, and the prosecutor herself. At one point Kerns glanced over at the defense table after Robert noisily flipped the legal pad to a fresh page, after which she stumbled through her next few points.

After a time, Byron realized with a shock that Robert's notes were nothing but long, scribbling lines meant to mimic cursive—a trick to throw off his opponent, as though critiquing every syllable without ever uttering a word in actual rebuttal. Brilliant.

Finally Robert nudged Byron and showed him a few actual words on the page: *Steak dinner later tonight? On me.*

THE OPENING STATEMENT, METICULOUS AND DRAMATIC on its own terms, took nearly two hours. Exhausting.

When Kerns was done, Byron glanced at the jury. He could see they had believed her. He was guilty of being a bad husband and a spendthrift. At times, yes. But when had selfish or thoughtless relationship behaviors become crimes? None of the jurors returned his glance.

"Counsel for the defense, do you wish to present an opening statement?" The judge seemed almost to be implying that after hearing what the prosecution had said, doing so would be a waste of time.

"We do, your Honor."

With that Robert turned to the jury. He went and stood in front of them a long, quiet moment. Throats cleared. The judge leaned over, her chair creaking.

"My client did not kill his wife." And then Robert returned to the defense table and sat down.

A murmur and bustle swept through the courtroom. Even the judge was caught off guard. The jurors looked at each other as if to say, that's it? Ms. Kern began to whisper in an agitated voice to her law clerk.

Meanwhile Robert sat smiling, calm as a sleeping cat. Byron thought Robert had either done the most brilliant opening statement ever, or this trial was over before it had begun. Robert Taylor's opening had taken exactly six seconds.

"All right-y, then," Judge Wright finally said, pursing her lips and moving papers around in an attempt to find her judicial footing. "Let the record show that the court sits duly impressed with counsel's brevity. The State may call its first witness." And Byron, confused, felt his head growing hot as the floor was again given to those who would put him in jail—who would put him to death, if they could.

BYRON SCANNED THE SPECTATORS. SIDNEY HAD

positioned herself so the cameras could get a full-face shot of her looking serious. When she turned away, she gave him a wink and a secret smile.

"The State calls Martha Temple."

"Objection, your honor. This witness has no relevant testimony to offer the jury." Robert half rose out of his chair, which at his size was far enough. He was conserving his energy for what was to come later. Like any good fighter, he knew trials were often won in the late rounds.

"Ms. Kerns, how do you respond to the defense objection?"

"The witness was Mr. Round's personal assistant for a number of years. I believe the evidence will show she was involved in an intimate relationship with the defendant."

"I would remind Ms. Kerns that we are not in family court, and this is not a divorce case." Robert seemed to enjoy his own witticism, as did several jurors who laughed. Robert had struck his first blow by making Ms. Kerns look foolish. "Since the state cannot prove Mr. Round murdered his wife by direct evidence, they hope to smear his reputation."

"It is the State's position that the defendant's affair with Ms. Temple was the motive for the murder of his wife." Now it was Ms. Kerns' turn to look superior.

"Objection overruled." Judge Wright lowered her glasses. "However, Ms. Kerns, I admonish the state not to speculate about this relationship without having some foundation for offering such rhetoric."

Ms. Kerns seemed excited by the prospect of revealing to the jury exactly what a lout Byron Round was. "If I'm allowed to get to it, we do, your honor."

On the stand, Martha, pretty with her hair pulled back but obvious in her anxiety, peered out at the courtroom through glasses Byron had never seen. He suspected Robert of coaching her on her appearance.

When she gave her name, her voice quivered. Byron realized how terrible all this must seem.

"I guess they're going to try you for adultery first, and then tack murder on later," Robert whispered. "Soap opera element for the rubes."

"Ms. Temple: do you know the defendant, Byron Round?"

"Yes."

"Please speak up, Ms. Temple, the jury can't hear you." Ms. Kerns was in her element now, bullying a frightened witness.

"Yes, I know Mr. Round."

"And how do you know him?"

"I was his executive assistant for six years."

"Did you enjoy working for him?"

Martha brightened up at the mention of that happy time in her life. "Yes, very much. He was a wonderful boss."

"Were you married when you first went to work for Mr. Round?"

"Yes, I was."

"And did you subsequently divorce your husband?"

"Yes—but that had nothing to do with my job. Or Byron. Mr. Round, I mean."

"I'm surprised to hear you say that." Kerns read through her notes briefly then asked, "Did you ever discuss your divorce with a Betty Rolston and a Paige Johnson, two fellow admin assistants in your department?"

"I may have." Byron could see Martha trying to remember what she might have said to the two women. "But I don't recall anything."

"Would it be a surprise if I were to tell you both women are prepared to come into court and testify you told them your feelings for Mr. Round was one of the reasons you divorced your husband?"

Martha's voice grew firm. "No, it wouldn't."

"And why is that?"

"Because I did have feelings for Mr. Round."

"And what were those feelings?"

"I enjoyed working with him."

"That's it?"

"I admired him."

"Anything else?" Ms. Kerns let the obvious insinuation in this question work its way towards the jury box.

"Yes—I felt sorry for him."

"And why was that?"

"Because his wife was so awful."

"Did Mr. Round tell you that?"

"He didn't have to. Everyone could see she was on something—pale, sweaty, nervous. She came in one time in her housecoat, wearing socks instead of shoes. And whenever she'd come to the office, I could hear her shouting at Mr. Round."

"And could you hear what they were arguing about?"

"Usually about money."

"What about it?"

"She usually needed some."

"So you felt sorry for Mr. Round, and you admired him. That hardly seems motivation sufficient to prompt someone to leave their spouse. Did you have other feelings for Mr. Round, feelings you haven't told us about?" Ms. Kerns turned towards the jury and shared a conspiratorial glance with them as if to say, *we are all adults here, we know what makes a woman leave her husband.*

"I did. I do have feelings for Mr. Round."

Byron was sure the jury was watching him to see how he reacted to Martha being grilled. Despite his best efforts to stay calm, once or twice he felt himself wince.

"And what were those other feelings? Are you in love with Byron Round?"

"I wouldn't say I was in love with him." Martha looked at Byron for the first time since she had begun to testify. Sheepish, she continued, "Not exactly."

"Why would you say not exactly?" Ms. Kern's sarcasm seemed like piling on, and Byron could see from the folded arms of the jury that they didn't care for this angle.

"I could have been in love with him, but we stayed friends. Good friends."

"And why was that?"

"I'm not sure. Bad timing? He was married. And yes, I was

getting over my own divorce." Martha stopped speaking. It was obvious she was overwhelmed by everything that had happened to her. "And I had vowed to stay single for a year or two."

"But you did stay in the same hotel with Mr. Round on many occasions, isn't that true?"

"Yes, on business trips."

"And he would come to your room on those trips?"

"Yes."

Kerns took a little breather. Strolled around making eye contact with various parties in her own display of theatricality, meanwhile Robert blazed through another page of his fake notes. "Ms. Temple, did you ever think that if Mrs. Round weren't there that your relationship with her husband might become more than you've described here today?"

"Yes. I thought about that possibility."

"The State has no more questions for this witness, your honor." Ms. Kerns collected her notes and returned to her seat.

"Has the defense any question for the witness, Mr. Taylor?"

"We do, your honor." The small mountain of Robert Taylor rose to greet the morning sun. "Ms. Temple, I apologize if my questions seem indelicate, but the State has tried to leave the jury with the impression that your relationship with Mr. Round might be the motive for the murder of his wife."

"Objection." Ms. Kerns sprang to her feet. "We object to counsel's mischaracterization for the State's purpose for introducing this testimony."

"Your honor, we would love to hear the reason the State thought it necessary to humiliate Martha Temple here in this way."

"The court, too, would also enjoy hearing the reason the State compelled Ms. Temple to testify."

"The State withdraws its objection." Ms. Kerns sat down. Byron had begun to see why the name Robert Taylor was so feared in the courtroom.

"Now, Ms. Temple, I must ask you some questions to correct an impression now left in the jurors' minds. Ms. Temple, have you ever been sexually intimate with the defendant?"

"I have not."

"Did Mr. Round ever tell you he was going to leave his wife?"

"No."

"Did he ever tell you he wished his wife were dead?"

"No, of course not."

"Why do you say, 'of course not'?"

"Because he thought she was still the girl he'd fallen in love with before he joined the army."

"Did you find that frustrating at times?"

"Yes."

"And why was that?"

"Because I couldn't understand why he stayed with her when… when we…"

"When the two of you got along so well?" Robert offered.

"Exactly."

"Objection," Kerns called out.

The judge was curt: "Reframe the question so she may answer in her own words, counsel." He did so.

"Thank you, Ms. Temple." He smirked with satisfaction. "The defense has no further questions for this witness, your honor."

Byron breathed a sigh of relief. But that would change.

"At this time the State calls Doctor Eric Segal of the county coroner's office." Ms. Kerns had had enough of Martha Temple and her unconsummated affection for the defendant.

Doctor Segal, poised and cheerful, settled into the witness chair with practiced ease. He had testified at hundreds of trials and was nearing retirement, but he hadn't lost his zeal for seeing to it that the guilty were properly punished. He swiveled around in the witness chair and smiled at the jurors. The king was in his counting house.

Recovering from the unpleasant turn Martha Temple's testimony had taken, Kerns smiled at the doctor. The two had played pitch-and-catch in other trials, and as such were quite familiar with each other's style. It was Segal's practice to offer the jury a kind of country doctor folksiness while hinting that modesty kept him from revealing what a brilliant man he really was. No one was more surprised than Segal, Robert had said to Byron during trial prep, at how often people were impressed by this performance.

"You're the Medical Examiner for Winsor County, are you not?"

Segal directed his answers to the jury. "Very much so. I have been entrusted with the role for over thirteen years."

"That's quite a long time in such an important role."

"Yes. County council has seen fit to renew my contract three times."

"You're too modest, Dr. Segal. Isn't it also true that for the last three years, the state medical examiners' association has seen fit to elect you as its president?"

"Well, yes, my colleagues—the *body* of the medical examiner's association, if you will," his dry joke causing a ripple of laughter that went all the way up to the judge, "have been kind enough to honor me with such a high office."

"Did you, in your capacity as medical examiner, have an opportunity to examine the body of Dianne Round?"

"I did."

"Describe those circumstances for us."

"*Well*," he said, sucking his teeth, "I was called by the state police and told that the remains of a caucasian woman in her early thirties had been found inside a vehicle in the parking lot of a shopping mall."

"Were you told anything else?"

"Undetermined cause of death was the report from officers at the scene."

"And upon arrival, did you examine the body?"

"I did."

"And can you tell us what you found?"

He described the scene, the position and condition of the body, the clothing Dianne wore, her approximate weight and height, and that she showed signs of malnutrition and prolonged drug use.

"When you say drug use, doctor, do you mean she was taking prescribed medications?"

"No, I mean she showed signs of a long history of drug abuse. We found traces of heroin and cocaine in her hair, nails and tissue. Her heart was enlarged, and she was close to renal failure. In her condition a near-term death, I will say, was likely, if not inevitable."

"Did you find anything else?"

"She displayed indications of having suffered at least one or more STDs. This is quite common among female drug users who become prostitutes to support their habits."

"Would Mrs. Round have been able to have children?"

"Absolutely not. The extensive scarring I saw, and caused by STDs, would have made conception impossible."

"Were you able to determine to a medical certainty what brought about Mrs. Round's death?"

"She died of acute narcotic intoxication that caused her to have what is essentially a heart attack."

"In layman's terms, she died of a drug overdose?"

"I don't prefer that term, but you are essentially correct. 'Medical complications from an injection of an unregulated street drug is vastly more accurate'."

Ms. Kerns watched the jurors scribbling notes every time the ME spoke. "What signs of prolonged drug use did you find on her body?"

"Both her right and left arm had puncture wounds caused by hypodermic injection. Additionally, the veins in her arms were near collapse from repeated injection. She had punctures between her toes as well, a common place for addicts to inject when the veins on their arms collapse."

"And to conceal drug use from loved ones as well."

"Yes, it's a typical subterfuge desperate addicts employ."

"Were you able to identify the injection sites that caused her death?"

"Yes. Addicts heal slowly, and thus I was able to identify the two most recent injection sites that certainly brought about her death."

"How were you able to identify those sites?" Ms. Kerns could barely get out her questions now. She was like a hound barking at a treed animal, breathless with anticipation of what was to come.

"The two most recent sites were still pink, and had not scabbed over. All the other injection sites were of a gray color."

"Were the two injection sites alike?" Here Ms. Kerns turned to the jury so she could watch their reaction to the answer that she already knew.

Segal glanced at his notes as if he were refreshing his memory. "*Well*—no. They were quite different."

"How so?"

"One was small and showed evidence of someone skilled in the use of a hypodermic needle."

"And the other?"

"The second injection site was larger and near the first site, but it was obviously made by someone unfamiliar with injection procedure. I found significant bruising around the site consistent with a difficult or unskilled injection."

"And that bruising indicated that the person who gave that second injection was either inexperienced with hypodermic needles, or nervous, perhaps?"

"Very definitely." Segal sat back in his chair. He looked over at Byron and smiled. "Additionally, the very fact that there was bruising around the second injection sight indicates the deceased was alive at the time the second injection was administered."

"How so, doctor?"

"If Mrs. Round had been dead at the time of the second injection, the flesh around that puncture would not have displayed the indicia of bruising in the way it did."

"Is that because only live tissue bruises in that way?"

Segal sat back in the witness chair. "Precisely."

Once or twice Byron tried to look at the jurors during Dr. Segal's testimony, but they returned his glance with a collective scowl. Byron's twelve 'peers' thought he had murdered his wife. That much remained clear.

ROBERT TOOK OVER THE FLOOR FOR HIS CROSS-examination of the wizened and charming medical examiner.

"Doctor, you earlier testified that to a medical certainty you believed Mrs. Round died from a drug overdose. Now, is medical certainty the standard for all expert testimony such as you offer us here today?"

"You know that it is."

"The question isn't what I know, it's what *you* know. Now I will ask you once again: is medical certainty the standard for expert medical testimony?" Robert's tone was that of a policeman ordering a driver to produce his license.

Embarrassed by Robert, the doctor tried to make light of the question by smiling at the jury. "Yes, as we all know, that is the standard."

"As you sit here today, is it your testimony that to a medical certainty Dianne Round was killed by a drug overdose?"

"That is my testimony, yes." Exasperation had crept into Segal's voice.

"So you know how Mrs. Round was killed, is that correct?"

"I do. I have already testified to that."

"So you have. I want to be sure we all understand exactly what it is that you're testifying to." Robert, casual, leaned on the edge of the defense table facing the jury. "Doctor, do you know for a medical certainty *who* injected those drugs into Dianne Round?"

Segal took his time answering, as if to say we all know who did that. "I could not know that from an examination of the injection site. No."

"Did you do a careful examination of Mrs. Round's body?"

"I most certainly did."

"And did you find any evidence thereupon that might indicate to a *medical certainty* that her husband had killed her?"

"I did not."

"So you have no opinion as you sit here today as the state's witness as to who killed Mrs. Round, do you?"

"That's correct."

"I believe you further testified that you spoke with the state police lieutenant leading the murder investigation before you did the autopsy on Mrs. Round—is that also true?"

"Yes, I may have spoken with him."

"Would you care to look at your notes to refresh your recollection?"

"No. I did speak briefly with him." Segal's reluctance to discuss his conversation with the police only served to excite everyone's curiosity, as everyone from jurors to the judge to Sidney Biddle all leaned forward with anticipation.

"When you were asked by Ms. Kerns about your conversation with the police, you testified that they simply told you they had discovered a body and needed your help in determining the cause of death, is that correct?"

"Yes, more or less."

"In fact, doctor, you and lieutenant Atkins talked a good bit more about the case—isn't that so?"

"He may have. I was focusing on the cause of death."

"I can certainly understand that. But, you will concede the lieutenant did discuss the case with you?"

"I believe he mentioned one or two details, yes."

"In fact, he told you he believed Mrs. Round's husband had murdered her, didn't he?"

"It's possible. I don't fully recall."

"Doctor, if you continue to be evasive, I will be forced to ask the court to instruct you to answer my questions truthfully."

Indignant, the doctor shot a look up to Judge Wright, who merely gave a small shrug.

Segal answered: "Yes, the lieutenant did say he thought the husband had killed his wife."

"Did he say how Mr. Round had killed his wife?"

"No." Segal's lips worked as though he fought not to say the next words. "He asked *me* to find out how the husband had killed her."

"Understood. Interesting. The police didn't ask you to determine the cause of death. They asked you to determine how her husband had killed her."

"It sounds that way when you say it, but the lieutenant merely meant for me to determine the cause of death. At least, that's how I understood the framing of the request."

"But even you will agree that's not exactly what he said, nor how he said it."

"I'm not sure I could characterize such a conversation with full accuracy. Not after so much time."

"I had no doubt you would eventually get around to saying that. Now: As a medical examiner, say one not so impartial as yourself, could such a medical examiner might have gotten the impression he was being asked to look for evidence to connect the husband to the crime, instead of looking at the evidence in an objective fashion? As is the charge of the office you hold?"

"I didn't take it that way. You're misrepresenting a standard request."

Robert raised a skeptical eyebrow. "But someone else might have taken it another way?"

"Someone else might have, I suppose."

Kerns, exasperated: "Objection! Speculation."

"Sustained."

Undeterred, Robert smirked and continued: "Dr. Segal, how many days after the body was discovered did this conversation with the police take place?"

"Two days after the body was found."

"So, two days after the body was found, the police had eliminated all other suspects, and were focused on the defendant?"

"The lieutenant told me the husband had killed her. That's all I can say."

The audience bustled. The judge bade them to quiet and settle.

Robert, brushing lint from his enormous suit jacket, returned to his seat. "We have no further questions for this witness."

"That's that for Monday, then. Court will be recessed until tomorrow morning at nine o'clock." Judge Wright dropped her gavel all nonchalant and businesslike, after which she stood and left the bench without looking at anyone.

Day one of Byron's trial was over, and he had no idea what any of it meant, or what the jurors were thinking. They checked into the hotel across the street from the courthouse so they could get an early start in the morning. Robert made good on his promise, and room service delivered a sizzling platter with a fine cut of meat to Robert's room, where they ate with gusto and shared a bottle of expensive red wine.

While spending most of the night gazing out the window waiting for sunrise, Byron could hear Robert snoring as loud as he spoke from the room on the other side of the wall, and often felt fleeting sympathy for the lawyer's wife and family. Luckily, he couldn't have slept if he tried. Not with his life on the line.

23

K erns seemed unfazed by the way Robert had limited the impact of the medical examiner's testimony on the previous day, and jumped right in by calling the lead cop to the stand.

"Lieutenant Atkins: you were the investigator in this case, were you not?"

The formal lieutenant's uniform lent added authority to what he had to say. "I was and am."

"Were you at the scene when the victim's body was discovered?"

"Every step of the way. I was called to the scene by Trooper LeClair, who first responded to the call of a body in a car in a mall parking lot."

"And what did you observe upon arriving at the scene?"

"A young, white female propped up against the door on the driver's side of the car. We quickly determined the woman had been placed in the car after she was murdered."

"And what led you to that conclusion?"

"Several things. First, the victim was wearing only one shoe. The other shoe was found in a woman's restroom in a nearby shopping mall. Secondly, the position of the body, her head was against the door and her legs were across the seat, as if someone had dragged her body into the car. Last, we found a syringe behind a toilet in the bathroom where the shoe was recovered. The syringe was found to contain heroin, the same drug that was found in the victim's body."

"Was the syringe empty?"

"It contained trace elements of heroin, but it was pretty well empty."

"And what, if anything, did you conclude from that?"

"That the victim had been injected with all the drugs in the syringe."

"Did you know the victim's husband?"

"I did. Before he went into banking, the defendant was a trooper under my command."

"Did he tell you about his plans to marry the victim?"

"He did, and some time later I told him about her arrests for possession of narcotics."

"And how did he respond to the news of her drug arrests?"

"He seemed angry. He said she was not using drugs anymore."

"Angry at whom?"

"At me for bringing up her drug use."

"Did you tell him about Dianne's arrests for prostitution?"

"I did not."

"And why not?"

"I thought that was a fact his future wife should tell him."

"Did you tell him that if he married Dianne, he would have to go before a board of inquiry to see if he could remain with the state police?"

"I did, and a few days later he handed me his resignation."

"When was the next time you saw the defendant?"

"Years. When I told him we had found his wife's body."

"And how did he react?"

"He didn't react much one way or the other."

"Did you think that was unusual?"

"Everyone's different receiving such hard news. I've seen tears; I've seen stony silence. But even so, right then I thought Round's demeanor might indicate involvement in his wife's death, so I asked him if he could tell me where he had been for the past few hours."

"His reply?"

"He said he was doing chores around the house. I asked him what chores those were, and he said he had been working in the yard, but I didn't see any evidence of that. I asked if we could look around the house and he said no, he was too upset for that."

"Was there anything else that made you suspicious of the defendant?"

"When I asked him if anyone could verify his story that he had been at home, he said he could not."

"What did you do then?"

"I waited for the results from the forensic tests done at the scene."

"And what did those tests show?"

"The DNA tests from the women's restroom were inconclusive. The lab people call a public restroom an adverse forensic environment because so many people use it, and because of the personal nature of that use. Additionally, the restroom had been cleaned by the store staff before the lab people took samples. They use commercial grade cleaners that leave very little for the lab technicians to sample."

"Did you find any evidence in the restroom?"

"We found the victim's shoe and the syringe I mentioned. We also subpoenaed the store's security camera tapes and have pictures of someone about the defendant's height and weight going into the restroom approximately seven and a half minutes after the victim entered the bathroom. Five minutes later the subject comes out of the bathroom pushing what appears to be a cleaning cart. The victim is never seen leaving the restroom."

"And what did you conclude from that?"

"That the victim was killed by the subject who followed her into the restroom, and then he took her body out in the cleaning cart."

"You say he took her body out." Ms. Kerns emphasized the

word he. "Was it a man who entered the restroom behind the victim?"

"We believe it was a man disguised as a woman, a man about the height and weight of the defendant."

"And what motive would the defendant have for killing his wife?"

"Our investigation revealed the victim had begun using drugs again. We believe her husband discovered her drug use and killed her so he could be with the woman who was his administrative assistant. Also, Mr. Round had severe financial problems, and had taken out a two million dollar life insurance policy on his wife."

"I have no further questions for this witness, your honor."

Judge Wright sipped a mug of coffee while glancing at the clock on the wall in the back of the courtroom. "Mr. Taylor, I suspect you have some questions for Lieutenant Atkins?"

"I do indeed, your honor. Questions, questions."

But instead of diving in, Robert arraigned his notes on the podium in front of him and stood silently looking at the lieutenant. He did this long enough for the jurors and spectators alike to twist with discomfort in their seats as they waited.

At last: "Lieutenant, you concluded Mr. Round had murdered his wife after your first interview with him, isn't that correct?"

"I concluded he may have been involved in his wife's death in some way, yes."

"So you were looking at other possible suspects at that time?"

"We didn't find evidence that would indicate anyone might be a suspect at that time."

"Did you even bother to look for that evidence, Lieutenant?" Robert's sarcastic tone appeared to rankle the lieutenant.

"Like I said, we didn't find any evidence that would lead us to any other suspect."

"Did you consider a gentleman named Lyman Schuler?"

"I did not."

"As a matter of fact, lieutenant, you didn't even know who Lyman Schuler was, did you?"

"That's correct."

"And you didn't know because you were obsessed with pinning this murder on Mr. Round—*isn't that so?*"

A red patch appeared on the side of the lieutenant's neck. "No, it is not. I had evidence to believe Mr. Round was involved in the death of his wife, and I followed up on that evidence."

"Well, let's see what that evidence entails, shall we? You testified that Mr. Round didn't show much emotion when you told him his wife had been found dead in her car, is that right?"

"That's correct. He just stood there. Didn't seem fazed. Didn't seem upset."

"And despite your earlier assertion about the variety of aggrieved responses, when Mr. Round appeared 'numbed' at the news of his wife's death, you testify that this was somehow odd. Isn't this a contradiction?"

"Some break down crying, some turn into granite. I testified as to what I observed."

"So looking back on it, wouldn't you say that Mr. Round acted the way some other people have when confronted with very bad news?"

"That would probably be more accurate, yes." The lieutenant looked like a fighter who has taken a hard body shot and was starting to wilt.

"So your impression that Mr. Round was indifferent to the news of his wife's death may well have been inaccurate?"

"I suppose that's possible."

"You also testified that you thought Mr. Round was lying when he said he had been working in his yard at the time of the murder?"

"That's correct. I didn't see any tools in the yard when I was there."

"But you also testified that Mr. Round declined to let you search his house, isn't that so?"

"Yes."

"Could you see Mr. Round's backyard from where you were standing by the front door?"

"Not very well, no."

"Have you since that first meeting had an opportunity to search the defendant's home?"

"I have."

"Is there a backyard at the house?"

"Yes, a large one with a pool and a covered picnic table."

"So, is it possible that Mr. Round was working in his backyard at the time of his wife's murder?"

"I suppose it is."

"And you knew that when you testified here this morning that you thought the defendant had lied about working in his yard."

"I said I didn't see any yard tools."

"And you said that because you wanted the jury to believe Mr. Round was lying, isn't that so?"

"I honestly reported on what I observed."

"But you didn't tell the jury that you subsequently learned there existed a backyard at the house and you couldn't see it, isn't that so?"

"That's correct."

"Did you, on that first interview, ask Mr. Round if he had been working in the front yard or backyard?"

"I did not."

"So you have no reason to believe that he was anything other than honest with you?"

"I still say I didn't see any yard tools."

"Lieutenant, you just testified that you never examined the backyard for tools, so you have no idea if there were tools laying out there or not, do you?"

"I do not."

"Yet, knowing that, you tried to give this jury the impression that Mr. Round lied to you."

"I could have been more complete, I suppose."

"You also testified that you were one of the first officers to arrive at the crime scene."

Sweat began to gather on the lieutenant's upper lip. "That's correct."

"Did you recover the cleaning cart that you theorized was used to move the victim's body from the restroom to her car?"

"We have not."

"Did you order the state police crime lab to test the car for evidence?

"I did."

"Did you find any evidence in that car linking Mr. Round to the crime?"

"We did not."

"And since you already suspected Mr. Round, I assume you instructed your lab people to look for evidence to tie him to the crime."

"I did."

"And even though you specifically ordered them to look for evidence that Mr. Round had murdered his wife, you still didn't find any?"

"We found plenty of evidence that he had been in that car."

"It was his wife's car so you would expect to find evidence that her husband had been in it at some time, wouldn't you?"

"Yes, of course."

"So there was nothing especially incriminating about that either, was there?"

"No."

"And did you test the restroom where Dianne was last seen for evidence that Mr. Round had been there?"

"We did."

"And did you find any evidence whatsoever that the defendant, Byron Round, had been in that restroom?"

"We did."

Here Robert turned to the jury and rolled his eyes as if to say, *here we go again.* "And what, pray tell, was that?"

"We found fibers from a red wig that we believe Mr. Round used as a disguise."

"Well, then the only thing you know from that evidence is that the red wig was in the woman's restroom, isn't that so?"

The jury laughed. They had lost all confidence in the lieutenant's testimony.

"We believe Mr. Round was wearing that wig when he entered the restroom to kill his wife."

"And why do you *believe* that?"

"Because the store security camera shows someone wearing a red wig going into the restroom after Mrs. Round went in."

"And you believe that person was Mr. Round."

"The person was the same height and build as Mr. Round."

"That's your evidence?"

"Yes."

They compared the heights and weights of Lyman Schuler and Byron Round, indeed quite similar in build.

"So it's fair to say that either one could fit into the uniform of the cleaning woman as seen in the security camera video."

"Is there a question, Mr. Taylor?"

"Oh, my, Judge Wright—yes." To the lieutenant Robert said, "Did you recover the red wig?"

"We did."

"I see." Taylor turned to the jury. Now in the late round of this trial, he'd told Byron he always remembered what his boxing coach at Yale taught: never try to knock a man out, get him to the point where he wants to be knocked out. And now Lieutenant Atkins waited to be KO'd. "And tell us where you found that red wig?"

"Above one of the air ducts in the store where Mrs. Round was killed."

"Where is Mr. Schuler employed?"

"At the same store."

"And in what capacity does he work there?"

"On the cleaning crew."

"And in that capacity would he have access to the canvas cart we saw in the security video?"

"Yes, he would." You could barely hear the lieutenant's voice, now.

"And I believe you testified the killer was disguised in the duster women on the cleaning staff wear—is that correct?'

"Yes."

"Would Mr. Schuler have access to those dusters as well?"

"Yes, he would."

"Objection." Ms. Kerns charged over and stood next to Robert. "Mr. Round is on trial here, not this Lyman Schuler person. This testimony has no relevance to this case, and we ask that the court instruct the jury to disregard all testimony about Mr. Schuler."

"I am inclined to agree with Ms. Kerns, Mr. Taylor. How do you respond to her objection?"

"Your honor, the state has offered Lieutenant Atkins as the lead investigator in its case against the defendant. We are entitled to show bias on the part of that witness."

"And how do you propose to do that, Mr. Taylor?"

"By demonstrating that the witness intentionally ignored any and all evidence that would have proved Mr. Round did not kill his wife."

"As this is a capital case, I will grant you some latitude in this area, but I will not allow you to use speculation as the basis for impeaching this witness."

"Now, lieutenant, did you test the wig for Mr. Schuler's DNA?"

"Not initially, no."

"In fact, you only tested for a match with Mr. Round's DNA, did you not?"

"That's correct."

"And did you find a match?"

"We did not."

"Did you subsequently test the wig for DNA matching that of Mr. Schuler?"

"We did."

"Please don't keep us waiting, lieutenant. What did you find?"

"Trace amounts of DNA that matches that of Mr. Schuler."

"And how did you come to do that?"

"The district attorney, Ms. Kerns called me and said you were complaining about my investigation of the case. She said you thought we should look at Lyman Schuler as a possible suspect."

"And did you investigate Ms. Schuler?" Robert looked over at

Ms. Kerns and pressed the corners of his mouth in a frown one would use to show disappointment with a child.

The lieutenant's downcast eyes drooped as he was dragged into the deep water of his investigation. "I did."

"Please tell the jury what that investigation uncovered?"

"That Mr. Schuler was at work on the day of the murder."

"Come, come, lieutenant, you are being far too modest. Your investigation uncovered that Mr. Schuler was not only at the scene of the murder, but himself has a long record of drug arrests and violence against women—isn't that true?"

"Yes."

"Was Mr. Schuler able to account for where he was at the time of the murder?"

"Yes, he was."

"And how exactly did he do that?"

"We interviewed the other people who were working on the cleaning staff with Mr. Schuler that day, and they remembered seeing him throughout the day."

"Throughout the day," Robert repeated the lieutenant's words with undisguised disdain. "That's hardly the same as saying they remember seeing him at exactly the time the murder was committed, isn't it?"

"It is not the same, no."

"And yet you accepted Mr. Schuler's alibi and rejected what was essentially the same alibi when Mr. Round's neighbors told you they remembered seeing him working in his yard on the day of the murder, isn't that also true?"

"You could say that, I suppose."

"Well, I'm not saying it, the internal investigation done by the state police says that." Robert waved a blue bound booklet over his head. "And, in fact, you were removed as lead investigator on this case for failing to investigate all the evidence in this case, were you not."

"Yes. Captain Elliot took over as lead investigator after you threatened to sue the state if I was allowed to stay on."

"And did that cause you to change you mind about Mr. Round?"

The lieutenant's old confidence returned. He had weathered all that the formidable litigator Robert Taylor could throw at him, and he was still standing. "No. We got the right guy. That man, Byron Round."

"Well let's see if that's true, shall we?"

The slightest murmur of sympathy for the hapless lieutenant swept among the jurors. Even they could see the storm that was coming his way.

"You have testified that you have no forensic evidence tying the defendant directly to this murder. You tell us that he behaved strangely on the day of the murder, but upon reflection you recanted that testimony. You told us the defendant lied about what he was doing at the time the murder was committed. But today, you admit that that conclusion was not supported by the evidence? You were good enough to admit you never even considered Lyman Schuler as a suspect even though he worked at the store where the murder took place, the red wig used to disguise the murderer was found in the store and Mr. Schuler's DNA was found on that wig. Is that all true, Lieutenant?"

"Yes."

"Please speak up. The jurors can't hear you."

"Yes it is true."

"Yet, you persist in your belief that Byron Round murdered his wife?"

"I do."

"One last question, Lieutenant. Did you ask Lyman Schuler if he could account for his time during the time when Dianne was murdered and dragged to her car?"

"I did."

"And what did he tell you?"

"He said he was working."

"Was anyone working with Mr. Schuler?"

"No. He was alone."

"Did you believe him?"

"I had no reason not to."

"You had no reason not to?" Robert, aghast, walked in a circle and repeated the lieutenant's words for the jury. "No reason not to." He rested his enormous hands on the railing in front of the jurors and hung his head as if in grief.

And then back over to the witness, a sudden, lunging gesture that seemed to startle Atkins. "And yet, and yet, you didn't believe Byron Round when he told you he had been working in the yard all day, did you?"

"No, I didn't and don't believe him."

"Do you have some kind of a built-in lie detector that tells you who's lying and who isn't?"

"Because it was a reasonable suspicion—in these cases when a wife shows up dead, it's almost always the husband who killed her."

"So, a statistic, if it pleases the court, is the evidence in this specific capital case against a citizen of the state of Connecticut. All right. Understood. If it is most often the husband who kills his wife, then why bother to look at anyone but the husband. Sir, is that what you're testifying today in a court of law?"

"I didn't say that. Not exactly. Not at all. It's usually the husband. And in this case, the evidence confirmed that."

"Lieutenant, would you concede that some of that so-called evidence against Mr. Round has been discredited by your own testimony here today?"

The lieutenant found his defiant voice again, managing to not sound grudging. "Not all of it."

"Oh, impressive. And would you further concede that by your standards, there exists at least as much of this so-called 'evidence' that points to Lyman Schuler as points to Byron Round?"

The cop held out his hands. "There's some evidence that you might say points to Mr. Schuler, but not as much as against the defendant."

"All right. But one last thing, lieutenant. What person on the cleaning staff cleaned the restroom where Dianne Round was murdered?"

"Lyman Schuler."

"Thank you very much, Lieutenant. Your honor, the defense has no further questions for this witness."

"Does the State wish to examine the witness on redirect?"

The prosecutor, troubled, appeared to consider asking the lieutenant more questions, but decided against it. "We have no further questions for this witness, your honor. The State rests."

Byron saw her and Robert exchange a glance, with her dropping eyes first. Her opponent had undermined every aspect of her case, and she looked like she could use a drink.

Judge Wright, eager to hear the rest, nonetheless called it for the day and looked to the next frame. "How many witnesses to you expect, Mr. Taylor?"

Robert gazed out over the courtroom. "The defense believes the state has not met its burden of proving beyond a reasonable doubt that the defendant murdered his wife. Therefore, we move for a directed verdict of not guilty. If the court is not inclined to grant our motion, the defense will call only one witness."

"And who will that witness be?" Judge Wright raised her pen to jot down the name of the witness.

"We will call Trooper Ted LeClair to the stand, your honor. Trooper LeClair met with the defendant when he first reported his wife missing, and he will testify as to Mr. Round's reaction to his wife's disappearance. The state has attempted to portray Mr. Round as being indifferent to his wife's murder. Trooper LeClair's testimony will rebut that false impression."

Robert led Byron outside amidst more jostling from spectators and various legal actors.

"We could rest our case now, but I don't like the jury thinking you had no feelings at all about your wife's disappearance."

Sidney Biddle came and shook Byron's hand. "Congratulations. You'll be a free man." Then she turned to the television camera crew waiting behind her to tell her audience of her certainty that the jury would decide Byron Round's fate in his favor.

BYRON SPENT THE WEEKEND THINKING ABOUT WHERE he would go on vacation when this was all over. There could be no question now of his exoneration. Robert had shredded every aspect of the state's case, especially the testimony of Lieutenant Atkins. All had worked out. A small miracle.

Byron almost felt sorry for the lieutenant. He had always thought of him as being a pretty good, if not especially bright policeman. But this case was clearly over his head. Anyway, he was close to retirement, so the fact that he had been removed as lead investigator wouldn't mean very much to him. There would be a reprimand in his file certainly and maybe even a reduction in rank, but nothing more. All in all, Byron thought the lieutenant had gotten off easy for trying to convict an innocent man.

He took a long motorcycle ride, far from the city, winding roads, and considered heading north until he hit Canada. The wind in his face, Byron tasted freedom. But not all the way. Not yet.

24

The courtroom settled as Judge Wright gaveled the trial back into session. "The court has considered your Motion for a Directed Verdict, but found the State has put forward sufficient evidence for the case to go to the jury. The Defense may call its first witness."

"We call Ted LeClair to the stand."

Trooper LeClair took the witness stand and smiled when he noticed Byron Round at the defense table. Byron returned his smile. Unlike Lieutenant Atkins, Trooper LeClair had always been polite to him.

"Trooper LeClair, did you receive a call to go to the home of the defendant regarding a possible missing person?"

"I did."

"And would you tell the jury what you found when you arrived at the defendant's home?"

"I found Mr. Round in his living room. He seemed very upset, and said his wife had gone shopping in the afternoon, and hadn't come home yet. It was approximately ten o'clock at night when I arrived at the Round residence."

"You said Mr. Round was upset. How did you know that?"

Robert was going to draw this out so the jury would have no doubt that Byron was distraught at his wife's disappearance.

"His face was flushed. He spoke very rapidly and he seemed angry when I told him I couldn't put out a missing person alert until his wife had been missing for twenty-four hours."

"Was there any question in your mind that Mr. Round was upset about the disappearance of his wife?"

"No, sir."

"And then what did you do?"

"I asked him to provide a description of his wife—what she was wearing when she went shopping, among other physical details. Then I asked if he had a recent photograph of Mrs. Round, which he produced."

"What did you do then?"

"I left the Round residence and went back to our office and started the paperwork for the missing person alert."

"Did you eventually issue a missing person alert?"

"Yes sir, Lieutenant Atkins issued it at exactly three o'clock the next afternoon. That was when Mrs. Round had been missing for twenty-four hours."

"Your honor, the defense has no further questions for this witness, and we rest our case."

"I believe the case is now ready to go to the jury, then."

"One moment, your honor." Ms. Kerns rose slowly to her feet. "I believe the state is entitled to ask questions of this witness as well."

Judge Wright looked impatient. It seemed State v. Round would not end as soon as she had imagined. "Forgive me, Ms. Kerns. I didn't mean to imply the state could not question the witness. The state may proceed."

"Trooper LeClair, you testified that you asked Mr. Round what his wife was wearing when she went off shopping on the day she was murdered, is that correct?"

"I did. I needed her description for the missing person alert."

"And did Mr. Round tell you what Dianne Round was wearing on the day she was murdered?"

"He did."

"Objection, your honor. What Mrs. Round was wearing or not wearing on the day of her murder is not in issue here today. This testimony is irrelevant to the guilt or innocence of the Defendant." For the first time since the trial had begun, Robert seemed to have an uneasy feeling about the direction this was taking. His face turned sour and troubled. He had stopped scribbling nonsense on his legal pad.

"Your honor, Mr. Taylor called Trooper LeClair as his witness to testify about his role in the investigation into the disappearance of Mrs. Round. As part of that investigation, Trooper LeClair testified that he asked the Defendant what his wife was wearing on the day she was murdered. The state is merely following up on that line of questions."

"Overruled. Proceed."

"Thank you, your honor." Ms. Kerns approached the witness again. "Trooper LeClair, did you make any notes during your interview with Mr. Round that evening?"

"Yes, I did."

"Did you bring them with you today?"

"Yes I did, just as you asked me to."

"Now, Trooper LeClair, please tell the jury what Mr. Round said to you in response to your question about what his wife was wearing when she left to go shopping on the last day of her life." Ms. Kerns stepped away from the witness so he could speak directly to the jury. "You may consult your notes if you wish."

Trooper LeClair studied his notepad for a moment and then looked up. "Mr. Round said she was wearing a light tan skirt and matching jacket, along with a white blouse and blue shoes."

"You are certain he said she was wearing blue shoes?"

"Yes. We have to be accurate in our missing person reports."

"And why is that?"

"Because that's all we have to go on to locate these people."

"Do your notes reflect the fact that Mr. Round said his wife was wearing blue shoes at the time she left the house on the day she was murdered?"

"They do." Trooper LeClair held up his notebook.

"Your honor, the state has made copies of the relevant pages of Trooper LeClair's notebook for counsel and the court. We would offer the original notebook into evidence at this time."

"Any objection, Mr. Taylor?"

"Not at this time, your honor." After Robert sat down, he leaned towards Byron and whispered, "What is this all about?"

"I have no idea."

"The notes of Trooper LeClair are accepted into evidence."

"I have no further questions for this witness, your honor, but the state wishes to recall Lieutenant Atkins to the stand."

"Objection." Robert leapt to his feet. "We have been remarkably patient with this line of questioning by the state, but even our patience has worn thin. So what if Mrs. Round was wearing blue shoes on the day of her murder? We all heard Trooper LeClair say Mr. Round told the police she was wearing those shoes."

"Mr. Taylor has almost asked the right question, your honor. The question isn't, what if Mrs. Round was wearing blue shoes when she left home that day, but what if she was not?" Ms. Kerns could feel the jurors lean forward in their seats. "Lieutenant Atkins can answer that question for the jury, your honor."

"I am going to let Ms. Kerns continue. Objection overruled." Judge Wright began to scribble notes on the margins of her witness list. And Byron Round now began to sweat.

Lieutenant Atkins made his way to the witness stand. In his right hand he carried an opaque plastic bag with an evidence sticker tied to it. Whatever was in the bag, it certainly had an odd shape and no one in the courtroom could guess what it was. All eyes were on that bag as the lieutenant prepared to testify.

"Lieutenant, did you hear the testimony of Trooper LeClair this morning?"

"I did."

"And when you learned on Friday that the defense planned to

call Trooper LeClair to the stand today, did you have occasion over the weekend to follow-up on certain evidence referred to in that testimony?"

"I did." Lieutenant Atkins rested his hand on the plastic bag that lay in front of him. "Something about what Mr. Round told Trooper LeClair bothered me."

"And what was that?"

"He said his wife was wearing blue shoes when she left the house."

"What was so unusual about that?"

"I asked every trooper at work what color shoes his wife was wearing that morning, and not one of them could tell me."

"What, if anything, did you conclude from that?"

"That Mr. Round has a remarkable memory or, more likely, he remembered the color of his wife's shoes because she flung one of them off as she was jerking to death in front of him in that bathroom stall. That's why he was able to tell Trooper LeClair what color shoes his wife was wearing. Like most husbands, he had no idea what color shoes she was really wearing when she left the house that morning. He assumed they were the same as she when he murdered her."

Ms. Kerns stepped to the side so the jurors could have an unobstructed view of the lieutenant. "Please tell the jury what the results of your investigation have been."

"When Mr. Taylor said he was going to call Trooper LeClair to the stand, I went over all of the notes he had taken when he interviewed Mr. Round. When we found Mrs. Round's body, she was dressed as her husband had said she was when she left the house on the day she was murdered."

"And how was that?"

"She was wearing a light tan skirt, match jacket, a white blouse and blue shoes, just the way Mr. Round said."

"And what did you conclude from that?"

"Well, nothing of significance. Not at first. But I was telling my wife about it at breakfast, and when she said it was unlikely a woman would wear blue shoes with a tan shirt and jacket, it stuck in my craw."

"But if that's exactly what Mrs. Round was wearing, I'm confused as to your intuition."

"But see, then I remembered there were almost no marks on the soles of those shoes."

"And what is the significance of that?"

"The shoes were new."

"You mean Mrs. Round bought them while she was shopping on the day of her murder?"

"At that point I thought that might be the case. When I checked Mrs. Round's credit card purchases for the day of her murder, I found she had bought a pair of shoes matching the ones we found at the time of her death."

"Were you able to locate the shoes she was wearing when she left home that day?"

"Yes, I was." Lieutenant Atkins opened the plastic evidence bag and lifted out a pair of brown loafers, scuffed, dirty, one with a loose heel. "When I followed up at the store where Mrs. Round bought the blue shoes, they told me she had come in and left the others to be repaired."

"You are referring to the shoes she was wearing on the day she left her home before being murdered?"

"I am."

"Did the store give Mrs. Round a ticket to use to redeem her old shoes?"

"Yes."

"And have you found that ticket?"

"No. When we found Mrs. Round's body, her purse and most of her jewelry were missing."

"You say, most of her jewelry was missing. What items, if any, were found on her body?"

"Just her wedding ring."

Lieutenant Atkins held up a clear plastic bag that contained a delicate gold ring. He continued holding it so all the jurors could see it. It wasn't difficult to see they were all thinking that ring had been on her finger when she had been murdered.

"Doesn't that indicate that the murder was a result of a robbery gone wrong?"

"No robber would have left that ring on her finger. It's real gold. Taking the purse was what someone would do who wanted us to think it was a robbery." He stared hard at Byron. "But leaving a gold wedding band behind was an action a husband might take. Sentiment."

"Objection," Robert all but shouted. "It's not sentiment at hand, it's rank speculation on the part of opposing counsel."

"All right, Mr. Taylor. Sustained. Proceed, Ms. Kerns," but it was clear the judge smelled smoke.

"Now, Lieutenant Atkins, I ask you: is there any way Mr. Round could have known his wife was wearing those blue shoes *unless he saw her wearing them in the bathroom at the time of her death*?"

"No. The mall security cameras show Mrs. Round leaving the shoe store and going directly into the restroom."

"Is there anything further linking the defendant to this crime?"

"Yes. When I pulled up Lyman Schuler's records, I found that one of the arresting officers was then-Trooper Byron Round. So Mr. Round knew all about Lyman's past arrests for drug possession and criminal domestic violence. Once he saw Lyman was working at the mall, he had someone he could pin the murder on."

"Can you prove Mr. Round has ever been to that mall?"

"The lady at the shoe store remembered seeing him with his wife there many times. They were big spenders."

"How do you account then for the fact that Mr. Schuler's DNA was found on the red wig you recovered?"

"When I interviewed Mr. Schuler, he told me his car had been broken into a week before the murder, but the person who did it only took the car ashtray. Mr. Schuler thought it was kids being stupid. But we suspect it was Mr. Round getting those cigarette butts with Schuler's DNA on them to rub against the wig. It's called transfer DNA. The lab technicians suggest the material had been smeared on the wig along with minute traces of carbon, what was most likely cigarette ash residue."

"Now, lieutenant: in your cross examination by Mr. Taylor, you heard the defense claim a rush to judgment in this case, that your single minded-pursuit of the defendant occurred without ever looking at other suspects."

"Mr. Round was a trooper before he joined the bank, so he knew in a murder investigation we always look at family members first."

"And what did you find?"

"We immediately found out that the defendant had taken out a two-million-dollar life insurance policy on his wife, that he had a girlfriend, that he had big money problems—all the tells that go into giving you probable cause to make an arrest."

"And did anything about that make you suspicious?"

"No, not at first. A few weeks after we found Mrs. Round's body, I applied to you for an arrest warrant for Mr. Round based on the early evidence I had found."

"And did you arrest Mr. Round?"

"We did. But it was only after his arrest that I started thinking about how all the evidence against him was laying there waiting for us. At first I thought he wasn't smart. But then I realized because I had arrested him so quickly, I hadn't bothered to investigate all the evidence."

"And you were given a reprimand for that?"

"I was."

"Did that make you rethink that evidence?"

"Yes, when I did a timeline, I spotted an anomaly—Mr. Round took out the life insurance policy on his wife eighteen months before his she died, and not when he bought the house as he first told me. According to the witnesses at the bank, it was around that same time that he started being rather affectionate to Martha Temple in public. I think this is when he decided he was going to kill his wife and leave a trail of evidence for us to follow straight back to him. He wanted us to arrest him right away. That way his attorney could point out all the details we had missed after we had reached the conclusions he wanted us to reach.”

“And is that what happened?”

“Only after Mr. Taylor said he would call Trooper LeClair as his witness did it occur to me that the evidence I needed to put the defendant in that bathroom with his wife at the time of her death was there in front of me. When my wife mentioned that blue shoes didn’t match Mrs. Round’s tan suit, I reread Trooper LeClair’s notes to be sure that’s what the defendant had told us she was wearing when she left the house. I went to get the blue shoes out of the evidence locker, and saw there were almost no marks on the soles. They were new. And the only opportunity the defendant had to see them was in that bathroom. After she was dead.” Lieutenant Peter Atkins left out a sigh that was audible all over the courtroom. “And that’s how we put it all together.”

“Thank you, Lieutenant.” Ms. Kerns turned to face Judge Wight. “The state has no further questions for this witness.”

“Does the Defense wish to cross examine the witness, Mr. Taylor?”

“We do, your honor, but I would like to confer with my client for a moment first.” Robert leaned to his right and whispered to Byron, “They can put you in that bathroom with your wife.”

“All they have is—nothing. I wasn’t there.”

“Stop that. No more lies. The shoes put you in that bathroom, and the jury is going to convict you of your wife’s murder. Now that’s where we are.”

“Let me take the stand.” Byron could explain why he had thought his wife had worn blue shoes that day. Perhaps she had other blue shoes at home, and he had simply confused them with the pair she was wearing.

He had already started rehearsing his lines: *It was a mere coincidence that she had bought a blue pair that day. You can’t convict someone for making a stupid mistake like that.*

“Do you hear what I’m saying?” Robert had begun to raise his voice.

“My mind had wandered.”

"Tremendous. Buddy, we've got to try for a plea deal. The jury will give you the death house, now."

And that's where it stood. Time to decide. The game, played out. The theatrical play at its end, the curtain hung heavy over his head. And so Byron decided.

25

Not long after the trial Martin Kingsbury died of a heart attack, after which Suzanne went to live alone in a cottage in Maine. The three of them, Dianne included, had gotten what was coming to them, but only Byron was made to truly pay for it—the Kingsbury's suffering had become his for all time.

And the worst part? He let them do it to him.

But maybe acknowledging such a fact helped him adjust to life in the penitentiary as a murderer, a hard-ass rep which helped keep him out of trouble. Small blessings.

A BORED GUARD WAVED ROBERT THROUGH TO THE sterile visiting room where Byron waited, scratching at a beard he had started to let grow out. It was already getting long.

Robert sat down on the visitor's side of a scratched but clear plastic partition. He carried more than the weight of his body, but his first words belied the fatigue of his slumping shoulders. "Got a bit of news."

Byron couldn't summon much enthusiasm for what Robert had to say. Their relationship had ended when he accepted the state's offer of life in prison without the possibility of parole. Appeals were useless. "I can't imagine what."

"The whistleblower judge decided you've no standing to bring the case, since apparently you were given shares in Sunwest by the same people you now accuse of securities fraud. It's called the Clean Hands Doctrine. The government doesn't want to reward someone who may have had a part in the wrongful act they're reporting." The attorney's smirk told a smug tale, especially since he wasn't trying to disguise it. "You can see the logic of that, can't you?"

"You know I had nothing to do with those shares of Sunwest."

"I know. You told me that. Sure. But the judge didn't agree."

"How did the judge come to find out about those shares?" Byron got the idea that Robert's visit wasn't merely a lawyer dropping by to see how life inside felt.

"Oh—as an officer of the court, I found myself duty-bound to report it."

"Duty. You."

Robert, every inch the righteous barrister. "If it came out later I'd concealed that info, I could be disbarred."

"Then it seems you have no whistleblower case." It gave Byron satisfaction, at least, that Robert wouldn't earn that multi-million dollar fee without him.

But no—and the lawyer couldn't have been more casual about how he said it: "Well, now. You know these cases are labyrinthine. Moving parts. Players. Actors. And as it turns out, I've found another one to take your place."

Byron was sure he had rehearsed this poetic speech, like before appearing in court. It sickened him.

He wondered who'd know enough about what Sunwest had done to replace him. "And who would that be?"

"Oh—Martha Temple, truth be told." Robert's breezy nonchalance now seemed to mask a hint of anxiety. Treachery always comes wreathed in nervous smiles. "Not that it matters now."

"I don't believe you."

"That's why I stopped by to give you a copy of the motion withdrawing your complaint and substituting that of hers." Taylor opened his briefcase.

Byron could smell the leather. The money. The deceit. "Martha would never do that."

"It's already been filed. Once she realized your only interest in her was as a kind of make-believe girlfriend, she had no trouble taking your place in the suit."

"I don't suppose the Whistleblower fee…?"

"Would a million dollars help you get over a romantic heartache? From a nonexistent fling? Or else being used to cover up a murderer's crime?"

"Why don't you all go to hell."

"You're the one who failed to think every last detail through. You impress me, Byron. You always did it. But it wasn't enough to fool us all."

"I suppose not."

Robert snapped shut his fine briefcase, signaled the guard. "I think this concludes our formal relationship. We'll always be friends, though, Byron. You can count on that."

"Friends? You bet, Bob. Take care. Best to the family."

AFTER TAYLOR LEFT, BYRON LOPED BACK TO HIS CELL. He caught himself in the small mirror above his sink as he went to lay back on the stiff cot he called home. His skin, one size too large, no longer fit. It hung at his cheekbones, and bagged along his arms down to elbows like crepe. His eyes were set inside two shadowy hollows. His growing beard was shot through with strands of gray. No one ages gracefully in prison.

Life without parole. As though there could ever have been such a possibility as parole for him. What possible release awaited from the lies the Kingsburys had told to get him to marry Dianne? How they must have laughed at his wedding. The only qualification that had made him a suitable match for Dianne had been that he had no idea who she was, or the myriad ways he would be used by them all.

Yeah—he had married the memory of his high school sweetheart, not the real-time version of her. She must have chaffed under the burden of that as much as he had. They were the couple that wakes up to find themselves in bed with a complete stranger. Perhaps if he had understood this better, Byron wouldn't be spending the rest of his days in a cold prison cell, beating himself up over a tiny detail like the color of a pair of shoes.

Maybe one day he'd get the chance to ask her, somewhere on the other side, why they had both made their choices in life. Maybe in death, he'd finally get to know the real Dianne.

From late summer 2014, following the author's tragic motorcycle accident:

Thirty-seven days ago, right about now, Mike saddled up, headed for the grid with Dave Pisak, Dave Semian, Steve Kidd, Jim Ray, Johny Waters and Brian. It was a short lap, and just the first of a very long session. He's still in that session, and has had a pretty good week.

As his life is now measured, it's filled with concern over fluctuations in heart rate and blood pressure, maintenance of oxygen saturation levels, independent breaths a minute, ability to withstand a thirty degree angle on the tilt table, indications of sensitivity or movement in his arms, pain and the nature and location of it, restlessness, sleeplessness, and so on.

There's not much excitement in Mike's world as far as I can tell, but he manages to gives those of us around him those moments, and in the process both encourage and aggravate his nurses and caregivers...sounds pretty much like Mike doesn't it?

But here's how he is 888 hours after his injury: he's on the ventilator pretty much full time, and will be for the foreseeable future. His heart rate and blood pressure are maintained with a small-dosage of drugs, he was not able to tolerate the tilt table for the period of time we hoped, but the pneumonia is gone, and there are no other incipient infections, the amount of fluid collecting in his lungs is greatly reduced, and the general edema is lessened. He's had a tracheal device inserted that will allow him to talk, but doesn't like it because it removes the ventilator support when he uses it. He'll get over that fear.

There is talk now of a step-down room, still in critical care, but a step toward rehab nonetheless. He's quite sick of the twenty four hour news talk shows, and is even bored with the music we play for him. The guys at the track sent over a small DVD player with some horrible B movies so we'll see what that does for him! I'm assuming what he'd really like is a walk with Mollie, and you can be sure that's at the top of her list as well.

HOSPITAL REPORT BY STEPHEN SCHAR

And from Michael's funeral comes this eulogy:

Mike Sullivan was a man, in every sense of the word. He was many things to many people. To Natt and Rani, he was a father. To the rest of us gathered here, he was a friend, a great friend. Every time we met, he didn't just greet us; he burst into our lives, suffusing them with the magic of his energy. He filled our lives with fun. Our good times were better because of his presence, and our hard times were softened by the support you knew you could count on. Every man who knew Mike well, appreciated the authenticity of his character–this was a man unafraid of the world and whatever it held in store. And every woman who knew him well, understood this one truth: no harm could ever come to her as long as he was around. He was a natural protector: a Marine, a policeman, and a lawyer with a strong affinity for the poor, the marginalized and the dispossessed. When I think of those roles he played, I am reminded of the first night we met, some 33 years ago. We were watching a championship heavyweight boxing match and began swapping stories about our days as Marines, cops and our own somewhat exaggerated martial prowess, when one of the other men present just shook his head and observed ruefully, "Ex-Marines age gracelessly". We took it as a compliment! Little did I suspect at the time the strong friendship that would evolve over the years and survive even the inevitability of death.

Mike instinctively liked people. He had a way of breaking through the barriers that too often separate us–race, gender, ethnicity and economic station. He'd walk into a restaurant for the first time and, by the time he left, every Black waitress in the place would be laughing and waving him goodbye. People loved him. He could see the humor in every situation. We all have a thousand stories illustrative of that lightening quick wit.

I remember one time he called me to say he had some legal work to attend to on the Outer Banks, and suggested I motorcycle down there to join him for dinner. We stayed at an off-season hotel and ate in its practically empty restaurant. We ordered steaks. I have never seen less appetizing steaks. When the waiter put Mike's in front of him and turned to walk away, Mike said, "Hey, wait a minute, where are the laces? You forgot the laces."

Self-deprecating and egalitarian, he disdained the pomposity of the proud. It evoked–not his animus–but his humor, the quality most feared by the proud and most revered by the humble.

He was also, perhaps, the least politically correct man I knew. He could not care less what others expected him to say or believe. That was just part of the ferocity of his independence. As communal and sociable as we know him to have been, he was also comfortable as a loner, an entrepreneur running his own business or law firm. He was a New Yorker who moved to Columbia, South Carolina where he knew no one, to start a solo practice with no safety net beneath him. This was not a man who shunned risk; he embraced it. It gave his life vitality. We did our first track day together up at Watkins Glen, we parachuted together, we kayaked across the Puget Sound. He was born for action. And if his lifestyle seemed to some as "graceless" for a man of his age, so be it. His body may have aged, but his spirit remained ever resolute, and up for any challenge.

There was another side to Mike, softer, but equally authentic. He was kind, and not in a showy way. He had shouldered his share of life's disappointments. He felt the hurt. He could see it in others and was quick to offer help. He earned the trust of his friends who, like I, sought and highly valued, his counsel. And there was a spiritual dimension, as well. He had a tattoo on his shoulder–not USMC, not a woman's name or a drawing of some sort, but a concept–"Kannegara no Michi"–Japanese for "a soul in search of God". And the inscription was in calligraphy. This was not a tattoo for others to see and appreciate. It was there simply as a reminder of our greatest challenge and destiny. His search would be unique because he always he sought the untrod path.

Mike spurned the ostentation of wealth and its possessions. Give him a motorcycle and a roof over his head and he was happy. That's all he needed. His "wealth" was the knowledge that he was in possession of himself. The pleasure he sought was not of the fleeting and perishable kind, but a more robust and virile type that derived from self-discipline and virtue. Cicero tells us that the word "virtue" comes from "vir" or man, and denotes manliness in action. That is how Mike lived and that is how he died. In his last three months as a quadriplegic, never did I hear him complain, never any self-pity.

He told me long ago that when he returned from Vietnam, he was billeted in a transit area in California, a decompression base, I gather. As a sergeant, he was assigned command of a platoon of 40-50 returning Marines. A more senior Sergeant told him to have his unit fall out in formation at 0600 the next morning. Mike informed him that some of those men had lost legs and others were pretty banged up. The sergeant replied, "When they get back out in the civilian world, others can treat them like victims or handicapped, but as long as they are in the Marine Corps, they will be treated as Marines and they will act like Marines." Mike got it, and he remembered it these past few months. It was all about nobility of character and toughness. He could endure the fear and the suffering involved because, through years of practice, he had steeled himself to defy the misfortunes to which human lives are subject.

From the moment of his accident, his survival was a long shot. But, as Seneca tells us, "The brave and wise man should not beat a hasty retreat from life; he should make a becoming exit". Death overcomes the coward as well as the brave, but it hounds the coward and merely liberates the brave. Mike neither feared death nor did he readily surrender to it. But when the time came, he was ready to die, with the strength born of a life of valor.

In closing, I would note that it is fitting that we lay him to rest on this, the 239th birthday of the Marine Corps. This Marine is not lost to us but merely posted ahead of us. We should not let the enjoyment of our friendship pass away with him. We should endeavor rather to rejoice because we possessed his friendship, than to lament because we have lost it.

The years ahead will roll on ineluctably, like the winter waves that wash away the footprints from the sands of summer. But the years will not wash away our memory of his friendship. He faced life with intelligence and honesty; with an open mind and an open heart. By his friendship, he shored up our self-respect. He saw the good in us before we even knew it was there. If this man cherished our friendship, then we could know that hidden deep inside us there must be the moral strength that engaged his respect. And so, in the years ahead, we carry forth the memory of that friendship and we honor it by doing our best to meet the standards he set for himself: to speak honestly, to act nobly and to love grandly.

EULOGY BY PETER CONNELL

Born on Staten Island in 1945 but much later settling in Columbia, South Carolina, Michael George Sullivan served as a United States Marine Corps rifle platoon sergeant deployed during the Vietnam conflict, as a Vermont State Trooper, and later an attorney specializing in commercial litigation until his retirement in 2012. 

Along the way he wrote or co-wrote a number of publications for the South Carolina Bar Association. An avid motorcyclist as well, he would further refine his authorial skills by publishing a regular column in *Motorcycle Consumer News Magazine*, reporting from racing schools in Atlanta, Virginia and Las Vegas. He also produced the all-but edited novel manuscript he entitled *Feint*, complete through several drafts, now in the reader's hands.

Thank you,

Michael